Suzannah Dunn

was born in 1963. She is a graduate of the creative writing course at East Anglia University. She has had short stories published in magazines, and Serpent's Tail published some of her stories and a novella, under the title *Darker Days Than Usual*, in their series for the 1990s. *Quite Contrary* is her first full-length published novel.

QUITE CONTRARY

SUZANNAH DUNN

Flamingo

An Imprint of HarperCollins*Publishers*

Flamingo
An Imprint of HarperCollins*Publishers*
77–85 Fulham Palace Road,
Hammersmith, London W6 8JB

Published by Flamingo 1992
9 8 7 6 5 4 3 2 1

First published in Great Britain by
Sinclair-Stevenson Limited 1991

ISBN 0 00 654479 7

Set in Bembo

Printed in Great Britain by
HarperCollinsManufacturing Glasgow

Acknowledgements

I am grateful for the assistance of the Kathleen Blundell Trust. Many thanks to Penelope Hoare and Emily Mallaby, Imogen Parker and Debra Isaacs for their enthusiasm and kindness.

CONTENTS

FOR
JO
AGAIN

FRIDAY
21 APRIL 1989

Semolina is palatable only when slurried with jam. Tapioca is nasty and sago is worse. Semolina is gritty. There are lumps in tapioca and clots in sago. Sago is rare. My mother bought a tin of it from the Co-op when I was four. She thought it was something from her childhood, like sarsaparilla.

'You'll like it,' she told me, sitting down at the kitchen table.

I climbed onto a chair to watch the tin opener twisting in her hands. The tin revolved, revealing the label: S-A-G-O. The lid punctured and fractured along the seam.

'It's like rice pudding,' she said when she lifted the lid, her fingertips soft against the serrations. 'See?'

It was creamy white, and dropped solid into the saucepan. She beat it with the back of a spoon.

'It's like rice pudding,' she said, 'and you like rice pudding.'

'It's lumpier than rice pudding,' I said.

She left the table with the saucepan. She insisted on puddings: usually we had *Angel Delight*, strawberry flavoured or lemon and lime, but on this occasion we were to have sago. She lit the gas ring and I moved from the table to the cooker to watch her stirring the sago with the spoon. After a few moments it bubbled, so she removed it from the heat and poured it into bowls. There were three bowls. One was for my father, who was not yet home. She placed his bowl in the oven and then carried the others to the table. We sat down together. I laid my spoon in the sago and it sank, collecting milk. At the sides of the spoon, and beneath it, there was a rapidly cooling paste in which the pieces of sago shivered. I raised the spoon and sipped. The pieces of sago slid around inside my mouth. I looked at my mother in alarm. She too had raised her eyes from her bowl.

She swallowed before she spoke.

'You don't like it?'

I swallowed too. 'No.'

For once she did not disagree; for once she smiled. She lifted the bowls from the table and crossed the room to the bin.

'Never mind,' she said.

I am twenty-five and I have not yet learned that the cupboard is empty by Friday. I cannot shop tomorrow because I will be at work. I bought a frozen lasagne this evening on my way home. The lasagne is now ready. The smell of it fills the flat. I am not hungry. I have turned off the oven. I am sitting in darkness. The lights had not been on when the 'phone rang. It had not been dark.

The telephone had rung as I placed the lasagne in the oven. I shut the oven door with my foot and reached for the 'phone with one hand and a pen with the other. The pens are in a box on a shelf above the work surface. The box rattled with blunt pencils. I found a biro and I wrote a reminder to myself on the notepad by the 'phone – *laundry, letter to bank* – while I recited my number.

Then the caller spoke: 'Elizabeth?'

The caller was my father.

My father telephones me only in emergencies. I took the receiver in both hands and sat down on the kitchen stool. I have been sitting here ever since. The conversation has long since finished. The receiver has long since been replaced. I am sitting here with my chin in my hands and my elbows on the worktop. I am thinking. It is important that I remember the details.

I had asked him immediately what was wrong.

'I tried to reach you earlier,' he said.

'I was at work.' I asked him again, 'What's wrong?'

He sighed. 'It's your mother: she's in hospital with stomach pains.'

'Stomach pains?'

'Stomach pains.'

'What kind of stomach pains?'

Severe, he said; they had lasted several days; they were worse last night. 'The GP suspected an infection.'

'An infection?'

'A pelvic infection.'

He told me that he had taken her to hospital; that she had been examined by a doctor without delay; that the doctor had been young, polite, well-spoken, thorough. 'He thinks she's too old for a pelvic infection,' he said. 'Is he right?'

I drew on the notepad: a flower with a heavy head and wavy stalk. I remember how I used to infuriate him with my *it depends* . . .

'What else did he say?' I asked.

'Only that she should be admitted and that we should bear in mind that it could be cancer.'

Yes, it could be cancer, of course it could be cancer. It could always be cancer. I am a doctor, I work in Casualty. My first patients this morning were a smoker with a headache and a teenager bleeding from the rectum. I arranged a scan for the smoker and examined the teenager. The smoker chatted in the waiting room about eye-strain and the teenager lay in silence in a cubicle on a couch. The teenager had piles and needed reassurance. The smoker was cough-free and proud of it, but he

5

did not know that he had a tumour in his lung and secondaries in his brain.

My father wanted me to tell him whether or not my mother has cancer. I asked him to telephone me with any news tomorrow. I told him the number of the hospital and explained that I would be at work from ten until nine. I heard him scratching the number in pencil across a notepad.

Eventually the scratching ceased.

'Who should I ask for?'

'Dr Hamilton.'

'Dr Hamilton.'

The scratching resumed.

He wanted to ask me whether or not she might have cancer. Should I answer him as a doctor or a daughter? I haven't seen the patient, nor read the notes, nor felt for the pain, and therefore, as a doctor, I can have no opinion. As a daughter, I haven't seen my mother for more than a year.

He challenged me at the end of the conversation: 'You know what you forgot?' he said to me. 'You know what you forgot, don't you?'

'No, what?'

'Yes, you do,' he insisted, 'you know. You forgot to send her a birthday card.'

I distracted him with a question, a seemingly innocent question, the kind of question a daughter might ask: 'Has Mum lost weight?'

'No,' he replied, 'she hasn't lost weight.'

'Good.'

'*Good?*' He sounded incredulous. '*Good?* Try telling her. She's been on a diet since Christmas.'

I laughed a little. 'Dad,' I said unsurely, 'she'll be fine.'

1975

I am standing at the fridge. The fridge door is open and a fog drifts among the shelves and out into the warm afternoon air. I look for the butter, reaching along the shelves: ham, sliced, best before yesterday; eggs, boxed brown, farmhouse fresh; cheese, cheddar, Canadian; and a fudge flavoured yoghurt. Behind the cheese is a tub of low fat spread new improved flavour. I turn my attention to the compartments, lifting a flap marked dairy: it is empty, we never use it. I examine the crisper: three tomatoes and a lettuce.

My feet, bare on the blue and white tiles, are cold despite the sunlight. I removed my socks and shoes when I came in from school. I arrived home as usual at half past four and Mum called to me as usual from the garden.

'Is that you?'

I had dropped my school bag at the foot of the stairs and kicked off my shoes – my school shoes, my no-slingbacks-or-peeptoes-or- heels- above- two- inches and please- note- that- wedge- heels-present-a-danger-to-wearers-on-the-stairs and therefore-must-not-be- worn shoes. And I had peeled off my socks and dropped them into the shoes and walked through the living room where the curtains were drawn and my sister sat on the sofa watching *Top Cat*. I had walked into the kitchen. Mum was in the garden. I knew she would be in the garden. Through the open door I saw her legs outstretched across the paving.

'Yes,' I replied, 'it's me.'

I drank lemonade, and then sat for a while at the kitchen table drinking tea and reading the newspaper. Now it is half past five and I am gathering the ingredients for my cookery class tomorrow. I have to make a Victoria sandwich: eight ounces of flour, four ounces each of sugar and butter, two eggs, and a tin in which to bring it home. The flour and sugar are in the cupboard, the eggs are in the fridge, and there is a tin in the drawer under the sink. But where is the butter? When have we *ever* run out of butter?

'Mum?'

Silence: she hates to be disturbed when sunbathing.

'Mum?'

Still no reply: her face, no doubt, in sunlight; her eyes closed, the sunlight seeping beneath the lids.

'Mum?'

She clicks her tongue against the roof of her mouth before replying:

'What?'

'Where's the butter?'

'*What* butter?'

'*The* butter.'

I hear her sigh with irritation. 'Where do you *think* it is?'

I scan the fridge shelves. 'It's not in the fridge.' I shut the fridge door with my foot.

'Not in the fridge?' She hates to be wrong: in the garden she will be raising herself onto one elbow and blinking blindly at the sun. 'Not in the fridge?'

'No.'

I cross the kitchen and stand at the table transferring sugar from the scales to a container.

She raises her voice. 'Are you sure?'

'Yes.'

'Have you looked?'

'Yes.'

She clicks her tongue again and I know that she is lying back on the towel. 'God knows,' she mutters; 'some bugger must have had the last of it, that's all I can say.'

I wonder for a moment about fatless sponges. I have heard of such things: can anyone tell the difference?

Mum is wondering about something too. Once disturbed, she never rests. Her voice drifts to me across the patio: 'Can't you use the Outline?'

Outline, according to the lettering on the lid, is not suitable for culinary purposes: the answer is no.

'What do you need it for?'

'Cookery.'

'Cookery?' She sits bolt upright: I know this by her tone. 'Cookery? I didn't know you had cookery.'

She didn't know because I didn't tell her. I forgot to tell her. She hates forgetfulness.

'You didn't tell me.' Her voice no longer drifts across the patio. She clambers to her feet, soles slapping the stone, and she approaches the door. 'Why didn't you tell me?' she shouts. She appears in the doorway, casting a shadow. In her hand is a towel, the favourite coffee-coloured towel on which she likes to lie. It has trailed in the soil; she will be cross when she notices. It trails close to her toes: her toenails are newly painted, a paste of resin and glitter solidifying on each nail. She wears a short yellow dress. Suntan oil runs down her legs. Her hair is immune from the sun, being black, but it is shapeless with sweat. I stare at her and press the sugar into a container. The sugar is soft and moist and brown: brown is best for the bowels.

'Cookery *when?*'

'Tomorrow, periods three and four.'

9

She raises a fistful of towel to her forehead. 'I thought you had metalwork for periods three and four tomorrow.'

'Not this term.'

This term we have cookery: Victoria sandwich in Lesson One; and then Quiche Lorraine; and then rissoles.

She sighs. 'How was I supposed to know?' She purses her lips. 'What am I, a mind reader?'

The hand drops to her side. She peers at me. I am standing in shade beside the table with flour and sugar in bags and containers. Her gaze softens.

'Anyway,' she says, crossing the kitchen towards me. 'What do you have to make?'

'A Victoria sandwich.' My eyes are suddenly hot with tears: Mrs Earles, the cookery teacher, will not forgive me forgetting an ingredient. She will keep me cakeless at my bench and will insist that I help someone else to cream their fat and sugar. The hardest task. The hardest fat. Mrs Earles does not like me. She gave me a D minus last year for needlework.

Mother stands beside me at the table, unaccustomed to shade, dizzy with darkness, her fingers running over the bags and containers; she is checking the ingredients. 'Victoria sandwich?' She sounds interested. People who lived through the War enjoy anything sweet: sugar was rationed; and now, sometimes, she eats sugar sandwiches. Her hand rests now on the bag of muscovado. 'Caster sugar,' she tells me. 'For a Victoria Sandwich it has to be caster sugar.'

She turns to the open cupboard and draws from the top shelf a bag of caster sugar. 'Here,' she says, dropping it into my hands: it is crunchier than muscovado, and white.

'It's after half past five,' she says; 'and the shop has shut; so what are you going to do about the butter?'

'I don't know.' I bite my lip.

Her eyes are level with mine. She knows I can do nothing; that without her I can do nothing.

She sighs wearily and turns from me to close the cupboard. 'Well, you had better go next door to Mrs Westler, hadn't you? And you had better tell her I'm very sorry and that I'll drop in on her tomorrow when I've been to the shops; and remember to thank her.'

I hurry to the door.

She calls after me: 'Elizabeth . . .'

I pause. 'Yes?'

'Is there anything else? What about the filling?'

'Jam or buttercream,' I tell her from the door, 'and Mrs Earles says it's to be done afterwards at home.'

I had asked my father about Carrie. Carrie is my youngest sister. She is eleven years old: fourteen years younger than me, eleven years younger than Verity.

'She's fine,' he said, 'she's coping. She came with me this evening to the hospital with a bag packed for your Mum and insisted that we stop en route to buy Lucozade.'

I smiled. 'Poor Carrie.'

'She's fine,' he said again. 'She's at Guides tonight until nine.'

I glance now at the clock on the kitchen wall. It is five past nine. Carrie will be arriving home, hurrying towards the house with my father behind her on the driveway. She will wait on the doorstep for him to unlock the door.

'Tea,' he will say, following her into the hallway and lifting the coat from her shoulders. 'Tea, and straight to bed, because it's late.'

Carrie has beans on toast for tea tonight, I suspect: my father's speciality. He prepares the beans in the kitchen while Carrie unlaces her shoes in the hallway. She hops on the doormat and searches for her slippers, and then goes upstairs to the bathroom to wash her hands. 'Wash your hands,' he shouts to her when he hears her on the stairs. He stands at the cooker scraping a spoon around a saucepan. The saucepan balances above a roaring flame. He starts to make the toast, reaching into the breadbin and lifting slices two-by-two from a bag. Carrie returns to the kitchen. Absentmindedly, he reminds her again to wash her hands. Again she disappears—to her bedroom this time, perhaps—and toast emerges from the toaster.

My father will insist in future on eating regularly at a restaurant; at the local branch of a chain restaurant where he can order steak and chips and peas.

A *proper meal, for a growing girl*.

If my mother dies and I don't move home, then the only vegetables Carrie will ever have will be peas, those small damp balls of pale green starch.

Tonight my father calls out to her and she appears sooner than anticipated because she is hungry. He ladles beans from the saucepan: they creep like red-hot lava across the plate. He adds grated cheese: a vital ingredient, a vital part of the speciality. Grated cheese is not usually allowed. Mum economises; cheese is not for adding, cheese is for sandwiches. Dad does not economise, or not until too late; he uses most of the cheese and then furtively wraps the remainder, placing it at the back of the fridge. He sits with Carrie at the table and they eat hungrily. A brown crust dries at the edge of each plate.

They will learn about the washing machine and for a time they will succeed. My father will prompt Carrie to bring the dirty laundry from her bedroom. But eventually someone will forget and the laundry basket will remain unemptied. Suddenly there will be no clean clothes. For the first time in her life Carrie will attend school in a dirty shirt. Her weekend clothes will become thin and shapeless and pale.

If my mother dies then Carrie will suffer because she cannot open tins.

When I was last at home, my father asked Carrie to open a tin of soup. He came into the kitchen from the living room, the signature tune of the BBC six o'clock news jangling in the background. Carrie had been sitting opposite me at the kitchen table with her knitting. I was sitting in front of a pile of books but reading the newspaper. I had been reading the television guide: *Nine o'clock, West Side Story*. Dad stood at the kitchen door with his coat over his arm.

'Open a tin,' he said to Carrie, 'and heat up some soup, because I'm going to the station to fetch your mother.' Car keys rattled in his hand as he turned away. He paused in the hallway. 'Tomato soup,' he said before closing the door behind him.

Tomato soup is my mother's favourite. She had been shopping in London. It was Christmas Eve, she was Christmas shopping, last minute Christmas shopping.

Carrie laid her knitting on the table. She rose and crossed the kitchen, and reached into a cupboard for a tin of tomato soup. She placed the tin on the work surface and took a tin opener from the cutlery drawer. Holding the tin opener in one hand, she clipped it over the rim of the tin and squeezed. Nothing happened: no cracking of tin, no hissing of air. She tried again but again nothing happened. She stood with her head bowed. Her hand remained around the tin opener, her fingers slender but strong. Her face was hidden by blonde hair swinging to her shoulders either side of a parting. I returned to the TV guide: *A story of love and death in a New York ghetto*. Carrie shuffled past me in wrinkled socks. She lifted a biscuit from my plate and popped it into her mouth on her way towards the door.

The tin and tin opener were discarded. The tin had not been opened. I left the table and went in search of Carrie. I went to the living room and stood unnoticed at the door. Carrie was sitting on the settee watching television; her feet on the carpet, her chin in her hands. She was staring at the screen, at soap opera characters flouncing from set to set. *Hopeless*, my mother would have said: *Carrie is hopeless, but sweet*. Carrie likes to sit with Mum in the evenings. Often they sit together, ostensibly

13

watching television: Mum on the settee, Carrie sprawled across the carpet; Carrie's head resting against Mum's knees, Mum playing absently with Carrie's hair.

Carrie is blonde. She is pale and soft and secret like the inside of an eyelid or the underside of an arm. She is slim and people say that she is beautiful but my mother does not agree. My mother wanted dark, striking daughters:

Carrie is *sweet*, she concedes.

Sweet, she means, unlike me and Verity.

Carrie is tall, tall for her age, as tall as me, but I am not tall. I am *slight*.

Bessie is slight, my mother used to say, encircling my wrist with her fingers. I was slight despite vitamins and protein and three square meals each day.

Neither am I dark.

Mousey, my mother used to tell me sympathetically, *you are mousey, your hair is mousey like mine before I dyed it*.

Her hair is long and straight and black. Mine has a kink. *Kinky*, my mother used to say, laughing, pulling at it with a brush.

My eyes are hazel. I never claim, as Verity claims untruthfully of hers, that they are green. They are hazel. My mother likes chocolate-coloured eyes, deep and hot and sweet.

If I was a disappointment to my mother, then Verity was an affront. As a child Verity was a pale, frizzy redhead: a mother's nightmare. She looked like a maggot or a worm. She blistered in sunshine and had to wear sunhats and T-shirts with sleeves. Whenever I played in sunshine in the garden, she sat in the shade and peered at me with narrowed eyes, her pupils slipping from side to side between the lids like blobs of mercury. Eventually she hardened until she was no longer soft and wriggly, and then my mother called her a *bag of bones*. This was apt not only because she was thin but because she was brittle and bleached. My mother was fascinated by Verity. People are fascinated by redheads: they ponder their origins and make jokes about the milkman.

Verity did not always look like a prawn; sometimes when she was small she was as sweet as sugar-candy, her hair spilling down her back like candy floss, her cheeks as rosy as Turkish Delight or as pink as coconut ice. Sometimes she was as pale as pear-drops or as soft as milk and honey. At other times she was yellow like something turning sour.

Verity, according to my mother, is *not to be trusted*. She was never to be trusted: not as a sugar-candy child in a seersucker dress with ribbons in her hair and bows on her shoes; nor as a sticky-fingered miscreant in school uniform, a veritable Marmalade MacAdams; nor, later, as a honey-hued sophisticate, a Queen Bee. When I last saw her she glowed with autumnal tones: her hair in turtle-shell combs, her lips a rustic rosy-apple red. Apart from the lipstick, and the pale paste of foundation and powder, she wore no make-up. And apart from topaz or tiger-eye on her earlobes, and a signet ring, she wore no jewellery. Dressed in tartan, she resembled the women in up-market clothes catalogues who wear green wellies and squint at the horizon. *Au naturelle*. At last it was fashionable to be plain, to be as pale as linen and to have freckles rising like bubbles in champagne. But this was not good enough for my mother. Verity is not merely an affront to my mother's aesthetic sensibilities: Verity is a liar.

A *compulsive liar*, my mother claims. But this is romanticism, a desperate attempt at consolation because Verity's lies are frequent but shrewd.

If my mother dies, Verity cannot be trusted to care for Carrie. Neither can my father. My father will try but fail. He will return home in the evenings, stepping into the hallway and switching on the light, Carrie stumbling from the living room, rubbing filmy eyes, the television glowing behind her. They will select a meal from the freezer, light the oven, set the timer, clear the table of schoolbooks; they will run baths, wash socks, iron shirts and once a week they will change the pillow cases. The routine will fill the emptiness of the evenings. They will tread nimbly around each other in the hallway or on the stairs. My father does not sit like my mother in slippers in the morning in the kitchen, or in the afternoons and evenings in the garden or the rocking chair by the boiler. He paces, running hands over windows and doors, checking for draughts; and pauses momentarily against radiators, his hands behind his back, his fingers drumming. He never sits in the evenings with Carrie.

1978

I am kneeling on the floor at my dressing table, peering into the mirror. The room is dark because the curtains are closed. I haven't had time yet to open them. The alarm clock reflects in the mirror: 7:52. I have to go downstairs at 7:56, take my sandwiches from the kitchen table at 7:57, and leave the house by 7:58. The school bus leaves from the top of the road at eight o'clock.

I shuffle closer to the mirror. I am kneeling because I don't have a stool. Grandma gave me her dressing table but not her stool: 'I've no more use for the dressing table,' she said, 'but, if you don't mind, I'd like to keep the stool because sometimes a spare stool comes in handy.' She suggested that Mum might buy me a stool, but Mum laughed: 'You must be joking, because Madam here will want one of those silly white furry ones. She can make do instead with the chair at her desk.'

On my dressing table are an eyeshadow and a mascara. The eyeshadow is blue, *midnight* blue. It used to belong to Mum but she gave it to me with the rest of her make-up when the dressing table arrived. She never wears make-up, not even to Parents' Evenings.

The mascara, however, is mine. I bought it on Saturday with the last of my birthday money. I arrived home from town on the six o'clock bus. Mum was in the kitchen spooning *Apricot and Rice Delight* into Carrie's mouth and scooping spillage from Carrie's quivering chin. She asked me what I'd bought.

'This and that,' I replied.

I made a pot of tea and joined her at the table. I showed her the contents of my bag – the cardigan, the hairslides, the address book – but kept the mascara in the paper bag in my pocket.

It is 7:53 and I have smoothed midnight blue across my eyelids. My fingertips need washing but I wipe them on my blazer. 7:54: I picked up the mascara, unscrew the cap, and pull the brush through the narrow neck of the tube. Holding the brush level with my right eye, I place it beneath my eyelashes; and then, very gently, I lift. The eye widens. I lower the brush. The eye stays widened and stares at me from the mirror. I turn to the other eye, small and colourless and heavy-lidded, and once again raise the brush. Suddenly from downstairs there is a shout: 'Where the hell are you?'

Mum has bustled in her candlewick dressing gown from the kitchen to the stairs.

Where does she *think* I am? I take a deep breath, my gaze fixed on the mirror, and I shout: 'I'm here.'

'Where *are* you? It's eight o'clock. Verity has already left.'

Carrie screams now in unison: she thinks it's a game.

'Where *are* you?'

'Here.' *Here, here, here.*

'Well, get downstairs.' The voice is hoarse. 'It's eight o'clock. Get down here.'

I push at the eyelashes of my left eye with the brush.

'Just a minute,' I shout.

I hear her thump the banister. Carrie screams with excitement.

'Don't tell *me* to *wait a minute*. Don't tell me what to do. Get yourself down here before I come up and get you.'

Why will she never leave me alone? I scramble to my feet and peer again into the mirror. I want to examine my eyes but my attention snags instead on my blazer: navy blue, crested, enormous. Four years ago Mum assured me that I'd grow into it: it came from the PTA secondhand uniform sale. We had arrived at the sale with the list addressed to all new parents: blazer, regulation; skirt, navy, A-line; blouse, regulation; pullover, navy, V-necked . . . The most expensive item on the list was the blazer so Mum had pencilled an asterisk next to it and scribbled *PTA?* The sale was taking place in the school gym. The clothes had been heaped onto trestle tables. Each article of clothing had been pinned with a ticket bearing the owner's name and the price. Mum delved into a pile of blazers.

'Try this one,' she said.

'But it's enormous.'

She sighed with irritation. 'All the better for you to grow into.'

I slipped my arms into the sleeves and began looking around the room for a mirror; but Mum gripped me and turned me to face her, tugging the lapels and shifting the blazer across my shoulders. I looked in vain for my fingertips at the end of each sleeve. Mum struck fluff and dust from my shoulders and stepped backwards. She stared hard at me and reached forward to knock a shock of hair from my eyes. Then she smiled and nodded with approval.

'It suits you,' she said.

Then she realised what she had said and a look of unease crossed her face because she hates uniforms. She knocked the hair back across my face and turned away. She turned towards the woman on the other side of the end of the table and raised her hand to attract attention. The woman dimpled in anticipation and moved towards us, her arms folded across her chest. 'Any good?' She looked me up and down.

'We'd like this one, please.' Mum was smiling as she unpinned the ticket from the lapel.

'Very smart,' said the woman, taking the ticket (*Harvey*, £2.50).

There were no mirrors; I stood in front of Mum and looked into her eyes but saw nothing. I stood with my arms extended,

19

and the sleeves extended even further. 'Isn't it a bit big?' I asked her finally.

She sighed. 'You'll grow into it,' she said.

Verity started school two years later and insisted on a brand new blazer.

'No one wears those crappy old ones any more,' she told Mum.

Mum told her to watch her language; and pointed out to her that her elder sister still wore one. She had made Verity's point, so Verity began a campaign, a no-crappy-old-blazer-like-crappy-old-Elizabeth's-blazer campaign, until Dad conceded in exasperation. Verity was bought a new blazer. Mum sighed and said things like *that child*. But Verity had a new, fitted blazer.

Most of my school clothes are new but limited and uniform: navy blue knickers, three pairs; hockey socks, one pair; pullover, regulation. Verity's are new, plentiful, and daring: her skirt is straight, not A-line; she never had a briefcase but a succession of canvas bags graffitied with biro; she has a Snoopy pencil case. She has never worn a school summer pinafore.

I had never seen a summer pinafore on any of the girls passing our house each day in the cloud of grammar school blue, but it appeared at the bottom of the list: *summer pinafore, optional*. I went with Mum and Verity on the Saturday afternoon before the start of my first term to buy my uniform from Paula Lee Ladies Fashion (recommended retail outlet).

Mum and Dad were going to a wedding reception in the evening and had been into town before lunch to buy a present. It had been hot and crowded and they had found nothing except a wooden cheeseboard and wooden mouse in which a cheeseknife was embedded. They arrived home at lunchtime with fish and chips tumbling from newspaper onto plates: cod for themselves, roe for us. Mum took her plate into the garden because she wanted to sit in the sun. Dad told Verity and me to sit at the table and placed plates in front of us – a cake of roe each and half a portion of chips – before joining Mum in the garden.

Mum was in her favourite place – the sunniest place on the steps beside the rose-bush – with her plate in her lap. Dad sat on a chair which he had lifted to the patio from the kitchen. Through the open door we could see his back in a white cotton shirt against the wooden frets of the chair. Above the clatter of their cutlery Mum and Dad talked together in heated voices about how much was to be done during the afternoon and how little time there was in which to do it. Mum was worried about getting ready for the wedding reception: an hour's drive, an hour and a half, and not only was there the weekly shopping to do and the tea to cook but there was the school uniform to buy. After a while she began to shave her legs. She has a battery operated lady shave. If I could hear it, then so surely could the neighbours.

Dad came back into the kitchen, stepping into the ripples of sunshine which shivered through the waters of the goldfish bowl and splashed around the cool blue tiles. He paused at the table to glare at us.

'Hurry up,' he said, 'and don't mess about. Get yourselves ready for your mother: she has a lot to do today.'

Then he left us alone again. Verity stared at me with her bulging, blinkless eyes. She lifted chips from her plate and folded them into her mouth. I mashed a forkful of roe into a pool of tomato sauce. 'Hurry up,' I said to her.

Dad agreed to drive us into town but not to come with us to Paula Lee: he had work to do, he said, at the office.

'As usual,' added Mum.

The car rolled from the driveway into the lane and paused at the junction with the main road. Dad reached into his pocket for his wallet. He handed four or five notes across the gearstick to Mum.

'Enough?'

She nodded and pressed them into her purse.

Pushing open the door at Paula Lee activated a buzzer. There was no browsing, nor any escape, because the buzzer activated the lady behind the counter: she appeared from the stock room, swinging through the curtains like a figure on a weather vane declaring fair or foul. It was fair because she was smiling and because she wore her hair in a bun. She took up her position behind the counter and I could see that the smile was a can-I-help-you smile. How could anyone be *helped* into buying a dress from Paula Lee? I had seen the dresses in the window: big, heavy, buttoned and belted, they descended onto dummies. The dummies were young once because they had the wide, flat, forward tilting hips of the 1950s and an open arabesque of arms.

Mum lingered at the door and then crossed the room behind me with the list held forwards.

'St Martin's Lane Grammar,' she said to the lady by way of explanation. 'School uniform,' she added hurriedly.

The lady took the list and leaned over the counter to smile at me. 'St Martin's,' she said, 'how *lovely.*'

Was she Paula Lee?

She turned to Mum. 'Is it your first?'

Mum smiled. 'Yes,' she said.

'Not your last, though?' She nodded, smiling still, towards Verity.

Mum followed her gaze. Verity was at a rack of coats, running her fingers through the fur. 'Probably not,' Mum replied, lunging across the room to pull Verity away. She drew her close and hissed into her ear — 'Behave!' — before releasing her.

I knew that Mum doubted whether Verity would gain a place at grammar school. She wanted five children, all grammar school students, but was convinced that Verity would be the first disappointment.

The lady had turned to the drawers lining the wall to gather an armful of white shirts. 'You must be very proud,' she said. Everyone always said this: and it must have been true because when Mum and Dad heard that I had been accepted at St Martin's they gave me a present of a fountain pen in a case.

The lady turned towards us with the shirts.

'Yes,' said Mum, with a smile, 'she's a clever girl; she takes after her mother.'

There followed a long half hour in which I shivered behind a dressing room curtain and appeared at intervals for Mum to push and pull in front of a mirror. Clothes slithered around me to the floor from hooks and hangers and the backs of chairs. Mum and the lady were delighted by each of my appearances: they grabbed my collars and cuffs and waistbands, pinching them between their fingers and agreeing with each other that the skirt was *good quality*, the shirts *well made*, the cardigan *warm*. The lady talked in general about school uniforms. 'They look best in navy, don't they? And in cotton, and in games kit? And don't they look smart in the raincoat?' Since when had I become *they*?

Verity played unnoticed, running a hand along the glass counter, humming quietly: I could tell that she was imagining herself as a shop assistant.

We approached the bottom of the list and Mum began to express doubts: 'Don't you think this should be a bit bigger? You don't think she's a *twelve*?'

The lady did not think so.

'But the PE skirt?'

'It's fine.'

Mum laughed; she had become bold: 'Well you *would* say that, wouldn't you?'

The lady laughed with her. Then she picked up the list. 'Summer pinafore?'

Behind the curtain I smiled to myself: we had reached the bottom of the list, we had finished, we could go home.

'The summer pinafore is very nice.'

'Is it?' Mum sounded interested.

I poked my head around the curtain and glared. The lady had turned to the drawers behind the counter. Mum looked at me and bit her lip. The lady turned back to her with a package, a summer pinafore folded in polythene.

Mum shrugged. 'We could have a look,' she said to me. 'I do so hate uniforms; you don't want to be wearing a great heavy uniform in the summer, do you?'

'Yes,' I replied through gritted teeth.

When I appeared from behind the curtain in the pinafore, Mum squealed with delight.

'Lillibeth! how lovely! You look just like a little French convent schoolgirl.'

What did she mean?

'So cool and clean.'

But she did not think of French people as clean: she had said as much on many occasions. I looked into her eyes to see what she was seeing: something from a childhood film, perhaps, or storybook. A Bernadette tripping through an orchard in Provence, perhaps, or a vineyard in Bordeaux, or a park in Paris, her eyes bright, her socks white, her hair braided, an apple in her schoolbag and a prayer in her heart. Mum is an atheist; but they are simple souls, her Bernadettes, they are happy and hopeful and faithful and they remain so because they die young.

Mum added the pinafore in the end to the pile of packages and we waited for Dad to arrive with more money: the amount he had given her in the car did not take account of optional extras.

7:57. I dart into the kitchen, lift my sandwiches from the table, and turn back towards the door. Mum twists on her stool and something slops from Carrie's spoon onto her dressing gown.

'What's that stuff around your eyes?' she demands.

I pause at the door, facing away, and press the sandwiches into my bag. I can ignore her or I can answer back (*what stuff?*) It depends, as usual, on whether or not she repeats the question (*I said, what's that stuff around your eyes?*) I push the sandwiches to the bottom of the bag; she says nothing more. I sidle into the hallway. Behind me in the kitchen, she sighs and whispers perhaps not to me but to herself: 'Well, don't come running to me when you get into trouble.'

I reach above my head, feeling along the shelf for the black plastic lead and slipping my hand down the length of it until the switch

24

is in my palm and the button rolls beneath my thumb: spotlight flares onto a white tile. In front of me on the worktop is the 'phone; hunched and pale and silent. Should I call someone? Lilly? Wendy? Jem? I straighten, lifting my elbows from the work surface and dropping my feet to the floor; standing and nudging the stool into its usual place beneath the work surface. *Breakfast bar*, my mother would call it. I call it a work surface because it is where I work; where I chop vegetables, slice bread, and make 'phone calls. There is nowhere else in this kitchen to work. I never eat breakfast.

The kitchen is windowless but not claustrophobic. It is separated from the living room by a sliding door which never closes, by a metal strip across the floor between lino and carpet. It is bright in daytime with light from the living room window. Electric light spills now across the metal strip onto the carpet. I step into the living room. The window is dark: a large sash window, a beautiful window; the glass dense and smooth and black and brilliant. The room is lit by a tangle of streetlamps and trees, and a glowing, acid, urban sky.

It is not a large room, but large enough. The bedroom across the hallway is slightly smaller. The kitchen and bathroom are tiny. This is the smallest flat in the house, on the top floor: servants' rooms, presumably, at one time, or a nursery. The conversion is not recent, unlike most in the street. The carpet on the communal staircase is frayed, the entry system archaic. Nor do the residents appear to commute, like others in the street, to London. Below me live a married couple and their eight-year-old daughter. 'She was born here,' the mother told me when she introduced herself on the stairs. 'Well, not here,' she retracted, embarrassed, 'but in hospital, while we were living here.' I have seen a woman on the ground floor with a baby. The couple with the eight-year-old daughter are *in retail*. All the flats except mine overlook the street at the front and the garden at the back. Mine overlooks the adjacent house: the bathroom window, the stairwell window, some guttering, and black bins like bats against the fence. My flat is as secluded during daytime as it is at night.

The sofa, although small, dominates the room. It squats against the back wall, sagging beneath layers of covers. The covers are cream coloured and printed with rosebuds. At the base of the sofa is a frill underneath which things roll and become forgotten: tumblers, magazines, cotton reels. The scatter cushions are scattered where I left them: there is no one else here to move them. I live here alone. I left my room in the hospital six weeks ago, less than three weeks after arriving: I sleep there only when I'm on call.

My landlady lives in Madrid, where she teaches English. She left England two years ago and returned briefly last month to find a new tenant. She showed me round the flat and told me that she had decided to stay in Spain. 'Why not? It's a good life.'

She wants to sell the flat and has suggested that I might buy it. 'Why not? If you were interested we could work something out.'

It is true that for the first time in my life I can afford to buy somewhere to live: I am a doctor, and doctors have no trouble finding mortgages even though they may have trouble paying them. She told me that the flat would be furnished, that I could keep whatever I liked and throw out the rest. She says that she has everything she needs in Madrid.

On the walls there are the ghosts of framed pictures, the shadows where they once hung. When I arrived, the bathroom cabinet was empty of everything except a bottle of iodine. A three-way socket adaptor held a lone plug. There were sprigs of dried grasses in jam jars or in runny-glazed pottery-class products. There are still spider plants in yoghurt pots, potted geraniums on saucers, and watermarks on window ledges. There is still the box of blunt pencils by the 'phone. I stand in the living room and wonder whether this feels like home.

Home is where the heart is.

Have I never had a home?

Last night, sitting here in lamplight, I felt for the first time in my life that my heart was somewhere other than locked thumping deep inside my ribs.

*

26

I step out of my shoes and push them with my toes beneath my bed; then I peel off my ankle socks and drop them onto the floor. Light falls from the bathroom door behind me and rolls banks of steam across the room. In the bathroom, water crashes into the bath. I wonder whether my mother took a nightdress with her to hospital. She never used to wear one at home. Her shoulders were always naked in bed above the sheets. Around the house during the day she wore a candlewick dressing gown. The only nightdresses I remember her wearing were those she bought for herself as belated Christmas presents during the January sales: nursing nightdresses with laced bodices which became tatty and stained. I remember the one in which she breastfed Carrie: it was coloured blue like denim because Carrie was born in the 1970s. I imagine her this morning rummaging through Carrie's cupboards for nightwear while my father shouted at her from downstairs: *Good God, woman, will you leave that, it's the very least of your worries, get down here and into the car.* Perhaps Carrie was there, too, pulling from white wooden drawers enormous nightshirts printed with cartoon characters and holding them against Mum and exclaiming that she looked sweet.

Throughout my childhood my mother's dresses were short and spangly and worn with chain belts, and her legs and feet were often bare. She never wore tights or high heels. Now she is older, colder, less slim. She wears clothes discarded by her children; clothes left by me in my wardrobe, or discoloured and misshapen by Verity's washing machine, or rejected by fashion-conscious Carrie. When I was last home, however, she had a new dress: big, baggy, belted, and printed with a pretty pattern. 'Your father bought it for me,' she told me, standing with her arms splayed. She tugged at the belt and craned over her shoulder to look down at the hem. She meant that he had complained that she had nothing to wear, or that he had complained that *she* had complained that she had nothing to wear, and he had taken her with his wallet to a store on a Saturday morning and insisted that she choose.

I must remember to ask about the nightdress during the next

'phone call. If Mum does not have one then perhaps Verity can go shopping for her: Verity lives in London and works in the West End; she can go shopping one evening. She has charge cards for all the stores and welcomes opportunities to use them. She likes shopping: something she does well, Mum says.

I lie in the bath and stare above me at the light bulb. I had never noticed that it is bare. It buds from the ceiling. Perhaps before it counts as bare it must dangle on a length of flex. It is bright, too, and surely bare bulbs are dim, and rooms with bare bulbs are dingy. I wonder what sort of shade it should have: most shades cannot be hung so close to the ceiling; and a shade made of cloth or paper would become damp because the room has no natural ventilation. Instead of a window there is an extractor fan which is activated by the light switch. I have to switch off the light if I want to bathe in peace. This evening I forgot, and the fan whines now above my head. I don't want to risk standing and reaching for the switch because I'll slip or electrocute myself. Most other bathrooms with a light bulb like this would have a perspex shade screwed to the ceiling and trapping flies.

Nothing Dad can tell me now will make a difference. Everything has already changed. Everything changed when Mum entered hospital, when she stepped onto the black ribbed mat in the sweep of the automatic doors and stood in an orbit of porters with trolleys. She will return home at some time, of course; but perhaps now only temporarily, as a visitor with a taste for elevenses acquired from ward routine, and a sleeplessness learned from night staff; and a bag packed with a nightdress at the bottom of her wardrobe.

In the bath I raise five toes slightly above the water. I presume that my mother is *comfortable*: a euphemism for *drugged*. I can rely on diamorphine. Pain control implies that it cannot be eradicated but can be tracked instead by a rising level of diamorphine. It implies vigilance. If necessary, my mother's nurses and doctors will have to be vigilant. And so will I.

I imagine her lying in bed, wrapped in linen, her arms bound by the sheet to her body, the bedcovers rising and falling as she dozes. Towards dawn she sees daylight pressing through the darkness, falling through the shadows and settling around her. She waits for the return of pain. During the night she watches the arrival of a patient who has needs temporarily more urgent than her own; she watches in darkness, as if through a keyhole, while the procession glides through the ward with hushed urgency; the intravenous drip swaying, the contents ticking into the blood-stream like sand.

I reach past my feet to the end of the bath for the soap. Mum used to say that baths were for washing in, not lying in. She doesn't like water: 'wet,' she says, laughing, 'and cold'.

She says that water is somehow cold even when it is hot.

She avoids baths in favour of what she terms a *cat's lick*: a cursory wipe with a flannel, similar perhaps to a bedbath.

Over the next few days she will become familiar with her surroundings: first, unconsciously, with the folds of the sheet around her body; and then, consciously, with the outline of her feet within the blankets and the deepening confetti of cards and flowers at her bedside. The nurses will begin to chide her for leaving untouched her drinking water, the water viscous in a pyrex jug and thickened with a silt of afternoon sunshine. She will be delighted, however, with the small box of tissues: at home there was never anything for wiping noses apart from toilet paper.

Nurses will come to her bedside when she calls, and also when she doesn't, and they will prise her from sleep. She will ask them questions and they will answer, or prevaricate, or consider, cajole, complain. Visitors arrive, drawing chairs across the floor, plastic chairs with hard legs and rubber trotters which shudder against the tiles. The visitors nestle at her bedside and crane towards the snowy bank of sheets on which she is balanced like a princess on a pea. She sits each day a little higher against her pillows, pointing out the new cards on her locker and the new patients on the ward, and repeating whatever the doctor told her with explanations and asides of her own. She is watchful throughout for those visiting after work, arriving later at the door in their clean change of clothes: she calls to them and they hurry towards her with apologetic smiles and hushed greetings, their hands wrapped like any other visitor's around pale envelopes and brightly boxed gifts.

If my mother dies, then I shall not have had time alone with her.

I remember visiting Mum in hospital after Carrie was born. Before we left home I waited at the front door while Dad combed a parting into Verity's hair. When we were young he combed our hair only rarely but carefully, whereas Mum whacked our heads with a hairbrush every morning. After combing Verity's hair he went into the garage to start the car. Verity and I waited for him at the end of the driveway. We watched as Mrs Owen dropped a letter into the postbox at the end of the lane and turned towards us.

'Hello, girls,' she called. She was Snowy Owl at Brownies. Her husband was a Councillor. She smiled and walked towards us. Her smile revealed teeth and gums. 'Has the baby arrived yet?'

'Yes,' said Verity.

The Owens were middle-aged and had no children of their own: no love lost between them, my mother used to confide darkly to me.

Verity had been standing closest to Mrs Owen and had presumably felt it her duty to answer. She smiled back at her, but the smile was weak by comparison so she squinted instead and chewed a fingernail.

Mrs Owen chuckled. She folded her arms across her chest. 'Well?' She looked from Verity to me; then from me to Verity and back again. 'Well?' She was chuckling still. She seemed mildly outraged. I wondered whether I had been looking for too long at her teeth. I looked away. She made an impatient sound with her tongue against the roof of her mouth: 'Goodness me, is it a *boy* or a *girl*?'

'A girl,' I replied. It had been my turn to answer.

'A little girl!' She unfolded her arms and raised a hand momentarily to her lips.

Her exclamation irritated me: surely the baby could not be other than *little*.

'A little girl!' she repeated. 'How lovely! What will you call her?'

It was not my choice.

'Carys.'

Carys Mahalia.

I remembered how my grandmother had said that Mahalia sounded like a negro's name.

Good, my mother had retorted, big-bellied and defiant.

'Carys,' I told Mrs Owen, resignedly. 'It's a Welsh name.'

'I know,' she said.

I looked at her. Her eyes were twinkling. I had forgotten that Owen was a Welsh name. 'I know,' she said: 'it means love.'

At the hospital we followed Dad down the corridors. We urged him with our shuffling of shoes to quicken his pace, but we did not run ahead. In other corridors, in places like airports, we would always run ahead; and he would shout directions behind us. Now, in the hospital, he was quiet and we walked through the corridors together, tripping over each other. When we arrived on the ward Mum was busy, although I forget what she was doing: knitting, perhaps, or reading, or even humming. She did not see us arrive. We began to cross the ward and she looked up at us and smiled. Her eyes were brilliant blue. I realised that I had rarely seen her smile. She sat motionless and smiling on the bed as we approached.

When we reached her, she nodded to Dad: a small nod, a greeting, a bow, sunlight dropping down her dark hair from her crown. Her lips were parted as if she had whispered; but perhaps not, because Dad had said nothing in return. Her lips were soft and red against the hardness of her small, white teeth.

'Lizzie and Verity,' she said, 'you look lovely today.' Her fingertips brushed close to Verity's recently combed hair.

'Where's the baby?' asked Verity.

Mum laughed. 'She's in the nursery, at the end of the ward. Do you want to see her?'

We both nodded.

She laughed again. 'Well,' she said, gently, 'off you go, then.' She indicated the nursery. 'One of the nurses will show you.'

SATURDAY
22 APRIL 1989

It is eleven o'clock on Saturday morning and Casualty is very busy; I am standing in relative peace and quiet at the end of a corridor and listening to the buzz of a disconnected 'phone line. A few moments ago my bleep sounded so I left my patient and walked up here to answer it. I walked here, to the 'phone at the end of the corridor, because I thought the caller might be my father.

'I have an outside call for you,' the switchboard operator told me, 'shall I put him through?'

'Yes, thanks.'

We are disconnected. I gaze down the corridor. Most of the cubicles are occupied. Apparently it was busy as usual last night after the pubs closed but then it failed to quieten: when Vivien, Chris and I arrived this morning at ten o'clock the average waiting time was already two and a half hours. We were informed of this by the electronic display in the waiting area. As far as I know it has not been altered. People sit immobilised beneath it on plastic chairs. It is not successful as a hint, warning, or threat: already this morning I have treated a sore throat ('Yes, Doctor, but if I waited for my GP I'd wait for ever').

It is Saturday morning; I expect people to be shopping, not sitting in hospital waiting for hours in Casualty to see a doctor about a sore throat or an ingrown toenail. Usually on Saturdays I want to be shopping. This morning I watched from the bus window while older women waddled with bags and younger women packed toddlers into trolleys alongside bulk buys and freezer packs. Usually on Saturdays I want to be shopping rather later than half past nine; usually on Saturdays at half past nine I want to be in bed. Perhaps the women were busy. Perhaps the people in the waiting room have already been shopping and are overcome with exhaustion. I contemplate removing my white coat: this is the only department in the hospital where it is permissible to do so.

'Beth?' A voice calls from the 'phone. The caller is not my father: it is Jem. The switchboard operator intrudes: 'You're through now.'
  'Beth?'
  'Jem, hello.'
  'Beth, hi, how are you?' A child is crying in the background; he speaks loudly. 'Look, I'm really sorry for calling you at work but I haven't been able to get hold of you lately at home.'
  'That's okay.'
  'I thought that I might be able to get you at work.'
  'Yes, of course.'
  'Is it okay? can you talk? just for a minute?'
  'Yes, that's okay.'

I am watching Carol, the Sister, at the end of the corridor. She is gesturing at me: a can-I-have-a-word-with-you-when-you've-finished gesture; and, despite the smile, it is an in-my-office gesture. I resist the urge to turn away from her to the wall; instead, I smile and nod and raise a hand: just-one-moment. This seems to satisfy her, and she turns and moves away. I wonder why she wants to see me. She did not look pleased. She was holding some X-rays, but they might not have been for me. She looked irritable. Her hair had fallen in wisps from under her hat, and her face was flushed. She is busy today and already she has had to spend half an hour in theatre supervising Chris's attempts to stitch the forehead of a reluctant child. The child's screams were ringing throughout the department all morning and the parents became aggressive. This often happens, but unfortunately Chris is not blessed with patience or tact. I watch the siblings of the injured child tottering up and down the corridor with fistfuls of crisps. I wonder whether Carol stitched the wound herself: rumour had it that she was unwilling to do so because it involved an eyebrow. In Casualty the senior nursing staff have had more experience than the junior doctor, who is often newly qualified and always temporarily employed, but they are allowed less responsibility: Chris is protected if he makes a mess, but not Carol. Carol's request was not-urgent-but-just-as-soon-as -you've-finished; in other words, hurry-up-and-finish.

'I can talk only for a couple of minutes,' I tell Jem.

'That's okay,' he replies, 'because I only want to find out when you'll be at home so that I can call you later; but, first of all, I don't suppose you're around tomorrow?'

'No,' I reply, 'I'm working; why?'

'Never mind, it doesn't matter, it was just that we had thought of invading you for the day.' When he says *we* he refers to himself and Diane and Diane's little girl, Alice. He met Diane when he moved to Highbury. His first teaching job was in Highbury and he moved there when we separated a year and a half ago. Recently he and Diane bought a terraced house in St Albans. She is a textile designer, working at home. 'We fancied a day by the sea,' he explains, 'and all that.'

'Oh dear, I'm sorry, that's a shame.'

He pauses.

'Beth, are you all right?'

He sounds puzzled.

I take a deep breath. 'Yes; why?' I am glancing behind me as I speak. In the distance Vivien drifts across the corridor, her eyes downcast, her arms around a pile of folders. Her white coat trails around her ankles. She is followed by a nurse who towers behind

37

her in a hat. The nurse wears blue, her tunic tightened at the waist by a belt.

'Beth? are you sure?'

I turn back to the wall to answer him: 'Yes, but Mum's in hospital.'

'Oh' – he sounds surprised and disappointed – 'oh, Beth, I *am* sorry; what's wrong?'

'Cancer, possibly.'

He draws breath sharply. 'Oh no.' He pauses for a moment. 'When?' He sounds suddenly miserable. 'I mean, when did she go in? When will you know?'

'Monday.' I know this because I know hospital procedure, not because I have been informed. 'We'll know on Monday; or we'll know *something*, we'll have *some* idea.'

He is silent. Alice is no longer crying in the background.

'Beth?'

'Yes?'

He sighs softly. 'Are *you* okay?'

I smile a small smile, a reassuring smile, but a smile unseen. 'Yes, thanks.'

'Is there anything I can do?'

'No, I don't think so, thanks.'

'And you promise you'll tell me? If there's anything I can do, you'll let me know?'

Perhaps we are both smiling. 'Of course I'll let you know.' Such smiles are small; mine fades. I shift my weight from one foot to the other.

'So,' he says, 'so, have you spoken to her?'

'No, but I've spoken to Dad.'

'Will you see her?'

'I've sent her some flowers.'

'Oh, good.'

'I sent them this morning.'

'Good.' He sounds cheerful. 'She'll like that.'

'Yes, she will.' We are both cheerful. Perhaps the thought of flowers is necessarily cheerful. Perhaps we both imagine the soft calls of surprise and admiration from others for the flowers still dewy beneath a glistening membrane of cellophane; the holding out of arms to receive them, the dipping of fingers into the tangle of ribbon and bows to draw out the card.

For a moment I can imagine my mother in her hospital bed, sitting, smiling, glowing, free from pain and misery and fear, saying: 'Aren't they lovely, they're from my daughter, my eldest, she's a doctor.' My mother loves flowers: they're *exotic*, she says. She loves gifts, too, and is genuinely surprised to receive them. She reads the accompanying card first because she likes to discover the message. When Verity and I were very young there was no tradition of buying presents for our parents; it was *unnecessary*. They told us this kindly, their faces close to ours, their voices low, as if acknowledging that because we were small we were inevitably subject to overwhelming and unintelligible urges. They left us without the means to submit to these urges: we were given no pocket money. Everything we needed was bought for us. Instead of presents we gave our parents homemade cards. Then, when I was older, I discovered that each parent was happy if asked to donate money so that a present could be bought for the other; and the other was happy to receive it. The sums were small, and the gifts token. My father – who inhabited a world unfamiliar to me, a world of trusty suits and polished shoes, of ignition keys and leather wallets – received key rings, comb cases, beer shampoo, wine gums. My mother received chocolates, flowers, earrings, notepaper, scarves, stockings, handkerchiefs, sachets for hanging in wardrobes, lotions for hands and elbows, and bottles of bubble bath which remain unopened but prominent in her bathroom cabinet.

'Jem, I'd better go.'
   'Yes,' he says, 'of course; but when can I call you?'
   I shrug. 'Tonight?'
   'Not tonight, I'm afraid; we're off out tonight.'

'Tomorrow?'

'Tomorrow night?'

Suddenly I realise that I should call him. 'I'll call you. Tomorrow night, after ten.'

'No, really, I'll call you.'

'Jem, that's silly, it's my turn.'

'No, I'll call you, tomorrow night, Sunday, after ten.'

I shrug once again. 'Okay; if you insist; thanks.'

'You take care of yourself in the meantime.'

I smile the small smile: 'I will.'

'And remember,' he adds, 'that I'm here if you need me; I'll be here all weekend.'

Except tonight. 'Okay,' I say; 'thanks.'

'Speak to you tomorrow, then.'

'Yes.' I am turning from the 'phone, preparing to replace the receiver, when I remember: 'Jem?'

'Yes?'

'How are you? You and Diane and Alice?'

'Oh.' He is surprised, dismissive. 'We're fine, thanks.'

There is no time for lunch today but I am sitting for ten minutes in the doctors' room with a cup of coffee and a sandwich. I am swopping duties afterwards with Vivien. She chose this morning to work in *majors*: she has been dealing with chest pains mostly, as usual. Chris and I have been in *minors*, working our way through bumps and bruises. No one likes to work all day in *minors*; so, routinely, we swop.

This morning, when I had finished speaking to Jem and begun hurrying towards Carol's office, the patient who had been waiting for me in a cubicle appeared in the corridor. His injured foot was bare, his trouser leg rolled to the knee. I had already passed the cubicle, so I looked back at him over my shoulder. He was smiling and shaking his head. 'Just checking to see if you were still around,' he explained apologetically, returning to the cubicle.

40

He turned very slowly in the doorway, his hands pressed either side of him against the doorframe.

'I'm sorry, Mr Pegrum,' I called. 'I'll be with you in a moment, I promise; I haven't forgotten you.'

'That's all right,' he said; and then he raised his head again: 'I just wondered,' he called after me, 'whether you could give me any idea how long it might take – the X-rays and everything – so that I can 'phone my son-in-law and ask him to fetch me?'

I turned to face him, stepping backwards across the tiles. I smiled brightly. 'Don't worry,' I said, 'there'll be no X-rays.'

'No X-rays?'

I had anticipated his response correctly: he was dismayed; he considered himself cheated.

'No X-rays,' I insisted, cheerfully. My backward steps became elongated.

'Why not?'

I shrugged. 'It's not broken.'

We both glanced at the foot, hanging large and red above the tiles. I began to move away.

'Doctor!'

'One minute, Mr Pegrum,' I said, prancing backwards along the corridor, 'I'll be back in one minute.'

'But how do you *know* it's not broken?'

I wanted to tell him that I have had five years of medical training and yet spend all day every day examining swollen ankles. Instead, I smiled. 'Trust me,' I said.

Now I am eating a sandwich and contemplating an afternoon in *majors* breathless and bloodless and my task is to diagnose and stabilise. Most of them arrive on trolleys: I stand over them and run my fingers across their bodies in the laying on of hands that is in fact a search for clues. I take evidence into syringes, divining for it across skin with sharp slivers of steel: blood reveals a lot by its quantity, quality and flow. This was known by the ancient anatomists who traced its circulation in vessels against the colourless tissue of corpses. Whenever I watch blood leaking into

41

syringes, I consider how it is everything that anyone has ever believed it to be: easily spilled, but regenerated; abundant, but eventually depleted; the stuff of nightmares, but also precious inside an oyster of flesh. I seal with my fingertips the wounds that I have made, and am reminded each time that it is only for the circulation of blood that a heart beats.

Blood loss in *majors* is not always invisible; not always internal, from injured and weeping organs. Nor is it always from open wounds. There are more spectacular ways of losing blood: haemoptysis and haemetemesis; coughing, and vomiting.

'*It hits the wall*,' a student nurse whispered to me, standing shocked in the corridor, recalling a quote from her textbook, directing me with a shudder towards a busy cubicle.

The aim of the Casualty officer is always the same: initial diagnosis, stabilisation, and then transfer into the care of a specialist. The specialist comes down to Casualty, distracted temporarily from ward routine. Sometimes the specialist is me, or one of the other Casualty officers, working a locum as a favour for the hard-pressed medical staffing officer.

I remember that Vivien and I were sitting in here during a quiet evening last week when she told me of a friend of hers, working in psychiatry, who is HIV antibody positive.

'And not only is he continuing to *work*,' she told me in dismay, 'but he's working for *exams*, and going for *promotion*. Can you believe that? Wouldn't you just want to leave, to give up your job, to travel or something?'

Travel: the magic word. 'Travel,' my parents say. 'With your qualifications, why don't you travel?'

They are not happy that I work in a corridor in a hospital in a seaside town in England. They are not happy that I spend Friday and Saturday nights as a spectator at drunken brawls in the waiting room; or the rest of my time between the legs of miscarrying women, easing rejected products of conception through the cervix.

'With your qualifications,' they tell me, 'you should travel.'

*

My parents travel. For them it means freedom: freedom from England, from childhood memories of pebble beaches, from rock and amusements and guest houses and rain. It means freedom from daytrippers who drift in clouds from coach parks onto the pier: the men braced in T-shirts; the women wielding pushchairs in the wind, their stiletto heels striking the pavement, their bare legs scarred by cold air, their cigarettes held between fingers like lucky charms.

My parents first travelled abroad when I was two years old, taking me with them to Spain, and since then they have travelled abroad each year; to Europe mostly, but once to the States, once to Kenya, once to Santa Lucia. When I was young we went every year to Spain and stayed in resorts like Salou and Tossa de Mar. We chose from brochures the hotels with the brightest pools and shortest walks to the beach, with babysitting facilities and flamenco evenings and coach trips to caves. I have only one memory of the early holidays, and it is of a town at night: mopeds droning in the hot, soft darkness; sunburn stinging beneath my poncho; Mum long-limbed in the street ahead of me, her heels rolling round and brown inside her sandals like chestnuts, and my father shimmering in white shirt sleeves with Verity bobbing at his side.

The holidays ended when I was nine years old and my parents bought a villa. Mum, Verity and I spent the summers thereafter in Spain, and Dad visited us each year for a week or so with a suitcase of suntan cream and a pair of sandals. Dad was a holidaymaker but Verity and I no longer had holidays; not like our classmates who went abroad each year with spending money to buy souvenirs, to eat ice cream and make friends at the airport with people from the Midlands.

The villa was on a hillside above a village; the sea five miles distant, bright but silent. It was new and whitewashed but surrounded by older buildings which had turned grey after several winters of Mediterranean rain. The residents of the older villas were mostly retired English people who drank gin and tonic during the afternoons and leaned over their balconies to ask my mother whether she might remember next year to bring them English biscuits: Peak Frean, Huntley and Palmer, Marks & Spencer; jaffa cakes, bourbons, custard creams.

From these residents we learned in time of the villagers who would mend cars for us, or plant gardens, or unblock drains. We learned of the market in the village on Fridays, and of the bus leaving daily for the coast. We learned that international telephone calls should be made in the evenings from the exchange, that bread should be ordered at the end of each week at the bakery, that the tap water was drinkable and replaceable in times of shortage with water from the spring. They told us that the village policeman was harmless, but his gun real; that the nearest hospital was without nurses, and the doctors smoked over open wounds, and the ambulance would not arrive unless you promised to pay cash for it in advance.

We had arrived at the villa, dizzy from our drive through the Pyrenees, to find it unfinished: the cooker and fridge undelivered, the bathroom untiled, the electricity supply unconnected. My parents had been assured that everything would be ready: they had received a letter saying so from Vicente.

'Ah, *Vicente,*' said a woman who was gardening in the grounds of a neighbouring villa. My father handed her the letter through the car window. She read it before handing it back with a shrug. 'You'll get no joy from Vicente,' she said.

She directed us to Vicente's office and we drove into the village to confront him, the car and roofrack edging uneasily through the narrow streets.

Vicente greeted us at his office with smiles and exclamations.

'Never mind *Buenas tardes,*' my mother said to him, stepping in front of my father; 'I have no kitchen and no bathroom and I have *niñas.*' She flapped her hand in our direction. 'What am I supposed to do with the *niñas?*' Her eyes were bright with panic.

We stared at Vicente: we were hungry *niñas,* grimy *niñas;* we had been camping for several days in France and were in desperate need of a kitchen and a bathroom.

Vicente smiled at us: 'Ah, *si,*' he said; '*si, niñas.*'

He reached across his desk and handed us lollipops. Then he turned again to my mother: '*Mañana,*' he said, with a broad smile; 'tomorrow.'

We lit candles that evening and every evening during the first week. Mum cooked on a calor gas camping stove, or served bread and biscuits; or Dad drove us to restaurants. The builders arrived in the mornings at half past seven.

'I expect you'll be ready soon,' the neighbour called to us each lunchtime from her kitchen window. Then she would raise her eyes skyward: 'They're so awfully unreliable.'

We watched her through a veil of insects.

'Wet cement attracts flies,' she explained to us one day, flapping them from her face as she walked with her dog below our balcony; 'but I expect that things will be better for you in a year or two.'

At the end of the first week, just before my father was due to return to England, the electricity supply was connected: a man climbed into a nearby tree and looped cables through the branches.

'The burning bush,' my mother joked.

She would stand on the balcony all night during summer storms to watch the sparks fly.

The villa was unfurnished: we shopped for furniture during the first week and during subsequent years whenever Dad visited us with the car. We travelled into town in the evenings when it was cool enough for us to slide across the car seats without burning. My parents shopped for beds, bedlinen, headboards, bedside tables, a dining table, a coffee table, a patio table, rugs, chairs, armchairs, patio chairs, crockery, cutlery, bath towels, hand towels, and tea towels. Verity and I were tempted along by the prospect of ice cream: there was a visit at the end of each evening to an ice cream parlour or a bar. In the furniture shops Mum and Dad whispered together in the distant gloom, easing drawers along runners, sitting gingerly on sofas and beds, writing figures in pencil on the backs of envelopes. Verity and I sat by the door in the dark sparkle of the plate glass windows, our feet in sandals on the icy tiles, and listened to the rotation of the ceiling fans.

At the end of the first week at the villa we were able to roll up our sleeping bags and sleep on beds. Much of the rest of the furniture took longer to arrive: we did not buy a sofa for two years, but in the meantime we learned the Spanish for *washable* and *flame retardent*. Similarly we learned the Spanish for *new flavour* and *improved formula* whilst shopping every day for provisions in the village. The village shop was known as Granny's. Granny stocked tins and jars on shelves above the counter; beneath it were boxes of vegetables. Mum queued every day whilst Verity and I explored, wandering below a ceiling hung with sausages, along aisles and past the refrigerator, recognised brand names (*Tulipan*, *Lechera*, *Nocilla*, *Bimbo*). At the back of the shop there were baby clothes and baskets of espadrilles placed next to several large containers of washing powder. The containers were bright with illustrations of Maria Elenas with clean laundry and ecstatic smiles. Granny's smile was timid. She wore black, but her three granddaughters wore pink and green and painted their nails: they appeared behind the counter in the evenings with their hair washed in henna and twisted dry in towels.

Verity and I spent most of our time swimming, our arms and legs burning in the hot sunshine and icy water as we splashed about on the splintered surface of the pool. When submerged, we held our breath hot and hard against the cold dense water which sank into our ears and bubbled in our noses. When emerging, we coughed chlorine. The water dried sour-smelling on our skin, dampening and discolouring our golden hair, our pink cuticles, the whites of our eyes. Mum sat dry and brown on the poolside. Baffled by the lack of fishfingers in the shops, and dizzy with heat, she let us eat as and when we pleased: in the evenings when the sun dropped behind the hills and the sky became the colour of diamond, when our bikinis hung stiff on the washing line like dead butterflies, Verity and I would sit at the poolside and chew on small loaves of cool white bread.

*

During the second summer, when Dad had long since returned to England and the heat continued to pile heavily into the valley, I developed earache.

'I think you should see the *médico*,' said Mum, eyeing me uneasily.

For several days I had been complaining of increasing pain; now I was sitting next to her at the poolside, trailing my fingers in the water and then pressing a cooled hand to my ear.

'Why?' I asked her. Usually we visited the *pharmacia*: the *pharmacia* was bright and cold with chrome and air-conditioning; it was my favourite shop. It stocked everything we had ever needed for our ailments (eye drops, cough mixture, rash cream). 'Why the *médico*? Why not the *pharmacia*?'

She sighed impatiently. 'Earache is different.'

'Why?'

She looked away from me with a shrug. 'More serious.'

I was surprised. 'Why?'

'Because it *is*.' She did not look at me.

'Why?'

She sighed again, irritated. 'Elizabeth . . .'

'Why?'

'Mastoids.' She stared hard at the hills.

'Mastoids?'

She did not move.

'What's mastoids?'

She continued to stare at the hills.

'Mum?'

She turned suddenly towards me. 'Elizabeth,' she said, angrily, her face flushed, 'you can *die* of mastoids.' She turned abruptly back to the hills.

I pressed harder with my hand against my ear. She lowered her eyes.

'Mum?'

She began to bite her nails. I left her and went to my bedroom.

The next day we went to the *médico*. Mum had discovered the surgery hours from a neighbour. As we walked towards the village she seemed more cheerful: 'I'm sure it's not a mastoid,' she said to me, smiling. 'You seem much better today; I'm sure it's not a mastoid; mastoids are very serious; you can die of a mastoid.'

We walked to the old school and then across the deserted playground in the direction indicated by the signpost. We were directed to a small room in which several elderly women sat together on a bench. They nodded greetings to us, unsmiling, and made room for us at the end of the bench before continuing to talk together in bitter voices. They fanned themselves with health certificates.

We waited for about an hour before seeing the doctor. He looked up at us briefly when we entered his room, and indicated to us with a flick of his wrist that we should sit on the two chairs in front of his desk. He was writing notes. Our doctor at home usually wrote notes long after we entered his room and sometimes even looked out of the window whilst mumbling strange medical words. Mum sat on one of the chairs, hauling Verity onto her lap, and I sat on the other. The Spanish doctor continued writing, his head bent low over his desk, his bald patch visible. He was not at all as I had imagined him: he was not tall and dark; he was short and red haired. Our doctor at home was also short and red haired.

Our doctor at home began each consultation by saying, 'And what can I do for you today?' to serve as a reminder that he could do just as he pleased: his patients had neither the knowledge nor the power to demand otherwise. This Spanish doctor slapped his pen onto the desk and stared at my mother. He said nothing because he knew that she was foreign.

'*Buenos tardes, Señor,*' she began falteringly; '*habla inglés?*'

'*Français,*' he said, rapidly. He picked up his pen. '*Peu,*' he added, spitting this word across the desk with such ferocity that for a moment I forgot the mastoid and stifled a giggle. Verity looked across at me, delighted. Mum did not flinch. '*Bon,*' she said.

Mum's knowledge of French used to fascinate Verity and me,

48

and we would beg her to say some until she obliged and pranced before us, reciting: *Bonjour, Monsieur, comment allez vous? Je vais bien, merci; je m'appelle Marie; j'habite à Londres; aujourd'hui, il fait beau*. She used to sing for us, too: *Alouette, gentille alouette, alouette, je te plumerai*. One day we asked her what the song meant and she fixed her gaze on the ceiling and thought carefully in an effort to translate: *Lark, kind lark, lark, I'm going to pluck you*. She looked down to find us staring at her: 'You're kidding,' said Verity in disgust. It was never sung again.

'*Mal à la oreille*,' said Mum to the doctor, pointing at my ear.

He sighed and lifted an instrument from his top drawer. He leaned across the desk and stuck the instrument into my ear. Peering into it, he sighed again: '*Piscine*,' he said, shrugging and withdrawing.

'Swimming pool,' Mum said to me, triumphantly. 'All that swimming has given you an ear infection.'

The *médico* sent us to the *pharmacia* with instructions to buy antibiotic eardrops; and thus I endured a week of lying prone three times each day with my face turned into my pillow whilst the drops slithered towards my eardrum. For several days I was not allowed to swim at all; and thereafter only when my mother had skewered cotton wool into my ears with her long fingernails.

There was never any swimming at Christmas. Spain at Christmas is cold; although not cold enough for snow. I hated the Christmases I spent every year in Spain: Christmases without snow, without parties, without friends and 'phone calls and marzipan and *Morecambe and Wise*. I hated Christmases spent on a sunless balcony with my father in sandals and my mother chatting to us in Spanish. *Como está usted? muy bien, gracias*.

1979, SPAIN

I am sitting at the top of the steps. Below me, at the foot of the valley, beyond miles of orange and grapefruit trees, is the sea: blue beneath a colourless sky. Verity is sitting beside me on the balcony in a deckchair, staring at the hills. She is holding a cup of milky tea. Occasionally she sips it, her nose touching the tea-bag which floats below the surface. My tea, black and weak, is in a glass beside me on the tiles.

Mum steps out onto the balcony. She glances at Verity's tea, and then at mine. She regards neither as normal. Her own tea, which she carries before her in a mug, is normal; the colour of caramel. She glances over the balcony into the valley. The village is quiet.

'It's cemetery day today,' she reminds us, brightly.

The village cemetery is open to the public on Sunday afternoons.

'All those lovely names,' she says, gazing at the village, recalling headstones: 'Jesus, Conception . . .'

Verity's eyes slip towards her. 'I'm not coming,' she says.

'Not coming?' Mum turns to her, frowning.

Verity returns her eyes to the hills. I raise my glass to my lips and drink.

'Why not?'

Verity shrugs. She cannot pretend that there is anything for her to do here at the villa this afternoon: it is December: it is impossible to sunbathe.

'Verity,' Mum urges, 'think of all the lovely names . . .'

Verity closes her eyes. 'I'm not interested,' she says.

I stare at the bottom of my upturned glass: weak, milkless tea streams towards me.

'Well, that's typical, isn't it,' says Mum.

Verity does not reply. I replace my glass on the tiles. Perhaps Carrie will finish her lunch; perhaps she will come out onto the balcony with her doll in national costume and ask me to play flamenco dancers; and then I can take her into my bedroom and sit her beside me on the bed whilst I flick through Verity's *Seventeen*.

'Absolutely typical.' Mum has turned towards the sea. 'You've no interest in anything.'

Verity's eyes are open again, her eyeballs like clear glass marbles embedded with a twist of colour.

'I gave you lovely names,' Mum continues, 'and you have never appreciated them.' *Verity Colette Sophia Eve. Elizabeth Alexandra Eugenia Delilah.* 'Romantic names,' she adds, 'strong names.'

She turns from the sea to face us. I know that she will now attempt to justify her choice of my apparently ordinary first name. 'Elizabeth,' she begins, with a frown, 'is a strong name, an old name, a rich name; a very *unusual* name – an unusual *sort of* name – if you think about it.' She pauses to think about it, examining her nails. 'It was popularised by Elizabeth the First,' she adds, dropping her hands to her sides. She turns to Verity. 'Elizabeth the First,' she hisses, 'was our greatest Queen.' Verity fails History each year.

'Elizabeth the First,' Verity replies, quietly and confidently, 'was a lesbian.'

*

I turn the glass in my hands. It is almost empty. The dregs are thick with tea leaves.

Mum raps her mug onto the top of the balcony wall. 'No, she wasn't,' she says loudly.

I look up at her, spilling my tea. She is glaring at Verity. Her hands, behind her, are gripping the balcony wall.

'Yes, she was,' replies Verity calmly.

'No, she wasn't.'

'Yes, she was.'

I look in vain towards the door for Carrie.

Verity sighs: 'Lizzie the Lezzie,' she mutters.

Why is Verity behaving like this? It can't be sunstroke; there is no sun. She once had sunstroke at the Brownie summer fayre and called Mrs Owen a tart.

'Verity. . .' Mum's tone is threatening.

Verity shrugs. 'It's true,' she says: 'disprove it.' She closes her eyes and tilts her face towards the sunless sky.

Mum turns in exasperation towards the door. 'Paul!' she calls, 'Paul!'

Dad appears almost immediately in the doorway. He holds a teaspoon from which yoghurt drips onto his feet. He thrusts the teaspoon towards Mum. 'Carrie says she doesn't like yoghurt,' he says, scowling.

Mum frowns. 'Never mind Carrie,' she says, 'and of course she likes it; tell her it's good for her.' She turns from him to Verity. 'And tell Verity. . .'

Dad also turns to Verity. 'Verity.'

'What?' asks Verity, without opening her eyes.

'Don't give me *what*. Just stop it.'

'Stop what?'

'Stop whatever it is that you're doing.'

He turns again towards the door. I decide to follow him and to offer to feed Carrie; I will spread the remaining yoghurt around her bowl so that it appears to have been eaten, or I will bribe her with sugared almonds. I stand, picking up my glass, but Verity opens her eyes and leans forward in her deckchair: she has something else to say.

'I was only saying,' she calls cheerfully to Dad as he reaches the door, 'that Elizabeth the First was a lesbian.'

Dad freezes. So do I. Mum purses her lips, folds her arms, and looks at Dad. So do I. He turns very slowly in the doorway.

Verity shrugs again and leans back into the deckchair. 'We did it in History,' she says.

This is a lie. Verity and I are both taught History by Mr Murray, and he has never said anything about Elizabeth the First being a lesbian; and, besides, Verity has not yet studied the Tudors.

Dad stares at her. 'Don't use words that you don't understand,' he says.

Verity catapults forward, eager to protest. 'But I do.'

Mum steps towards her. 'You understand nothing,' she says quietly into Verity's face, 'because you're just a silly little girl.'

Dad turns again towards the door. 'That's right,' he says, loudly; 'and she can stay here alone this afternoon as she obviously can't behave herself.'

Mum straightens and glances over her shoulder at him. She watches him step away through the doorway, and then bends closer to Verity: 'Lesbian or no lesbian,' she spits at her, 'Elizabeth was a better queen than you'll ever be.'

Then she unfolds her arms and follows Dad from the patio. 'Betsy,' she calls to me as she leaves, 'are you coming?'

I look at Verity. Verity looks at the hills. In her hands is her teacup: the tea undrunk, the teabag bloated beneath the surface. Her eyes are open but sore with uncried tears.

'Yes,' I say, moving away, 'I'm coming.'

✳   ✳   ✳

I am standing again at the phone at the end of the corridor: I have been trying for the past twenty minutes to find a bed for a patient. I have telephoned all the hospitals in town. I have spoken to House Physicians and Senior House Officers and tried desperately to interest them: 'I've a woman here, sixty-three. . .'

No, they told me: not appropriate, or no beds, or try again later. The SHO at the St Mary Annexe was particularly nasty; but Hazel Williams at St Botolphe's was nice and we chatted for a while, swopping news of mutual friends. Then I rang the chest ward again: 'Sorry,' said Simon, 'but we decided not to transfer our patient: so there's no bed. . .'

So I prepare to dial the hospital in the next town, but instead I dial Lilly's number. The ringing tone breathes into my ear for a few seconds and then stops.

'Yes?' answers Lilly.

We once argued about her telephone manner: I mentioned to her that I found it abrupt. *It's straightforward*, she exclaimed. *It's aggressive*, I told her. She asked me whether I would prefer *Hello-this-is-Lilly, your-friendly-answering-service, let's-talk-about-how-you're-feeling-today*. . .

As a child I had been instructed to answer the 'phone by chanting *Double-five-three-four-nine-two*.

'Lilly, it's Beth.'

Music is playing loudly in the background.

'Beth! How are you?'

'I'm at work.' I keep my voice low.

She sighs noisily: 'You poor bastard.'

'Lilly,' I say, distracted by the music, 'what are you doing?'

'Dusting,' she replies.

'No, seriously. . .'

'Seriously, I'm dusting. It's Saturday: I'm dusting; it has to be done sometime.' She pauses dramatically. 'Someone has to do it,' she adds very loudly. Rudy, her boyfriend, laughs in the background in response.

'I wish I was doing mine,' I say wistfully.

'No, you don't,' she cajoles.

'No, you're right,' I tell her, more cheerfully, 'I don't: I wish you were doing mine.'

'Anyway,' she says, 'let's not talk dusting. When can we meet?'

'That's why I'm calling: what are you doing tonight?'

'Tonight . . .?' suddenly she falters '. . . tonight I was going to Rudy's new play. . .'

'Rudy's new play?'

'Mmm.' She does not want to talk to me about Rudy's play. 'Why?' she asks me, puzzled, 'why do you want to see me tonight?'

'It doesn't matter.'

'Yes, it does,' she coaxes. 'Why?'

I shrug. 'Why not?'

'Because it's sudden. Because you're working.'

'So?'

'So you don't usually want to come out after work; not at the weekends. You work late at the weekends, don't you?'

'Until nine.'

'So, what's wrong?'

I glance behind me down the corridor. In the distance, an ambulance driver leans against the wall. He tips the liquid contents of a plastic cup down his throat. 'I can't tell you now,' I say; 'I'll tell you later. I'll call you later.'

'Tell me now.'

'No.'

'Look,' she says, lowering her voice, 'I can be at your flat by midnight. The play is in Battersea: I'll catch a train from Victoria as soon as it finishes.'

'That's ridiculous.'

She is indignant: 'No, it isn't.'

'Yes, it is.'

'No, it isn't.'

'Yes, it *is*: it's too late to be travelling alone on trains.'

She is grudgingly silent.

'I'll call you later,' I tell her.

'I'll call *you*, after the play.'

'But what about the *first night party*?' I am smirking.

'Sod the party,' she says cheerfully. 'Have you any idea how awful these theatrical types are? Have you any idea how I suffer for Rudy's art?'

I laugh quietly. 'How *is* Rudy?'

She turns away from the 'phone. 'Rudy's cool.'

I hear him laughing and calling out to me: 'Beth, baby!'

'He sends you a kiss,' she says, returning to the mouthpiece.

'Wish him luck with the play.'

'I will,' she says.

'Tonight, then,' I remind her; 'I'll speak to you tonight.'

'Are you sure you'll be okay?'

'Yes, of course.'

'Your Mum,' she adds suddenly, cheerfully. 'How's your Mum?'

I shudder.

'My *Mum*?'

'Yes, your Mum.' She continues happily. 'Is she still in love with the paper boy?'

My mother is considered a source of amusement by my friends, which puzzled me until I became used to it.

'The *paper boy*? Which paper boy?'

Suddenly we laugh and say together: '*How many paper boys are there?*'

Lilly considers for a moment: 'Jeffrey, I think.'

'Jeffrey!' I am amused. 'When did she tell you this?'

She considers again: 'The last time I spoke to her: ages ago; perhaps a year and a half ago.'

'Jeffrey is the vicar's son.'

Lilly is pleased. 'Your mother is an atheist,' she reminds me:

The Antichrist, she calls her. She regards herself as my mother's friend. She is unaware that my mother disagrees: my mother considers Lilly to be a *bad influence*.

Loud, coarse, crude, lewd, she used to say of Lilly: *unfeminine*.

'Jeffrey's *lithe*,' says Lilly.

'He's *what*?'

'He's *lithe*.' Lilly laughs wildly. Her earrings clatter against the receiver. 'That's what your Mum said: *He's lithe from all that cycling.*'

I shake with silent laughter and a sheet of paper shakes free from the bundle of notes in my hand. It glides to the floor. 'I don't believe she said that.'

Lilly's laughter becomes a cough. 'Yes, you do,' she says.

'What I believe,' I say, bending to retrieve the paper, 'is that you put her up to it.'

'Beth,' says Lilly, emphatically, 'your mother doesn't need encouragement, she needs supervision.'

I see the nursing manager approaching me along the corridor. Nursing managers used to be matrons: they were supposed to thunder through wards in stout shoes and starched linen. Nowadays nursing is supposed to be a career; and our nursing manager, young and male, specialises in *Accident and Emergency*. He walks briskly towards me in the short white gown that he wears whilst helping in the department. The gown looks like something a dentist might wear, or perhaps a straitjacket.

'I have to go,' I tell Lilly hurriedly. 'I'll speak to you tonight.'

We say goodbye, and I replace the receiver before the demented dentist reaches me.

'Dr Hamilton,' he says with a brief smile, glancing at the papers in my hand, 'my staff are concerned about the patient hyperventilating in cubicle two: he is becoming agitated and aggressive. Could you take a look for us straight away, please?'

'Right,' I mutter, sorting papers, beginning to move down the corridor.

'There is some Sparine ready,' he adds.

I look up at him, glowering: *my job, not yours.*

He turns and continues along the corridor towards his office.

'Mr Clements,' I call to him, 'I can't find a bed for Mrs O'Brien.' I follow him and thrust the papers into his hands: *your job, not mine.*

He looks startled. 'Right,' he says, awkwardly. He stares at the papers. 'Right,' he mutters, 'I'll get onto it right away.'

My mother once left me a message about the paper boy: it was on my telephone answering machine the night Jem came to collect his bike. Jem had moved out of the flat three weeks earlier; I was staying until the end of the month. That evening, he was waiting for me in the porch, when I returned from work, sitting hunched in darkness on the floor, sheltering from the drizzle.

'You made me jump,' I said.

'Sorry,' he replied, standing, blowing warm breath onto his hands.

'Why didn't you let yourself in?'

He still had a key. He was still paying rent.

He shrugged, laying a hand very lightly on my shoulder, bending to kiss my cheek. 'How are you?'

'Fine.' I continued looking into my bag for my keys.

Inside, we hung our wet coats over the backs of chairs in the kitchen and Jem went into the living room.

'It's good to see you,' he said from the window. He was looking across the street. I began to fill the kettle. 'How was your day?'

'Not bad.' I turned off the tap and lifted the kettle from the sink. 'Yours?'

'Not bad.'

I plugged the kettle into the wall and flicked the switch. 'You must be freezing.'

'I'm fine,' he said. He was now at the unlit fireplace, running his fingertips along the mantelpiece. He raised his eyes and smiled faintly. 'Darren Donovan split his head open today on the corner of a desk.'

I wrinkled my nose: 'Yuk.' I turned and reached into the cupboard above my head for two cups.

'Five stitches.'

'And a lot of tears?' I reached onto the top shelf for the teabags.

'And a lot of tears.'

I dropped a teabag into each cup and then turned to lean back against the table. The kettle began to whine and rattle. Jem walked towards me into the hallway and stopped at the answering machine. Glancing at the message indicator, he pressed the rewind button. The tape rushed noisily from one spool to the other. Then, suddenly, he withdrew his finger and the tape stopped. 'Beth,' he said, horrified, pressing his hand against his forehead. 'I'm sorry; I wasn't thinking.' He had forgotten that the messages would not be for him.

I shrugged. 'It's okay, I need to hear them.' I reached behind me for the kettle. 'You can take it with you when you go.'

He raised his head and stared at me. 'What? This?' He tapped the machine.

'Yes.' I turned and lifted the kettle, pouring boiling water into the cups.

'Why?' he asked.

'Why not?'

'But you need it more than I do: you're the one who's never at home.'

I replaced the kettle on the table. 'No, but I'm always at work. Everyone knows where I am.'

Jem pressed the play button.

I came into the hallway and handed him a cup of tea.

'Lizzie?' My mother's voice crackled from the machine.

We stood in anticipation by the 'phone.

'Lizzie, this is. . .'

She paused and then started again. 'Hello. The paper boy has an abscess.'

59

Jem and I exchanged amused glances.

'On his BCG.' There was a further pause. 'Carrie is due to have her BCG next week.' There was the sound of the receiver being replaced.

We giggled.

I tried to steady my cup. 'I think she wants advice,' I explained.

His face folded into a smile. 'It sounds as if she needs it.'

There were no more messages so we went together into the living room and I switched on the lamp and drew the curtains. Jem sat on the sofa and I sat opposite him in the armchair.

'How is she?' he asked, placing his cup on the floor at his feet and leaning back against the cushions.

'Who? Mum?' I cradled my cup in my hands. I shrugged. 'She's okay.' Then I remembered. 'But it's almost November.' I grinned.

He ran his fingers through his damp, dark hair. 'So?'

'Almost Remembrance Day.' I sipped my tea. 'On Remembrance Day she goes to church, to the Scout and Guide service – to Carrie's this year, mine and Verity's in the past – and she *becomes emotional.*'

He frowned: '*Becomes emotional?*'

'Causes a scene.'

His frown began to lift. 'What kind of a scene?' He looked down and reached towards his feet for his cup.

'Oh, you know: *millions of young men were sent unnecessarily to their deaths. . .*'

'Yes,' he raised his head, levelled his eyes with mine, 'but to whom?'

I shrugged. 'To Hitler, I suppose.'

'No,' he laughed, leaning back, his hair rubbed against the cushions, 'to whom does she say it?'

'Oh . . .' I crossed my legs, 'the vicar . . . the Guides, the Brownies . . . everyone.'

He laughed again. 'How?'

'What?'

'How? I mean, *aloud*?'

I laughed with him. 'How else can someone say something?'

'Beth,' he insisted with impatience, 'does she *disrupt* the service?'

'No, of course not. The vicar *would never forgive her*. She waits until everyone is *unsuspecting* on the village green.'

Laughing, he swallowed a mouthful of tea with difficulty. 'Lilly says that your Mum has taken to wearing Carrie's old National Health specs.'

I folded my legs beneath me in the chair. 'When did you see Lilly?'

'When did I see Lilly?' He shrugged. 'It was half term last week. We met for a drink. Anyway, she says that your Mum is borrowing Carrie's specs.' He smiles. 'They must be rather small for her: Carrie can't have worn them since she was . . . what.?'

'Five.' I balanced my cup beside me on the arm of the chair.

'Five.' He is delighted. His gaze flicked around the room.

'But did Lilly tell you *why*?'

He raised his cup. 'No?' He took another mouthful of tea.

'It's because Mum drove over her own pair.'

'Drove over them?' He lowered the cup to his lap. 'How can anyone *drive over* their glasses?' His eyes were small and bright inside his smile. 'Sit on them, yes,' he said; 'tread on them; stamp on them, perhaps; but drive over them? How? Why?'

'I don't know, she didn't say.'

'She doesn't drive,' he protested. He paused and looked down into his cup. 'Evidently not,' he said to himself, quietly, with another smile.

When I applied for a place at medical school, my mother peered over my shoulder at the application form.

'*Distinguishing marks: none*,' she chanted.

Distracted, I lifted my pen and glanced down the form: there was no mention of distinguishing marks; she had been joking. I lowered my pen again onto the paper.

She peered closer. '*Sex,*' she quoted. She laughed loudly. 'Not yet, eh, Lizzie?' she said, tapping my shoulder. 'Tell them *not yet*, eh, Liz?' Laughing, she left the room in search of my father. I heard her calling to him in the hallway, eager to share the joke: *Hey, Paul; hey!* Over the next week she told her joke to everyone we met.

Not in my house, my father used to threaten me, suspecting corruption and decadence. He imagined that in his absence I would smoke, drink, and watch late night films. He was wrong: I did not smoke; I rarely drank (and not at home, and never to excess); and I liked to be asleep by midnight. He did not mention sex. I was having sex with Kieran, my boyfriend, in the afternoons; lying with him on his bed in the warm air that drifted through the window from the garden when the cool evening shadows began to press across the lawn.

Kieran's room was the smallest in the house, the most sparse, a boy's bedroom. On the floor there were training shoes and a few pellets of rolled sock. On the wall above the bed there were two shelves stacked with books: slim paperbacks of modern fiction; an economics textbook with a cover photograph of a cascade of coins; a treasured lemon *Wisden*. On the bedside table there was a Mickey Mouse alarm clock. Mickey was old and unreliable, stiff and ungainly, balancing on the clockface with outstretched arms. At the base of the alarm clock there were aspirins wrapped individually in foil and scattered like pieces of silver; and a tube of deep heat ointment, and an unwound bandage: the detritus of rugby matches.

His parents referred to rugby as his *first love*.

We were alone together each day after school until half past five. At half past five his mother arrived home from the local library where she was the part-time assistant librarian. We were alone together after a day of lessons, assembly and register, form

62

meetings and house meetings, duties, rotas, assignments. I could slip free from my clothes. The clothes were an adaptation of the *regulations for sixth formers*: the dark blue *knee-length* skirt that was a tight band around my legs; the *flesh-coloured* nylons that were dewy pale or inky black; the *low-heeled* shoes that were stilettos. For an hour each day my clothes lay scattered like posies on Kieran's bedroom floor.

We lay together on the soft mother-laundered sheet. Fine hair glimmered on Kieran's forearms like a sprinkle of brown sugar. His mouth was peppermint flavoured. He slipped easily into me; it surprised me each time how easily he slipped into me. I eased him gently inside me and held him tightly so that he did not slip away as we rocked together on the rippling sheet. Afterwards, we dozed; literally, we slept together. It was our secret, not to be guessed by others from the way we kissed lightly when meeting or parting. It was a secret, but surely it was not wrong; how could it have been wrong? Childhood friends, adolescent lovers: our lovemaking had nothing to do with envy, despair, violence, apathy, or greed. It will perhaps never be so easy or so pleasurable for me again.

No-one explains to girls about sex. Girls are told about conception and contraception; boys are told about wet dreams and erections. Boys are reassured that size is irrelevant. No-one reassures girls. Size is relevant for girls, too: I worried secretly for years that *it wouldn't fit*.

Mrs Pincott, our Biology teacher, once mistakenly described the average contraceptive diaphragm as having a diameter of eight kilometres.

'Centimetres,' corrected Lilly, absently, beside me.

'*Lilly . . .*' snapped Mrs Pincott, craning over the benches, aware that Lilly had spoken but unaware of her own mistake. Like many teachers, Mrs Pincott welcomed any opportunity to berate Lilly.

'But . . .'

'Lilly! Don't answer back!'

As soon as Mrs Pincott was busy with condoms, Lilly turned

to me: 'Can you imagine going to the clinic,' she whispered, 'and being fitted with a cap eight kilometres wide and *not answering back*?'

Kieran was not my first lover: loss of virginity is a traumatic event for a girl so she chooses someone with experience. I chose Patrick. Patrick was in the upper sixth form when I was in the fifth. He was everyone's favourite sixth former. He was Deputy Head Boy, not Head Boy: Head Boy was an authoritarian position, and Patrick was not authoritarian. Patrick appeared on stage each day at the end of assembly to read the notices. ('Members of the orchestra are reminded that today's rehearsal has been postponed until Friday; the science building will be out of bounds this afternoon and alternative arrangements are posted on the notice-board in the hall; applications forms for places on the ski trip are now available from Mr Rintoul.') He stood nervously at the lectern, shuffling papers, smiling shyly at any unintended humour. He was gangly in his blazer and his hair curled slightly on his collar. Many of the notices were relevant to him: he supervised Junior Chess Club at lunchtimes, and Junior Drama Club after school, and Sailing Club on Saturday afternoons; he was a member of the rugby and cricket teams, and of the brass band. At House Meetings it was his responsibility to thank everyone at the end of term for their efforts, and to present any departing members of staff with a gift. Whenever he was on tuck shop duty the sales of chocolate and crisps increased threefold.

His long-term relationship with Rachel Harding, Head Girl, had recently ended, distressing the older members of staff who regarded it as an institution. He described it to me as a *mutual separation*. When they passed each other in the corridors they smiled and raised hands or exchanged greetings. He referred to her as Rache. She called him Pat. She would call to him down the corridor, causing the crowd of attendant fifth form girls to ripple uneasily around him: Pat, can you check the common room tea money this afternoon? Pat, could you take Orienteering Club for me today? Pat, we've got the squash court booked for half past three. She had to call out to him because he was always pinned against the wall by fifth form girls whilst she jogged along corridors. She wore short skirts, T-shirts, and snowy sweat bands: she was permanently dressed for games. She was more stunning in games kit than in school uniform, so she ensured that there was always a game or a match for her to play. She reminded me of the characters in advertisements for tampons: active, energetic, hygienic. In the evenings she was meeting one of the teachers, but no one was supposed to know: Mr Rintoul, Metalwork and Woodwork.

Often during Patrick's last summer at school I found him ambling in the corridors in cricket whites, drunk on sunshine, sweet with grass stains. Sometimes we sat chatting together on the field. After the end of term we met with others in the evenings at the local pub, sitting outside at the wooden picnic tables, cars swinging past us into the car park. He was waiting, with the others, for A level results. He was hoping to go to University in Swansea to read Geography. During the day he worked at a local market garden, packaging vegetables, and in the evenings he drove his mother's car to the pub. I was waiting for O level results.

At the pub I drank fruit juices, bright orange and yellow fluid dropping from small bottles into my glass.

'You, Kiddiwinkle, are too young to drink,' Patrick would remind me, buying me another.

He and his friends were eighteen. Rachel rarely joined them. 'It's different for Rachel,' Patrick explained to me whenever we watched her arriving late, flushed and apologetic, hurriedly easing her small purse from her pocket: she had decided to return to school in the autumn to study for the Oxbridge entrance exams. There was a joke muttered among Patrick's friends when he was absent: 'I didn't know they offered Metalwork and Woodwork at Oxford.'

BMW, they called her: *Bachelor of Metalwork and Woodwork*.

In August, Patrick discovered that his exam results were acceptable to Swansea: two Bs and a C.

'The world's your oyster when you've got two Bs and a C,' his friends teased.

Patrick was thrilled. Packing courgettes was suddenly less arduous. He whistled to himself when he gave me lifts home in the evenings. I was still nervously awaiting my O level results. I had been told that they would be the vital factor in the decision of a medical school to offer me a place.

'Why don't we go back to your house for coffee?' I asked him as we walked together across the car park towards the car after celebrating my O level results. He had bought me three Bloody Marys during the course of the evening: *vitamin C*, we had agreed, laughing and tipping the tomato juice from the bottle into my glass; *vitamin K*, I had corrected. He touched my arm, guiding me gently past a pothole. The car park was poorly lit.

'Are you sure?' he asked.

He was surprised. He knew that I knew that his parents were away. He knew what was expected of him.

'Are you sure that you want to do this?' he asked me later, lying on top of me in the hot darkness of his bedroom. He had lifted his lips momentarily from mine. In the darkness he was looking closely at me. He was giving me a chance to say no.

I paused so that I could listen to his breathing. There was never any doubt on my part. We slept together once more before the end of the week, and once again a week later. Then his parents returned from Ibiza, and eventually he left home for Swansea.

I liked Patrick very much but I was not in love with him. I was already in love with Kieran. Kieran had begun picking flowers for me from the school caretaker's garden and performing the corniest *Doctor-Hamilton-will-you-cure-my-broken-heart* bended-knee pleas in the classroom. He was an old friend who had always enjoyed complaining to me about his girlfriends: quiet Kate, faithless Fadia, disinterested Deborah. I felt differently about him from the moment that he interrupted a conversation between the Headmaster and the local MP at Speech Day to insist that nuclear power was 'not a feasible option'. I was impressed when he eschewed his traditional allegiance to the Labour Party so that he could stand as the Ecology candidate in the school elections under the slogan *Kieran Grace walks on water*. One day, when he staggered injured from the rugby field, snorting on his gum shield, I took his cut and bruised head in my hands; and one night soon afterwards I surprised him not in a pub car park but at the school bus stop, and not with a proposition but a kiss.

I conducted my affair with Patrick with pretence. He behaved accordingly, expecting nothing. But nevertheless he telephoned me each day for a chat; and I sat cross-legged on the floor with the receiver in my hands, laughing at his jokes until I cried. He called me on the morning that he left for Swansea.

'Who was that?' asked Kieran when I reappeared in the kitchen. He ceased jiggling Carrie on his knee.

'Patrick,' I replied. I do not like to lie.

'Oh,' he said. He resumed jiggling Carrie.

Over the next few years Patrick and I met among friends at the pub on several occasions, usually on Christmas Eve.

There was no mystery about Patrick; or, rather, the only mystery about him was Rachel. I found it difficult to imagine him with Rachel. Later I realised that for other people the mystery about Patrick was *me*. When they saw us together on Christmas Eve, sharing memories, they wondered, as I have sometimes wondered about others, whether or not we had ever shared anything else. Lilly knew, of course. Kieran never asked: girls mature faster than boys, and boys who go out with girls their own age are careful not to ask questions. Kieran and I did not sleep together until after several months of sofa seductions whilst babysitting on Saturday nights. We slept together after he had passed his driving test. We celebrated with an orange juice at the pub, and then drove to his house. His parents were in London at a dinner party. I did not need to catch the last bus home. I knew that he was a virgin. There was nothing as tangible as a hymen; but inexperience is obvious.

The first time I had sex, penetration was not as painful as I had anticipated. I was punctured, not torn. It was bloodless. If I had waited until marriage I would have waited in vain: I would have been found guilty of promiscuity on the evidence of lack of blood. There was one sharp pain at the time and nothing more. Eventually, with Kieran, there were other pains: candiasis, vaginitis, cystitis. Soft young tissue bruises easily: it swells and splits and becomes infected. I have heard cystitis called honeymoon disease. I was lucky to escape the pain of abortion. The unspoken fears of my parents were founded: I was taking risks. Lying on Kieran's bed in the afternoons, tense with the prospect of pleasure, I would trust to the power of his whispered incantation: 'I'll be careful, I promise I'll be careful.'

My parents were determined that I should not have sex before marriage. They impressed this upon me when I was young, when sex was the subject of *sex education*. I could not imagine at the time that I would ever be at all interested in sex: eggs and sperm. My mother was anxious that someone would *take advantage* of me. My father wanted me to *save myself*. *Save yourself for your wedding night*, he used to say; but I used to worry that I would have other things to think about on my wedding night: the buffet, the going away outfit, the honeymoon. My parents never had going away outfits or a honeymoon. They married when they were both nineteen: they left school and started work, they married and started a family. By the time I was sixteen I had realised that if I wanted to wait for sex until marriage, I would have to wait for a long time.

My parents have always been disparaging about *nowadays*. I have had to resist an urge to tell them that people have been having sex for centuries. They were worried at one time about *unwanted pregnancy*. I want to tell them that a pregnancy can be unwanted within marriage or otherwise. A pregnancy would have been unwanted by me at seventeen, but it would have been equally unwanted when I was living with Jem, and equally unwanted now. At the time I said nothing because I did not want them to know where I was going in the afternoons and evenings or what I was doing. When I returned home after school each day or at the end of the evening, they regarded me with suspicion. I stood across the kitchen from them in silence, making my cup of tea or cocoa, eager to escape upstairs to my bedroom, worrying whether my clothes were mistakenly inside out or back-to-front and whether the buttons were unfastened or fastened incorrectly. I worried that their silence would precede questions. I wanted to avoid questions. I was desperate to escape detection. Be careful, Lilly had warned me: but how?

It was Verity who finally ended the secrecy.

I had come home from college to revise for my first year exams: I was following the example set by my friends who were enthusiastic about returning home for the week prior to the exams for *peace and quiet*. This had not so far been my experience of home. That afternoon, however, was unusually subdued: I was alone upstairs in my bedroom, reading my notes on respiration and quietly chanting formulae. Verity, who was at home during the day when not sitting O levels, had spent the afternoon downstairs playing records: three-minute bursts of American rap, of New York City street-strutting bravado. Now Carrie was home, and there was a distant babble of television voices: puppets and Australian soap opera stars. My bedroom windows were wide open. The garden was hazy beyond net curtains. Below me in the kitchen there was an occasional rustle that was sometimes more precisely identifiable as the shuffle of bare feet on tiles, the thud of the fridge door, the sharp hiss of the cold water tap, the pop of the biscuit tin lid. In the neighbouring garden there was a conversation, the words wriggling uncomfortably from Mrs Westler's plummy mouth.

Suddenly, downstairs, my mother shrieked: 'Bette!' There was a note of alarm in her voice; she was requesting assistance.

I closed my folder of notes; I stood up at my desk and walked from my bedroom into the hallway. 'What?'

'Bette!' It came back to me like an echo.

I stepped onto the stairs. 'What?' I began to move rapidly but steadily down the staircase.

She called out again, revealing to me that she was in the kitchen.

I pushed open the kitchen door. Mum and Verity were sitting in opposite corners of the room. They turned from each other to face me. They were glowering. Verity folded her arms across her chest. I wondered whether she was seeking a confrontation with me.

Mum sighed wearily. 'Libby,' she explained, 'your sister –' she spat the word across the room '– has announced that she wants to go on the pill.'

Heavy periods, I thought: Verity wants the pill to alleviate heavy periods. It was obvious, however, that this was not the case: Verity's eyes, focused on mine, were burning with the reflection of the flush of triumph in her face. The argument was not about the pill, but about sex. I found it difficult to imagine that Verity had anything to do with sex. I tended to think of her as an immaculate conception become less immaculate with the passage of time. I reminded myself that she was sixteen, and that she had a boyfriend: Terry came to the house on Saturday evenings and sat braced on the edge of the sofa, knees apart, clearing his throat by ejecting his bulky Adam's apple higher into his long skinny neck. He wore bright white socks tucked into bright black shoes: small areas of black and white smooth and bright side by side like onyx eggs.

Why had Verity raised the subject? Why had she not sneaked to the Family Planning clinic for a prescription? What did she hope to achieve by attempting to discuss it with Mum? Did she intend me to be her ally or her foe? I wondered whether she was pleased with the response: it was something that she could not have failed to anticipate. She gave nothing away; her arms remained folded. I looked reluctantly at Mum. Mum was pleading silently with me. I wondered whether she wanted me to offer filial support or medical advice.

'Oh,' I said.

'"Oh"? Is that all you can say?' Mum was horrified.

I was supposed to have expressed dismay.

Verity protested quietly: 'It's *my* life. . . .'

Mum turned on her. 'It's *not* your life. You're too young to make decisions, you're still my responsibility. It's *my* life, and I don't want it ruined by a pregnant sixteen-year-old daughter.'

Verity's eyebrows fluttered to the top of her brow. 'There's no need for me to get pregnant,' she said indignantly.

'There's no need for any of it,' snapped Mum. Then she sighed, and sagged. 'I never needed to do anything like this when I was sixteen,' she mumbled grudgingly.

'No,' flashed Verity, 'but you wanted to.' She smiled briefly and stroked her spidery fingers through her hair.

Mum snarled at her: 'Don't tell me what I wanted, Verity. At sixteen I didn't know the first thing about anything.'

Verity's smile slid further across her face, revealing rows of milky teeth: 'Ignorance!' she exclaimed, delighted. Mum hates ignorance: it is something of which she regularly accuses Verity.

Mum pursed her lips. '*Ignorance*, Verity, is sometimes *bliss*: there is a time and place for everything, including knowledge.'

Verity spoke rapidly: 'But you were old enough at sixteen to know that you wanted to marry Dad.'

Mum raised her voice: 'Forget *me* . . .'

Verity shrugged. 'That's what I'm trying to do.' She looked away, staring through the window into the garden.

I closed the kitchen door.

71

Mum turned to me, eager to continue the argument. '"Oh?"' she repeated with sarcasm; '"Oh?" is that all you can say?' She folded her arms. 'Are you going to train for another four years just so that you can dole out pills to anyone who asks for them?'

I crossed the room to the kettle. 'I wouldn't *dole out pills*,' I said quietly.

'Oh no?' She twisted in her chair, following me with her indignant gaze. 'Oh no? Well, what *would* you do?'

I shrugged. I lifted the kettle into the sink and held it beneath the tap. 'I'd help her to make a decision, I suppose.' I was disinterested; I had no ambition to become a GP, especially not Verity's GP.

'Oh,' said Mum, almost speechless with delight, 'oh, so *that*'s what they teach you at your college!' She turned again in her chair, tracking my path from the sink to the worktop. 'Well, let me tell you that you won't find the answer to this problem in any of your textbooks.'

I plugged the kettle into the wall and flicked the switch.

'Let me tell you,' she continued, 'that there's no point in studying for all those exams if you can't deal with a situation like this: medicine, medicine, medicine, but what about common sense?'

The kettle spluttered and steam rose from the spout.

'The decision is a simple one,' she concluded; 'the decision is *no*.'

I looked at Verity. She was staring through the window.

I turned my attention back to Mum. 'But isn't it better to acknowledge. . .'

'There shouldn't be any need to *acknowledge*,' she rejoined. 'There shouldn't be anything *to* acknowledge. She's a *child*.'

'But if there was something to acknowledge, wouldn't it be sensible for her to know about the pill?'

'Go ahead, then.' Mum gesticulated grandly towards Verity. 'Tell madam about the pill.'

Verity was positioned in the corner of the room like a pink

fibreglass sculpture. I realised that I knew very little about the pill. Suddenly Verity turned, her eyes as dull as nickel coins. 'I know about the pill,' she said flatly.

'Oh, I bet you do,' interjected Mum gleefully, 'and you know about thrombosis, do you? And cervical cancer, do you?' She stared at Verity with wide eyes. 'Do you, Verity? Do you know about those things?'

Verity sighed wearily. 'Mum . . .'

'Don't "Mum" me.'

When Dad arrived home at the end of the afternoon she told him everything.

'Verity,' he said, striding from the kitchen into the living room, 'you cannot be trusted.' He crossed the room to the television and lunged at the controls: the soundtrack faded; cartoon characters chased across the screen in silence. 'You will not be treated like an adult in this house until you prove that you can act like one.'

Verity tilted her face towards him. 'That's not fair,' she replied petulantly.

'Not fair? Not fair?' he brayed excitedly.

Carrie transferred her attention to him, lifting her eyes from the screen and twisting round in her armchair; her tiny red shoes dangling like a pair of cherries.

'It seems perfectly fair to me.' He took a step towards Verity: 'How exactly is it not fair?' he challenged.

Her words failed her. She opened and closed her mouth several times, watched intently by Carrie.

'It's *Catch 22*,' I said.

I am no longer in love with Kieran Grace: my parents were right; it did not last. I have not seen him since I was twenty.

Better to have loved and lost than never to have loved at all: this is what my parents believe on Christmas Eve when they sit

73

together on the sofa watching *West Side Story*; when they watch Natalie Wood stepping away from the body of her dead lover. *The course of true love never did run smooth*, and especially not for Natalie; but *innocence lost is experience gained*, and Natalie gained. She loved. And I loved. I loved Kieran for two years. And he loved me, he must have loved me, because he made me happier during those two years than I have ever been.

I might have married him. And I might have divorced him. Instead, I went to medical school.

He did not want to go to university. His sister, Jacinta, was at Oxford.

'If Jacinta can do it,' his parents admonished him, 'and Elizabeth, too, then why can't you?'

Jacinta was reading PPE: Philosophy, Politics, and Economics. Kieran's interest was Economics.

'I want to work in the City,' he would tell them angrily, 'not sit around for three years in Oxford.'

He told my parents that he was *impatient*, and seeking *hands-on experience*: an unfortunate expression, I thought.

'I want to be a banker,' he told me, 'not a wanker.'

Lilly reminded him that the two categories were not mutually exclusive. She was baffled by his recent change of heart. He had ceased joining her in the compilation of the top ten quotes from *Macbeth* that they had begun the previous term during the bus journey home from school at the end of each afternoon. He was now claiming that literature was bourgeois. 'Bourgeois, my arse,' said Lilly.

He told Mr Allan, the Careers Master, that he did not want to spend three years cavorting around Oxford in a college scarf. Mr Allen asked him whether he was perhaps being rather short-sighted.

'No,' he replied, 'because everything is changing: there's money out there to be made and I'm going to make it.'

He applied for a job with a broker in the City. He asked me

to marry him when he heard that his application had been successful.

I last saw him four years ago. He was sitting alone in a pub in the City with a pint of beer.

'Kieran,' I called softly through the crowds, 'Kieran.'

He looked up at me, surprised, delighted, smiling his crooked smile: 'Elizabeth!' He patted the seat next to him. 'Elizabeth! Sit down! How are you? Can I buy you a drink?'

I shook my head. 'No thanks.' I indicated my group of friends across the room. It was my twentieth birthday and we were having a brief celebratory drink.

His gaze followed mine. 'Christ,' he muttered cheerfully, 'what's the student population of Britain doing in here at lunchtime?' He turned to me again with his smile. 'Don't they give you enough to do? Aren't you supposed to be saving lives?'

'Aren't you supposed to be making money?'

His smile broadened. 'I'm spending it.' He looked exactly the same as he had looked in the sixth form at school; he wore a suit and an untidy tie.

'I'm having a well-earned break. I'm escaping my minions: the new graduates come to work under me for the first six months and they drive me mad because they're bloody clueless.'

His hair was shorter than it had been at school, or perhaps better cut. It was also blonder, but discoloured on this occasion by a halo of lamplight from a brass lantern on the wall. It had always been very blond. It became blonder in sunshine. I wondered where he had been on holiday. He was telling me that he had graduated from the school rugby team to the local club and had broken his leg during his first match. 'A minor setback,' he said, laughing, lifting his trouser leg to show me a scar. 'Pins or plates or whatever,' he said: 'I *rattle*.' Then he told me briefly about his two operations. 'And guess what? Angelina Demarco was a nurse on the ward.'

Angelina Demarco had been a year above us at school: *The Pasta Princess*, the boys had called her.

'Really?' I said. 'How was she?'

He laughed: 'Fat.' Then he bit his lip, exaggeratedly shame-faced: 'No, sorry, she wasn't *fat*, she was *a presence*.' The smile crept back again across his face. 'She slapped our wrists when Sister was around, but when Sister was gone she was wonderful. She let us get away with murder.'

I was held at the table by the weight of the crowd of drinkers behind me at the bar. Surrounded by dark grey suits, I had lost sight of my friends. 'Sit down,' Kieran was saying again, patting the seat again. He was smiling pleasantly. His crooked teeth were glinting; uneven but small and neat. I thought of *toothy-pegs*: his teeth were bright pegs of smooth ivory pressed into his gum. I realised with surprise that he was slightly drunk; I was surprised that I had not previously noticed this. 'How's your family?' I asked him. I did not sit down.

His smile widened. I thought of *eye-teeth*: his teeth were eye-catching.

'Fine, fine.' He nodded his head as he answered. 'And yours?'

'Fine.'

'Your Mum?'

'Fine.'

His eyes gleamed blue-green like petrol on tarmac: 'And the little one?'

I laughed briefly. 'Carrie's not so little now: she's almost seven.'

'Seven!' He groaned. 'I remember the day she was born. Why do I always think that she's three or four?'

'Because *time flies*.'

He laughed: he recognised this as one of the two favourite utterances of my mother; the other was *as sure as eggs*.

'Poor Carrie,' I said. 'Everyone always assumes that she's still three or four. Lilly calls her *Oskar*.'

He laughed again. 'How is Lilly? I've heard that she's living in domestic bliss.' He would have heard this from his mother, who would have heard it from Lilly's mother: both mothers were active together in the local branch of the WEA.

I laughed quietly with him. 'Lilly has always lived in domestic bliss.'

'Yes,' he said good-naturedly, 'but you know what I mean.'

'Yes,' I replied, 'I know exactly what you mean: you mean with a man.'

He frowned. 'Oh, *Elizabeth*.' The sigh was intended to be soft with sadness but instead it was full of reproach: to anyone else it might have meant *let's not argue* but to me it meant *don't start, don't start picking on me*. Exasperated, I looked away. I glanced around for my friends. I could not see them. 'Yes,' I replied absently, grudgingly.

'Who would have thought it?' He sounded pleased.

You, I thought, you would have thought it.

He told me that he was going out with Alison MacKenzie. I remember Alison MacKenzie as a little girl in the fourth form when we were in the upper sixth. She used to stand with other little girls at the entrance to the sixth form common room.

'Loitering with intent,' Lilly would claim, crashing past them through the door.

Kieran would protest: Lilly was cruel, he said; the girls were merely waiting for the key to the careers library, for the register of Junior House cross country runners, for permission to stay in a classroom at lunchtime; they were organising a fun run, finishing a project.

'Yeah, and I'm the fucking Virgin Mary,' said Lilly.

Kieran said that he was *going out* with Alison MacKenzie. He had spent most of his time with me in his *bedroom*.

He asked me whether I was involved with anyone: 'And you?'

'And me what?' I returned my attention reluctantly to him. I had been looking past padded grey shoulders for my friends: I was wondering whether Jem had arrived: he had said that he would be late; he had been at his college for the first of a series of revision seminars for finalists. 'Unlike you, you bright young thing,' he had teased, 'I can't spend all day in the pub.'

'Are you involved with anyone?'

I stared at Kieran.

'A medic?'

'No.'

'No Dr Kildare?' Kieran laughed.

'No.' I smiled and leaned towards him. 'Let me offer you some friendly advice, Kieran: never get involved with a medic; someone once told me that they have a despicable habit of leaving home for medical school.'

I watched his smile glimmer and fade.

When Alison MacKenzie was a fourth former she wore white ankle socks. Five years later, when she married Kieran, her ankles were hidden beneath a full-length ivory taffeta dress.

'It was a *traditional wedding*,' my mother told me after she had stood at the lych gate to watch the bride and groom leave the church.

When Alison MacKenzie was a fourth former her calves were as round and smooth and brown above her ankle socks as if they had been carved from wood.

1968

I am sitting on the doorstep scooping rose petals from a pile at my feet and pressing them with my fingers into empty jam jars. I collected the petals this morning from the flower beds beneath the rose bushes. I found the jars in a kitchen cupboard full of thermos flasks and jelly moulds. This afternoon I plan to add water to the jars to make rosewater.

Suddenly a dog's bark rattles on the other side of the garden fence. A neighbour admonishes the dog – 'Felix!' – and a cat lands at the top of the fence, parading briefly, tail raised, before dropping into our garden. It trots from the flower bed onto the lawn and then slinks through the grass. Mum is naked in the middle of the lawn, lying on a towel. She sighs and mutters – 'That sodding dog!' – and then stretches the arm that has been shielding her eyes from the sun. She sits upright, blinking. Her hair is stiff with sweat. She glances around the garden and then turns towards me. She draws her knees towards her chest and hugs her shins.

'It must be time for lunch,' she says. 'What do you want?'

I shrug: 'A sandwich?' I press my fingertips into a newly filled jar.

She frowns and rubs her eyes. Then she stands and walks towards me across the lawn. 'I can't remember the last time you had liver,' she mutters, frowning still.

I shift to one side so that she can pass me. She stands beside me on the step. 'I'll wake Verity when we've eaten,' she says. Verity is asleep upstairs in her cot.

I fill another jar: the eighth of ten. I place it with the others and then look up at her. She is staring across the garden, shielding her eyes with her hand. 'Perhaps we should go into town this afternoon,' she says. 'It's not good for us to hang around here all the time.' Her hand drops to her side. 'There's a play scheme run by the Council every afternoon in the park.' She steps into the kitchen. 'I picked up a leaflet at the library.'

She returns with a sheet of paper, crossing the patio and squatting on the garden steps, wearing nothing except a pair of flip-flops. She disapproves of walking barefoot in the garden: dangerous. She begins to read aloud from the sheet of paper: 'Summertime activities in the Philip Creighton Memorial Park for children aged five to twelve.' She lowers the sheet of paper: 'You're five,' she reminds me, 'so you're eligible.' She lifts the paper again and reads silently. 'Oh dear,' she says, after a while, biting her lip, 'we seem to have missed all the best things: Punch and Judy, and a magician last week, and a Treasure Hunt, a Talent Contest, some Country Dancing, and . . .' she frowns, '. . . inflatables?' She glances at me.

'Bouncy things.'

She shrugs. 'Today . . .' she says, running her finger down the list. She pauses, and places the paper beside her on the step. 'Today is Sports Day,' she admits.

An hour or so later we are sitting on the pavement, listening for the sound of the bus at the foot of the hill. Verity is parked behind us in her pushchair in the shade of the lych gate. Across the road the village shop is empty of customers. The ice cream sign hangs motionless outside the door. Terry Price and Christopher Law came out a few moments ago with ice pops, splitting the packaging with their teeth and spitting mouthfuls of polythene into the gutter. Terry Price's ice pop was red; Christopher Law's was green. Raspberry flavoured; lime.

Mum has said that I can have an ice cream in town when we have been to the library. Later. There is always an ice cream van in the park. She has said that I will not have to run in any races: A *Sports Day needs spectators*.

'The bus is late,' she says, stretching and twisting to face the clock on the church tower. 'Ten minutes late.' She turns back towards the road. Her legs are stretched across the pavement, sunlight glinting on the dark skin between the thick hem of her cotton dress and the straps of her flip-flops. She wriggles her toes and then bends her leg, leaning forward to inspect a varicose vein at the back of her knee. She traces the small, coiled rope with her fingertip; touching it very gently as if touching a bruise.

'Look at this,' she mutters sadly, turning towards Verity.

Verity stares, sunlight dropping between the slats of the roof and slicing across her face.

Mum taps the vein with her fingertip: 'You did this,' she reproves. 'I had lovely legs before you were born.'

Outside, in the library car park, cars sizzle in the sunshine. I am inside, sitting on a wooden stool in the children's corner, turning the pages of a book about hamsters. The book was on display in the rack with others: books about parrots, gem stones, travelling to Holland, baking cakes. My favourite, about pirates, with a picture of a gang plank, is not here; neither is the one about the ballerina who breaks her back and learns to dance in a wheelchair. I have chosen four others and piled them at my feet. I pass the time with the hamsters whilst waiting for Mum.

Suddenly Mum is across the room at the counter: 'Busy Lizzy,' she calls softly to me, 'are you ready?'

I nod, slipping from the stool and slotting the hamsters back into the rack; lifting my four books and hurrying to the counter.

She takes the books from my hands and begins to arrange them on the counter in front of the librarian. Then she frowns. 'You've had this one before,' she says, concerned. She opens the book and turns the pages. 'There are no words in this one, Bette,' she says; 'did you realise?'

I nod: 'Yes.'

She smiles briefly at the librarian and then crouches beside me. She shows me the open book: 'Look.' She turns the page: on this page, as on all the others, there is a drawing of Madeleine at the end of a long line of schoolgirls. The schoolgirls are being led across Paris by a nun. On one page they pass the Eiffel Tower; on another, the Arc de Triomphe. I like the Madeleine book. The nun has her nose in the air; the schoolgirls giggle. They walk through the Tuileries; Mum told me about the tuileries when we last looked at the book. Mum visited Paris once with Dad before I was born. She closes the book and looks into my eyes. 'You like reading,' she says quietly, 'but this one has no words in it, so Mummy can't read it to you; is that all right?'

I nod.

She sighs and stands, shrugging and muttering at the librarian: '*Little minds of their own.*'

We pack the books into the shopping bag and leave the counter. Mum manoeuvres Verity in her pushchair through the doorway into the porch. I follow, the soles of my sandals no longer slapping against black and white tiles but thudding instead onto the doormat. We stop and gaze as usual at the posters littering the walls.

'Can you read any of these words?' Mum asks me.

I look around. 'This–' I point to a poster '– says *under 5s.*'

'5 is a number,' she replies, 'not a word; but, yes, *under 5s*: do you know what that means?'

I shrug: 'No.'

'It means *playgroup*. Verity goes to playgroup on Mondays and Fridays.'

Verity's head twists like a mop below us in the pushchair: she stares up at Mum and I stare down into her open mouth.

'Did I go to playgroup?' I ask Mum.

'No, you went to nursery school: remember?'

I remember navy blue berets and grey pleated skirts. I remember Mrs Padley, the principal; her chins folded beneath her wet mouth and bristling with blunt black hairs. I remember Mrs

Senton, who was not the principal, and who was kinder. Mrs Senton patted papier-mâché onto balloons to make piggy banks. And there was Emily, who was seventeen and a student: she came from college to help. She knelt at our feet in the cloakroom, tying or untying our shoelaces; head bowed, blonde hair swinging over pink-tipped fingers. She told us that she had a sister called Dizzy, whose real name was Deborah, and a pony called Zach. She called me Libby.

Mum straightens the bow in my hair. 'There weren't any playgroups when you were small.' She lifts a sunhat from the shopping bag and drops it onto Verity's head. 'You began to learn to read at Nursery School: remember?'

I remember Mrs Padley standing at the front of the room, pointing to a poster; her arm raised and the skin swinging beneath it as her finger skipped from word to word: *the cat sat on the mat.*

'When will Verity learn to read?' I ask her.

Mum sighs and brushes her hand over Verity's sunhat. 'God knows.'

I point to another poster: 'What does this one say?' There is a picture of a telephone.

'The Samaritans.'

'What does *Samaritans* mean?'

'Kind people.'

'And this one?' I point to another.

'That says *Post-Natal Depression Support Group.*'

Mum pushes Verity's pushchair along the gravel path into the park. Verity is rattled. Mum nods towards the Sports Day spectators in the distance. 'There's Sally Penrose,' she murmurs to me. 'Do you think I should go and say hello to her?'

Mrs Penrose is watching an egg and spoon race through dark glasses; her hands behind her on the ground, her bracelets sinking into the grass; her legs crossed at the ankle, stretching out from a tight cream skirt. She turns towards us, sunlight flashing on her glasses. She smiles and waves. Bracelets tip down her arm. She beckons. Mum turns the pushchair towards her, shoving it from the path into the tufts of grass; driving it through the grass. Verity bounces. 'Hello!' Mum calls to Mrs Penrose; then she turns and whispers to me: 'Let's hope those bloody awful kids of hers aren't around.'

Mrs Penrose's smile broadens. 'Hello,' she says, patting the ground, indicating that we should sit. 'I thought you were still away on holiday.'

Mum lifts Verity from the pushchair: Verity's legs are white and limp below the stiff, shiny folds of her plastic pants. Each thigh is marked by the ring of elastic. Mum places her on the grass. 'We came back on Friday.'

'Was it good?'

Mum sits beside her. 'Lovely: *ninety degrees in the shade*.'

Why does she say this? The shade is unimportant; no-one spent any time in the shade.

'You look marvellous,' says Mrs Penrose.

Mum smiles. 'Thank you.' She tugs my arm and I sit beside her on the grass. 'And how are you?'

Mrs Penrose's teeth glint in the sunshine. 'Great, thanks; we had a super fortnight in Greece.'

'Greece?' Mum squints across the park: a rosette is being awarded in the distance to the winner of the egg and spoon race.

'Yes.' The winner appears on Mrs Penrose's dark glasses; fist raised, victorious. 'Super.'

Mrs Penrose turns to me, smiling widely: 'And how are these two lovely little girls?'

Mum smooths my hair from my face with her hand, smiling briefly in reply: 'They're fine.' She glances around the park. 'Where are your boys?'

Mrs Penrose laughs. 'Over there.' She waves a hand towards the duck pond. 'Making nuisances of themselves.'

Michael and Simon Penrose dart amongst friends, brandishing pea shooters.

'Goodness me,' muses Mum. 'I can hardly believe that your eldest will be starting secondary school next week.'

Mrs Penrose shrugs. 'I can hardly believe that my youngest will be following him next year.'

Girls crowd with skipping ropes at the starting line in the distance. 'I'm looking forward to the start of term,' says Mum.

The girls gather their ropes behind them; poising with arms open and wrists raised.

'Kids,' she continues: 'don't they just drive you mad, stuck at home all day, under your feet, with nothing to do, bored out of their tiny minds.'

Mrs Penrose nods towards the starting line. 'But this is a marvellous idea,' she says. 'The boys have been down here most days: magicians, Punch and Judy, inflatables.' She takes a sheet of paper from her handbag and reads: 'Skipping race.' She hands it to Mum. 'The programme of events,' she explains.

Mum peers at it: 'Skipping race,' she repeats. Then she runs a finger down the page. 'Sack race.' She looks at me: 'Sack races are a laugh, Lizzy; you'll like the sack race.' She glances again at the page: 'For children aged five to eight.' She looks at me again: 'You're eligible.' She hands the sheet back to Mrs Penrose.

'No,' I tell her, hurriedly. The girls with the ropes are towering at the starting line.

'Oh, Lizzy,' she says with exaggerated sadness, 'don't be a *spoilsport*.'

Mrs Penrose cranes towards us, interested.

'Sally,' Mum explains, turning towards her, 'Elizabeth doesn't want to enter the sack race.'

Mrs Penrose smiles at me. 'The sack race is a lot of fun,' she says.

'Come on, Lizzibeth,' says Mum, cheerily.

'You might win a rosette,' Mrs Penrose adds.

Mum waves a hand dismissively: 'It doesn't matter if you don't win.' She glances at the crowd at the starting line. 'You're bound not to come last.'

Mrs Penrose nods in agreement: 'You're an agile little thing.'

'Yes,' adds Mum, 'you're lucky: those great big girls will get caught up in their sacks.'

I fold my arms. 'No.'

'Yes,' says Mum, emphatically. 'You don't want to sit here doing nothing all afternoon, do you?'

'Yes.'

Verity shifts on the grass beside me, pants creaking; searching for daisies, scratching with her fingers through the clover.

I look beyond the race track towards the paddling pool. 'I could go paddling,' I suggest frantically.

Mum wrinkles her nose. 'No: you'll get wet.'

Mrs Penrose looks doubtfully at my skirt. 'It's a pity she's not wearing shorts.'

Mum shrugs. 'She can run in her knickers.' She grabs my waistband. 'Come on,' she says to me. 'Togs off.'

I roll away from her and bump into Verity; Verity looks up, startled.

'*Now* look,' shouts Mum.

Verity frowns.

'*Now* look what you've done.'

Verity opens her mouth.

'That's *all* I need.'

Verity breathes rapidly, and Mrs Penrose reaches swiftly for her: 'There, there,' she mutters, hauling her into her lap. Verity ceases breathing for a moment and stares at Mrs Penrose.

Mum sighs. 'Elizabeth is so self-conscious.'

Mrs Penrose's eyebrows rise above her glasses. 'Self-conscious?'

'And at this age!' Mum looks sideways at me. I am kneeling on the grass some distance away from her.

'Self-conscious about what?' Mrs Penrose's eyebrows hover.

Mum turns away from me. 'Everything. Her legs.'

'Her legs?'

Mum shrugs again. 'She thinks they're too skinny.'

'Too skinny!' Mrs Penrose roars with laughter. 'I wish *my* legs were too skinny.'

'Exactly.' Mum lifts Verity from Mrs Penrose's lap and places her on the grass.

Mrs Penrose leans towards me. 'You have lovely little legs,' she calls.

I wonder whether I am supposed to thank her.

Mum sighs again. 'And she thinks she has knock-knees.'

Mrs Penrose straightens, still smiling, and smooths her skirt with her hands: 'Goodness me, what a lot of silly nonsense.'

'Yes,' says Mum. 'And, anyway, who will see them when they're hidden in a sack?'

I pick daisies from the grass around my knees and throw them one by one at Verity. She gathers them in her lap, occasionally patting the pile with her hands. Competitors line in sacks at the race track. Mum and Mrs Penrose are swopping news: 'Sainsbury's is open now until seven on Fridays; did you know?' A whistle blows and the line of sacks explodes. I reach behind me to pick a buttercup. I hold it beneath Verity's chin, examining the evidence: 'You like butter,' I tell her. She folds her chin into her neck and clutches at the buttercup. I hand it to her and she lifts it to her mouth. 'No!' I knock it from her grasp, and then place it in her lap. 'You're not supposed to eat it.'

'Mum,' I whisper, leaning across the grass. 'Mum, can I have an ice cream now?'

She turns towards me, her face tightened in the sunlight. 'An ice cream?' She reaches across the grass for the shopping bag. 'Yes, I suppose so.' She searches inside the bag for her purse and lifts it from beneath some library books. She turns to Mrs Penrose: 'Ice cream, Sally?'

Mrs Penrose laughs: 'I've already had one, thanks.' She glances away, smiling.

Mum opens the purse and takes two coins. 'Here.' She drops the coins into my palm and closes the purse. 'Two cones,' she instructs. 'Small ones. Verity can have some of mine.'

The coins are cold in my hands. The van gleams in the distance; boys are playing football in front of it. 'Aren't you coming?' I ask her.

She replaces the purse inside the bag. 'No, Elizabeth.' She sighs, and dark hair tumbles across her face.

The footballers roar: someone has scored a goal. The man in the van pauses at the hatch with a fistful of cornets. He raises his head, frowning.

Mum has turned back to Mrs Penrose and begun a discussion about airports: 'Luton's a blessing,' she says. Then she looks at me again, squinting: 'Elizabeth,' she says, *run along*. What is the matter with you today?' The footballers in the distance chant: 'Two, four, six, eight, who do we appreciate?'

I fold my fingers around the coins. 'Can't you come with me?'

She sighs noisily, rolling her eyes and shrugging her shoulders. 'No, I can't; can't you see I'm busy?' She flaps a hand in the direction of Mrs Penrose. 'If you don't hurry, we'll all go without.'

In the distance the man in the van leans from the hatch with some cornets: *Tony's Ices*. A girl reaches towards him: she is taller than me; she grasps the cornets. Sometimes when I have an ice cream from Tony, he pretends to be unable to hear me – 'Eh? Eh? What's that?' – and he leans from the hatch, grinning and winking at Mum, his hand cupped behind his ear. Sometimes he pretends to be unable to see me: 'Hello? Hello? Is anybody there?' Sometimes he insists, 'No Italiano, no ice-a-cream-a'; leaning from the hatch with hands raised, demanding that I ask for 'gelati, due gelati, do-ay, doooo-ay.'

'Cockney git,' Mum calls him, laughing.

Now she laughs and nods in the direction of the van, telling Mrs Penrose, 'I'm not in the mood today for fun and games.'

It is late afternoon. I am standing in a corridor at a window, leaning over the sill, pressing myself against the cold capillaries of an unused radiator. Below me, in the streets surrounding the hospital, shoppers are returning two-by-two to their cars. They cradle carrier bags full of groceries: bottles, tins, cans, packets, jars, produce-to-be-weighed-at-the-counter; vacuum-packed, heat-sealed, freshly frozen. Children are fractious on the pavement behind them and mollified with sweets and buns. I look down at my watch: five twenty-five. In the distance, beyond the shoppers, is the sea; smooth and pale like the surface of a new jar of honey.

On Saturday evenings when I was a child I watched television: *Dr Who* and *The Generation Game*. Verity and I would sit in our pyjamas on the sofa and watch Bruce Forsyth encouraging Anthea Redfern to *give us a twirl*. This had been described beforehand by the BBC continuity announcer as *family entertainment*. We were waiting for *Starsky and Hutch*. We had Starsky cardigans. If Mum and Dad were planning a dinner party, then they were in the kitchen, appearing only briefly in the living room to plump cushions; their breath shallow and scented with aperitifs found in the sideboard and mixed in tumblers with the contents of tiny bottles labelled Indian Tonic Water and Canada Dry. If they were planning to go out, then they were upstairs: my father in the bathroom, steam pressed beneath the locked door into the hallway; my mother in the bedroom, dressing.

My mother's dress collection grew dense in her wardrobe: a bristling mass of material to be sifted expertly when choosing something to wear. Some of the dresses arrived home from the occasional long day she spent in London without me; whilst others had been stiffening in the wardrobe since before I was born. On her return from shopping expeditions we met her at the station; my father and I peering through the windscreen as she sparkled in the distance across the forecourt under streetlamps. When we were back home, reinstated in the kitchen with the kettle wheezing, she would lift purchases from the whispering carrier bags and invite me to admire them; removing each price tag with a sharp bite of her teeth.

On Saturday evenings a selection of dresses lay on her bed. These dresses were not the dresses that she wore in the daytime at home: not cotton dresses fragranced with washing powder and bleached by frequent flutters on the washing line; not dresses tacked with short hems and strung with broken zips. The dresses on the bed on Saturday evenings were the robes worn by her on occasions when she was less my mother than someone else's wife or daughter or friend; on occasions when she left me at home with a babysitter. I would stand unseen on Saturday evenings at her bedroom door and watch her as she prepared to leave. Having placed the dresses behind her on the bed, she would stand at her dressing table in her underwear. The soft dull brown skin on her shoulders bore the marks of fluorescent white bra straps; and her hips and thighs were cloaked in the white satin of her slip. The room smelled of bath salts. Lifting her foot onto the end of the bed, she would stroke her shin; her cupped palm oozing lotion. I could see that her toe nails had been clipped: the tip of each yellow nail sliced white. When she turned finally and looked into the mirror, lifting her hands to the nape of her neck to fasten buttons or beads, she would see me. She would frown, with disapproval perhaps, or puzzlement, and speak quietly to my reflection; reminding me to go downstairs to wait for the babysitter.

Other cars are arriving in the hospital car park, slotting side by side into parking spaces, nosing into the privet: visitors arrive early on Saturdays, perfuming the wards with the scent of eau de cologne and cigarettes, bringing gifts of chocolates and flowers. Casualty has visitors, in a sense, when friends and relatives accompany patients; but there are no chocolates or flowers. I turn from the window. The sea has become white with yachts returning to shore. If my mother does not have long to live then she should travel; it is what she has always wanted to do. She has always wanted to visit Australia. Perth, in particular; the city on the shores of the ocean at the end of the world.

When receiving a diagnosis of cancer, a person usually expresses a wish: *I want to walk with my daughter down the aisle at her wedding in July; I want to be waiting in the playground for my grandchild after her first day at school; I want to visit my sister in Florida; I want to run in a marathon.* If the prognosis is optimistic, a wish can express hope and courage; if the prognosis is poor, a wish can express an acceptance of death. Wishes, however, deny sickness; and cancer entails sickness. My mother is already in hospital; she is already sick; too sick to go to Perth. Cancer usually entails treatment; and treatment entails sickness, surgery, radiotherapy, chemotherapy. Treatment takes time; and so does sickness; and death, too. The heart and lungs of a young and previously healthy person will flail hopelessly for a long time like fish out of water.

Two years ago, after five years of training, I began working. For the first six months of my pre-registration year I worked for Mr Farquharson, a surgeon. I was Mr Farquharson's Houseman. Jokingly referred to by others on the ward as *the boy*, I was required to undertake routine tasks: to clerk patients and provide them with pre- and post-operative care; to be present on the ward before eight o'clock in the morning and to stay until the end of the ward round in the evening, and to work alternate nights and weekends. I was an apprentice; serving an apprenticeship.

One of my first patients was Janet Curtis. She had been referred to Mr Farquharson nine months previously with a breast lump. Her file rustled with a pile of letters, deep and white and patterned darkly with words: *Thank you very much for referring this woman.* Mr Farquharson had removed the lump, which was malignant, and prescribed a course of chemotherapy. It was my job to administer chemotherapy. Janet Curtis required three remaining treatments. On the morning that she was due to arrive for the first treatment I read through the notes: *fifty-six, nurse, unmarried, no children.* The ward sister peered over my shoulder. 'Janet Curtis,' she told me. 'Worked over the road on one of the gynae wards.'

Janet was sitting on a chair in the corridor outside the nurses' room. Head bowed; hands folded; feet aligned on the tiles in sensible shoes. At first she did not see me. Headscarf; cardigan; drip-dry dress in a floral print: Lilly would have described her as *a mother.* On the floor at her feet was a shopping bag containing a stiff cone of rolled up magazine, and two knitting needles risen and crossed like swords on a heraldic crest. She looked up and saw me walking towards her. She smiled; she had been waiting for me. The new young doctor. I was unmistakably the doctor because I was wearing a white coat: the insignia of my profession. Mr Farquharson, like many consultants, never wore a white coat: he judged his superiority to be self-evident.

'Miss Curtis?' I did not know what to call her. I extended my hand. 'I'm Dr Hamilton.'

She smiled and slipped her hand into mine.

Presumably I asked her how she was feeling; but I can only remember glancing at the empty chairs and asking whether she had come alone.

'No,' she told me, smiling kindly. 'A friend brought me; and she'll be coming back for me later.'

'Are you sure that you won't want to stay overnight?' I had anticipated that she would be very sick; I had reserved a bed.

She wrinkled her nose. 'No, thank you: I'd prefer to go home.' She smiled sheepishly: 'I don't much like hospitals, if you know what I mean.'

We laughed quietly together.

'Yes,' I said, 'I know exactly what you mean.'

Throughout the morning she lay on a bed with her hand pinned at her side and a tube fed into her vein. I had worn goggles and gloves when administering the drug: it is necessary to protect against splashes because the drug burns. It burned inside Janet's body, stripping layers of cells from her scalp, mouth, gut, womb. She had lost her hair during the course of treatment, and her appetite; whilst the warm air shimmered in the ward, nurses went regularly into Janet's room to wipe her forehead with a moist sponge. Janet's sickness was worse this time: I saw it welling in her eyes whenever I entered the room. Her gaze was reproachful, damaged. I prescribed against this side effect with a drug which caused another: dizziness.

'Why don't you stay here tonight?' I suggested gently from her bedside.

*

Janet stayed in hospital that night and then each night following treatment.

'So far so good,' Mr Farquharson said to me when the course of treatment was finally complete; and he went to her bedside to explain that she should not hesitate to come back if necessary before her next appointment.

She telephoned the ward a month later. The ward sister shrugged, baffled and sceptical, as I entered the office. 'Janet Curtis,' she whispered, smothering the receiver: 'She wants an anti-emetic.'

I took the receiver from her and called quietly into the dark mouthpiece: 'Hello? Janet?'

I heard a distant sing-song of greeting in reply.

'Janet, how have you been?'

Her words ran towards me down the line: 'Fine, thanks, Beth, but I've been rather sick this last week or so, and I wondered if I could have something for it.'

Sister rose from the desk; a bustle of glimmering nylon.

'Of course you can have something for it,' I said. 'But do you have any idea why you're so sick?'

Sister carried empty cups from the room.

'Oh, it's just a bug; everyone has it, it's just that I'm not yet strong enough to cope.'

I reached across the room and closed the door. 'How long have you had this bug?'

'Not long. I suppose it's either a bug or a result of the chemotherapy. Do you think it could be a result of the chemotherapy?'

I shuffled the waste paper bin beneath the desk with my feet. 'I don't know: why don't you come to the ward and let me have a look at you?'

She sighed. 'I'd rather try the drug.'

'So you don't want to come in?'

'No; not yet.'

* * *

I had never seen a dead body before I began training. No-one special to me had ever died. Except my grandfather. My grandparents lived in London on a hill. At the bottom of the hill there were gas cylinders beside the railway track, squatting amid rubble like rockets on the moon. The hill was North London: Kings Cross at the bottom, Hampstead Heath at the top. I have friends now in North London, but no family: my grandmother moved to Suffolk when my grandfather died.

'Why not the South Coast?' my mother asked her. 'You like the South Coast.'

My grandmother shuddered: 'Yes, but I don't want to live South of the river.'

My grandparents lived in a quiet street. In the afternoons children sat on the kerb between parked cars. Sometimes the boys played football in the road; running at each other, dodging, shouting encouragement. The girls played sevenses with tennis balls against garden walls. At the end of each afternoon an ice-cream van arrived, chiming *Lara's Theme* or *Greensleeves* whilst it rattled stationary and driverless at the roadside. A man dispensed ice creams from a machine in the back. The ice cream dropped from a nozzle into cones. The man reached occasionally into a freezer for Sky Rays and Funny Faces, lifting them cold and bright from beneath a dust of snow.

After eating ice cream, my grandfather and I would sit together at the piano in the front room and play Chopsticks, exhilarated, our fingers clattering over the keys. My mother and grandmother appeared occasionally in the doorway; their hands in rubber gloves, their waists bound with apron strings. Sometimes I had watched them earlier in the kitchen as they removed their rings, easing a dab of washing-up liquid along the length of the finger. The rings were placed on the windowsill *for safekeeping*. They were *engagement* rings, with *precious stones*: sapphires, diamonds, but not rubies because *rubies mean blood and sweat and tears*. Wedding rings remained: a plump gold freckle on the third finger of each left hand. My mother and grandmother were *spoken for*.

94

After Chopsticks I would fetch cups and saucers and plates from the kitchen.

'A cup of tea,' my grandmother called it, 'and a bite to eat.'

My mother would hand me a plate of sandwiches.

'On the coffee table, please, Bess, in the front room.'

The sandwiches were small and white and naked of crusts. They were accompanied by scones; soft little pillows stiff and yellow in the middle with butter.

'Don't touch,' my mother would warn, handing me the plate of scones. 'Not yet, not until everyone else is ready.'

Then she would lick her fingers. Grandma was still at the sink with her hands gloved, fluorescent, cupped around the potatoes that she was peeling for the evening meal.

In the evenings my grandmother and I sat in armchairs in the front room. She would knit, slapping together the knitting needles whilst I drank my milky bedtime drink. Sometimes we watched television, *Dixon of Dock Green*; and at other times the dial on the radiogram smouldered in the darkness and piano music chimed softly around the room. Where was everybody else? Where were my mother and father? I do not remember. Perhaps they went home without me; perhaps they went into town for the evening, perhaps my grandmother was babysitting. Where was Verity? In bed, or not yet born? Did my parents drive into London on Sunday mornings to fetch me? Or did my visits end when I was lifted from my bed and carried through darkness to the car? Where was my grandfather?

My grandmother was very kind: 'That's lovely,' she would say, bending over me whenever I brought her something or showed her something special; and then she would straighten and step away, saying 'Isn't that lovely?' to her companions: passing the buck.

Like her own mother she had only one child: a daughter, *an only child*. Like her own mother she was married young, and widowed young. Her mother, newly widowed, moved in with her at the beginning of the war; she was known to my mother, who was very young, as Nana.

'Nana always wore a hat,' my mother would tell me. 'Always.'

In my grandparents' house there was a photograph of Nana on the mantelpiece in the front room. When my grandmother sat knitting in the evenings I could study the resemblance: I could see similarities between the two small, pale, silent faces. My grandmother was older than the woman in the photograph; and she was hatless. The two women had been similarly named: Thomasina and Josephine; feminine forms of male names; diminutions.

My mother was named Mary.

When she was four years old she was evacuated from London at the beginning of the war. She went with Nana to Wales. My grandmother stayed in London, at home: waiting for my grandfather, she claimed; waiting *just in case*. After a year in Wales, Nana drowned one night in a lake. *There is nothing to tell*, my mother says to me whenever I quiz her. Sometimes she says that she *knows nothing*, sometimes that she *remembers nothing*, and always that she was *too young*. She says only that her mother came to fetch her and they returned together to London. When I was a child I wondered whether the hat had floated on the surface of the water.

My grandfather died of cancer when I was four, or so I am told: he died at home, the doctor visiting him once each week. I imagine the doctor as a man in his forties with a gladstone bag; I imagine his steps conspicuous on the lino in the hallway outside my grandfather's room. I imagine that he brought diamorphine with him; and I believe that he instructed my grandmother to pour it down the sink when it was no longer needed, but perhaps I am wrong, perhaps that is someone else's story. I remember that my grandmother served Lucozade to my grandfather at teatime in a tea cup: 'Something nice and cool for you on a long hot afternoon.'

My grandfather spent a fortnight in a convalescent home; the bill was paid by the union. When telling me this, my mother says *union* with respect: suddenly union means chivalry, not inconvenience. During his convalescence, she told me, he walked with me often on Hampstead Heath. I remember walking with him above London: our voices lost in the cold wind that rushed around us, numbing our throats and steaming from our mouths; our eyes smarting in the sunlight which scalded the low cloud. We stood together on the hill and looked down into the city: *Turn again, Dick Whittington*. When we returned to the house we were met at the door by my mother. Hurrying us into the hallway, peeling the mittens from my hands, she would ask questions: Had I had a nice time? What had I done? Had I fed the ducks? Had I seen the squirrels? At the time I was irritated, but now I realise that her fascination was genuine: her own childhood with him had been denied by the war.

He thought the world of you, they tell me: my grandmother, her friends and acquaintances.

He spent all his time with you, my mother says: *both of you in your own little world*.

I remember nothing except his storytelling whisper – *fee fo fi fum* – when I sat on his knee; and I remember that there were quieter days when my mother or grandmother took me into the kitchen or garden and he was left alone in the front room, his head resting against an antimacassar. No-one ever told him that he was dying. Secrecy about death was considered important in those days, like towels and hot water for childbirth. *I think he guessed*, my mother tells me.

Now he is gone; and Hampstead Heath remains above London like a cold star.

Janet Curtis came back into hospital when the sickness worsened. A scan revealed secondaries in her liver. It was my job to tell her: usually it was my job or Mr Farquharson's, and in this case it was mine.

'I don't want to be disturbed,' I told the nurses; and then I entered Janet's room. At her invitation I sat on the edge of the bed. My hand stayed inside my pocket, over my bleeper, ensuring silence. Hand on heart, I told her the news. I told her that there was *nothing more to be done.* Sometimes I am misunderstood when I say this, when someone understands that their condition will not improve but does not understand that it will deteriorate. Janet did not misunderstand me. Neither did she ask me for treatment; more treatment, different treatment, treatment recommended in newspapers, alternative and revolutionary treatments. Nor did she ask me for drugs or rays or surgery to shrink, burn, cut and seal the swollen tissue. She did not demand to know why her own story should suddenly be so very different from the success stories.

She did not ask me how long she might live. She knew the answer: that there is no answer. Predictions are for lay people. Predictions become incantations whispered incessantly and insistently amongst family and friends – *six months, six months* – and then, later, they become myths: *six months to live, they said.* Janet was able to estimate: she knew that she might live for another month, perhaps; or perhaps a little longer.

It was more important to her to know that she could die not in hospital but at home.

We talked about it; we made plans. She would be nursed by willing friends; she would have diamorphine for pain, stemetil for sickness, lactulose for constipation. I would not replace the drip; she would return home, temporarily rehydrated, when the last of the fluid had passed from the bright silky bag into her veins.

I remember the night that it ran dry. I was sitting alone in the office at the end of the ward, writing notes and drinking coffee. The ward was quiet, the patients asleep. Rain swelled with a hiss at the window, thrown against the glass by the wind like a handful of sand. I glanced up from the notes to see Susan, one of the nurses, standing in the doorway. She had been watching me.

'Beth . . .' she began kindly, quietly. She stepped towards me. She was young, twenty-one; newly qualified, recently married. She was tall and thin, gangly. One of her long pale arms stretched across the room for a chair, slipping it soundlessly over the tiles to the desk. She sat lightly and closed her eyes as she spoke.

'Janet's drip has finished.'

I laid my pen very quietly on the desk. 'Are you sure?'

She sighed wearily. 'Of course I'm sure.' She slumped, her backbone folding against the back of the chair. 'Well, no,' she muttered, 'perhaps not.' She sighed again. 'Perhaps you can fix it.'

I closed the folder of notes. 'I doubt it.'

'No, really.'

I stood behind the desk. 'If you say it's finished, then I'm sure it's finished.'

Her eyes were as spherical and luminous as the clock on the wall.

I shrugged. 'But I'll go and see.'

So I walked through the ward in the dead of night to Janet's bedside and fixed the drip so that she received fluid until morning.

Fifteen minutes ago I sat in a side room with the Gifford family: Mrs Gifford, her daughter, her son-in-law, and her teenage granddaughter. Mr Gifford had been taken from Casualty to the Coronary Care Unit. He had been at a wedding reception with his family earlier this afternoon when he collapsed. In the side room the women's dresses rustled as they crossed and uncrossed their legs. The teenager's shoes scraped against the tiles: stilettos, large and white. The son-in-law sat silently in a suit, staring at his hands. I was explaining the situation. The women were turned towards me, their faces luminous beneath make-up. Their lips were still and smeared with lipstick.

Dark eyeshadow lay gritty in the younger women's eye sockets but Mrs Gifford's inky green eyeshadow had melted into the folds on her eyelids. In her lap she twisted a hat between her hands; a pill box hat bristling with a veil. After listening for several minutes, she rose from her chair. The hat brushed against her skirt, and the veil scratched against the pleats.

'Thank you, doctor,' she said, placing a hand on the back of her daughter's chair. The daughter reached to the floor for her bag. The teenager followed, tucking forward and then rising. The son-in-law remained sitting, dabbing at his nose with the back of his hand. Mrs Gifford sighed: 'If there's nothing more we can do, then I suppose we should all go home and get some rest.' She turned towards the door. The son-in-law rose behind her. 'If there's any change,' she reassured her family, 'then I'm sure the doctor will let us know.'

She had misunderstood me.

I glanced hurriedly around the room: the two younger women were preoccupied, hooking handbags onto forearms and tucking handkerchiefs into sleeves; the son-in-law reached past them towards the door. No-one returned my gaze. Everyone followed Mrs Gifford. As she stepped towards the door I repeated under my breath the details that I had told her, and concluded that nothing had been omitted. How had I been misunderstood? What had I done wrong, and what more could I do?

I knew that I had to stop her leaving the room so I stood, resisting the urge to grab her and to shout at her to *stay*.

'No,' I said faintly, hesitantly, wincing as she stopped at the door.

She turned and stared at me; daring me to continue.

I faltered: 'He might need you.' I bit my lip: I had promised myself never to prevaricate.

Mrs Gifford's face contracted into a frown.

I leaned against my chair. I knew that she was staring at me because I was staring at her but I did not know whether to lower my eyes. I could not remember what to do. It seemed to me that to look away would be cruel: dismissive, evasive, unsupportive. Yet I did not want to look at her. So I spoke, my gaze moving

100

with my words across four blank faces: 'Mr Gifford is very seriously ill.'

I heard fluttering on the other side of the door and saw the simultaneous depression of the door handle. Suddenly the door was ajar; and the face of Loulou, a nurse, was pressed into the opening. She glanced anxiously around the room. The Giffords slid their baffled gazes towards her. 'I'm sorry,' she whispered. Then she turned to me: 'Beth?' She opened the door wider: a wordless plea for me to leave the room. I muttered apologies to the Giffords and snatched the folder of notes from my chair as I left.

I followed Loulou into the corridor and closed the door behind me. 'What?' I hissed furiously.

'Mr Gifford,' she whispered, her small face drawn tight and pale around her mouth.

I jerked my head towards the door: 'That's Mr Gifford's family in there.'

Her eyes were milky in the middle with light grey irises. I tightened my grip on the folder of notes.

She spoke very quietly: 'Beth, Mr Gifford arrested a few minutes ago on CCU.'

A trolley rattled past, the attendant porter whistling the *Marseillaise*. The trolley slid in front of him across the tiles, rolling through the banks of fluorescent fog collecting in the corridor beneath the striplights.

'Well?' I was belligerent.

Loulou remained calm, and shrugged unhappily: 'No.'

'No *what*?'

'No, they couldn't *bring him round*,' she explained rapidly, her voice suddenly raised. 'He's dead.'

I wanted to shout: *Why didn't you tell me?* Suddenly, the absurdity of my rage became apparent to me, and I lowered my eyes.

Loulou lifted a hand and dropped a finger lightly onto my folder: 'Are you all right?' Her voice was soft again.

I sighed miserably. 'Yes.'

'Sure?' She bent towards me, her grey gaze swooping beneath mine.

'Yes.'

She nodded towards the door. 'Do you want me to tell them?'

'No.' I glanced at the door. 'I'll do it.'

Janet Curtis was dying in hospital. The drip had been taken away, she had been freed, but she did not leave.

Not yet, she said each day when I came to her bedside; *I'm not yet strong enough*.

She wanted to be strong enough to return home to die. She lay in bed, sucking ice cubes.

Not yet, she pleaded.

Like any other dying patient, she was pleading for more time; but there was no more time; I tried to tell her, but words failed me. She believed in the right to a good death but she was dying for the cause.

One more day, she said each day.

After six days I moved, as planned, to a neighbouring hospital for the second half of my pre-registration year. Janet Curtis died five days later, on the ward.

Few doctors welcome the prospect of patients who are dying. Opportunities for treatment are regarded as limited or non-existent.

I'll treat you, my mother used to say; beaming at me across a table, brandishing a menu card, hinting at buttered muffins; or standing with me in a dress shop, perusing the rails.

How can you treat me like this? she used to shout when I left my laundry on my bedroom floor or scraped uneaten meals from my plate into the bin.

102

It seems to me that to *treat* means to *pay special attention*. I pay special attention to my dying patients.

'Loulou?' I hear her behind me, walking down the corridor with her flat black rubber-soled shoes slapping the tiles like small flippers. 'Loulou?' She halts and then joins me at the window, folding herself over the sill; forearms aligned, hands together. We both gaze into the street below. 'Loulou, I'm sorry for having been so awful.'

She looks sideways at me with a neatly pressed smile. 'My fault,' she says, returning her attention to the street. In profile her dark hair curves onto her cheekbone like the tail of a comma: she is nicknamed Loulou, I was told on my first day by the others, because of her resemblance to Louise Brooks.

'No,' I insist, 'it wasn't your fault.'

In the street a thin young woman spins amongst shoppers. I recognise her: she often comes into Casualty. Today she is laughing. Shoppers step around her; the hands of adults gloving the hands of children. They probably think of the woman as a *drunk*; but she does not often drink. Nor is she *homeless*: she has a home; or, at least, an address. *On the streets* means something specific when it is said of a woman; *tramp*, too: this woman is not on the streets, she is not a tramp; *the lady is not a tramp*.

Today she is dressed in well-kept clothes; recent hand-outs from the Salvation Army, perhaps. A tank top, the patchwork of bright woollen blotches strung low across a brown shirt, and trousers, salmon pink, hanging from an elasticated waistband. I cannot see the shoes but they are probably men's shoes: big, black, leather, laced, utilitarian; Dad's shoes. She reaches along the pavement with her feet. Her arms rise at her sides. She is floating: *swimming*, so often said when meaning *drowning*.

I turn to Loulou, and tell a lie: 'I don't know what's wrong with me today.'

Loulou flicks a grin at me: 'No worse than usual, surely, *Dr Hamilton*.' She turns from the window and smooths her hands across her apron. 'Blame the job,' she encourages cheerfully.

She leans suddenly and conspiratorially towards me: 'Did you ever know Jonathan Wilson?'

I nod: Jonathan Wilson's job in Casualty ended shortly after mine began. He now works in Anaesthetics in Croydon.

'Well,' Loulou continues, 'he was working here on New Year's Eve, and you know what they're like here on New Year's Eve.' She inclines her head towards the busy end of the corridor.

I don't; but I can guess, so I nod.

'Well, some of them were wearing fancy dress,' she whispers, 'and at one time Jonathan Wilson found himself breaking unexpected bad news to relatives while dressed *as Batman*.'

Shamefacedly, we stifle giggles.

'It's true,' she insists, a hand pressed to her mouth. 'He was even wearing his underpants outside his trousers.'

We walk slowly together down the corridor.

'Of course,' I add, 'Chris has a habit of wearing patients' glasses: did you see him this afternoon in Mr Connor's bi-focals?'

We giggle again.

'How long have you been working here?' I ask.

'About a year and a half.' She unfolds her arms and reaches absently for her hat. It is secured with difficulty to her sleek black hair.

'Do you like it here?'

She shrugs: 'I can't imagine working anywhere else.' She wrinkles her nose: 'I can't imagine returning to work on a ward.' She digs at her head with a hairgrip. 'And you?'

'I don't have any choice,' I remind her. 'Six months of shifts, and then back to the grindstone. Obstetrics next, probably.'

She snorts derisively. 'You're not exactly making it easy for yourself, are you?' The hairgrip slides onto the hat; the hat is as stiff and white and superfluous as icing sugar. 'Babies don't make a habit of waiting until morning to be born.'

I have been less keen lately to work in Obstetrics. It has always appealed to me but it is inseparable from Gynaecology, and specialists in Obstetrics and Gynaecology are surgeons: it would be necessary for me to train as a surgeon. In hospitals there are surgeons and physicians, surgical and medical wards. The surgeons are Fellows of the Royal College of Surgeons, and the physicians are Members of the Royal College of Physicians. It is rare for anyone to study for both the FRCS and MRCP exams.

Surgeons are titled Mr or Miss: an accolade, but historically due to the denial of the title Doctor. Surgeons are experts in the skills of hacking and sewing. Surgery means *work with hands*. I do not want to be a surgeon. It seems to me that surgeons do not understand bodies. They do not know how to restore and maintain equilibrium. They do not know what *makes a person tick*.

Like most people, my mother makes no distinction between medicine and surgery. If she has surgery, her conversation afterwards will be full of doctors: kind doctors, young doctors, foreign doctors, lady doctors. If she has no surgery, the visit to hospital will have been a false alarm, or a lucky escape, or perhaps even in some sense a failure. For most people, hospital means gowns and masks. On television, hospitals are lush with surgeons. The screen is a mosaic of sealed hands and hidden mouths. The surgeons are the heroes – and, rarely, the heroines – of the show.

I want to be a doctor, a physician, working with *physis*, with nature. Every day I see surgeons requesting physicians to monitor and diagnose, to stabilise the rhythms and fluids and sugars of their patients. Surgeons remove, repair, or transplant. They are technicians. After performing a renal transplant, the surgeon will leave the patient with a physician. 'Look around you,' my tutor at medical school once told me. 'The surgeons stride down the middle of the corridor; the physicians walk slowly, close to the wall, hanging their heads and trailing their fingertips on the paintwork, thinking.'

In hospital there is infection, inflammation, obstruction, degeneration, failure of hearts, lungs, livers, kidneys, brains, blood.

There are diseases and syndromes: Crohn's, Addison's, Cushing's, Parkinson's; Charcot-Marie-Tooth, Guillain-Barre. There are complications: diabetes with necrobiosis lipoidica diabeticorum, diabetic retinopathy, peripheral neuropathy, gangrene, acidosis, coma. There is cancer. Physicians are problem solvers and healers. They staff the Intensive Care Unit and form the Cardiac Arrest Team. I see them crashing into Casualty with their monitors and currents and drugs. With their electrocardiograms, their defibrillators, their lignocaine, bicarbonate, bretylium tosylate, atropine, adrenaline and isoprenaline, physicians possess the power to resurrect.

Loulou and I stand together at the end of the corridor.
    'What time are you finishing tonight?' she asks me.
    'Nine.'
    'Well, why don't you come over to the Plough for a drink? We'll all be there, all the usual crowd: me, Sandra, Liam, Anne; and Benjie, I expect; and Maria; and Mo – do you know Mo? – and Jane Simmons, Steve Gray, Heather; and Tim Keiller.' She looks at me. 'I don't think you've met Tim, he's new, the new radiology SHO; he's nice, you'll like him.'
    I sigh, and shrug: 'I'm sorry, Loulou, but I can't.'
    She regards me closely. 'Busy?'
    'Yes.' Another lie.

We are both silent for a moment.
    'Are you working tomorrow?' I ask her.
    'No.'
    'Doing anything nice?'
    She smiles and lowers her eyes. 'Yes, I'm taking my little girl out for the day.'
    'How nice,' I enthuse. 'Where will you go?'
    'Richmond, I think.'
    'How nice. I didn't know you had a little girl. How old is she?'
    'Three,' Loulou answers quickly, her smile bright: 'Chloe.'
    'Chloe,' I repeat appreciably. 'And who looks after her when

you're at work?' I am always interested in child care arrangements.

Loulou breaths a short, hushed laugh and flicks her gaze towards the ceiling: 'She stays under the desk in Reception,' she jokes. Then she shrugs. 'No,' she says quickly, quietly, cheerfully, 'she'd bite the receptionists' ankles. Actually, she doesn't live with me; she lives with her father.'

Loulou walks away from me down the corridor. Vivien sits nearby, writing, hunched at the desk; a desk without drawers, a table; a table with space for a sole occupant. She is writing hurriedly: *notes*. Her letters are rounded, loopy, large: *girls' writing*, bearing traces of *neat writing, best writing*; of writing learned from *A-for-Apple* charts in classrooms with Wendy Houses and Pet Corners; of writing doodled on notepads and perfected. *Girls' writing* bears the trace of the bold and regular curves of *girls' drawings*: suns and crescent moons, ribbons tied in bows, hearts and flowers, fat cats shaped like cottage loaves. At the top of Vivien's page of notes is a sketch, a matchstick man: X marks the spot, lacerations.

I lean over her shoulder. 'Who's working tonight?' I ask her.

She does not look up. 'Ginny.'

In the distance I see Mr Henry, the Consultant, reaching behind the reception desk towards the shelves above the heads of the receptionists. His shirt sleeves are rolled to his elbows and he wears light coloured trousers: his concession to informality because today is Saturday. Perhaps it is warm outside. A fuzzy gleam of fluorescent light rests now like a frost on the thinning patch in his hair. I wonder whether his three young children are waiting outside in the car. He often comes into the hospital on Saturdays, sometimes with the children, but not usually in the afternoon: usually he comes in the morning before leaving with his family for a weekend in the country or a day on the sea. The receptionists are chatting to him, asking after his children, his wife, his garden, his boat; and possibly they are also teasing him ('Can't keep away from us, can you, Mr Henry?') They duck exaggeratedly beneath his raised arms, their eyes flitting upwards to his face: paying him plenty of attention. He is well liked here.

I wonder whether he will give me time off, if I need it, to go home.

1976, SPAIN

I am sitting on a sun lounger on a sun terrace. At the other side
of the terrace, the swimming pool water scalds the surrounding
tiles. Mum is sitting beside me in a reclining chair; and beside
Mum sits aunty Carol. We have come from our villa in the hills
to spend the day with aunty Carol and uncle Tony. They are not
my real aunty and uncle; I do not have an aunty or an uncle;
they are *family friends*. We arrived here at lunchtime. Lunch
was paella. I hate seafood. I left the prawns and mussels on the
side of my plate.

'Don't you like seafood?' asked aunty Carol.

This evening we are having a barbeque. I hate meat. The
pieces of meat are wrapped in foil in the fridge. I found them
when I was searching for the lettuce at lunchtime.

'Foiled you, huh?' Mum called lightly to me, glancing from
the chopping board, glimpsing my predicament.

The pieces were wrapped closely, protecting against indecency;
wrapped individually, like severed limbs.

Mum called anxiously across the kitchen to aunty Carol: 'I
should warn you that Elli's fussy about meat.'

'Oh, goodness,' said aunty Carol.

'But take no notice,' Mum continued, 'because she can fill up
on bread, and she'll love the melon starter.'

Mum is wearing a dress, a short dress. Her legs are exposed to the sun. Her skin is dark and wet with oil. She applies oil to her body each day as if she is servicing an expensive piece of machinery.

'Stretch marks,' she says uninformatively, but with an air of foreboding, whenever she sees my eyes following her moist and perfumed hand across her flawless skin.

She is six months pregnant.

This morning, after breakfast, she lumbered naked from the balcony towards her bedroom, and smirked over her shoulder at Dad: 'I'd better get myself covered up,' she said to him, 'if I don't want to offend your super-duper aunty Carol.'

Dad is playing golf somewhere this afternoon with uncle Tony. He has never played golf before. Uncle Tony plays all the time.

'Aunty Carol is a golf widow,' Mum told me last night on the balcony.

I was staring at the stars and trying to tune the radio to Radio Luxemburg.

'A merry golf widow,' she continued, 'because she has never had much time for uncle Tony.'

'Why did she marry him, then?' I asked.

'Yes, why?' echoed Verity, from the darkness below us. 'Why, why, why, why, why?'

When she interrupts in this infuriating manner, Verity is unaware of the topic of conversation.

'Why what, Verity?' goaded Mum, calling mildly into the darkness.

There was no reply.

Mum leaned conspiratorially towards me. 'She married him because he asked and because he was tall, because girls of five-foot-ten couldn't be choosers in those days.'

Aunty Carol and uncle Tony have rented the villa for a fortnight.

'It'll be ideal for my kids,' aunty Carol told Mum when she chose it from a brochure.

We drove to it along a road lined with gardens.

'It's not the same as having your own place, though, is it?' Mum said to us from the front passenger seat.

No, I thought to myself, looking through the window at lawns sparkling with sprinklers: it's nicer.

It is in a town, on a beach. In the town there is a bar called Smith's. On the beach there are pony rides. In the villa there is a maid.

'Twice daily after meals,' said aunty Carol, indicating the busy maid. 'The perfect tonic.'

I am watching aunty Carol's children, Jane and Alistair, in the pool. Verity is bobbing between them in a rubber ring. They have tried to persuade her to play piggy-in-the-middle but she is uncooperative. She has probably told them that she can't swim, which is untrue. She is drifting aimlessly, following the ball closely with her eyes but making no attempt to reach for it. She has probably told them that she is blind. Mum's voice distracts me. She is complaining to aunty Carol: 'Kids – you break your back for them, and do they care? You give them everything, and what do they give you in return?'

What does she want?

I take the opportunity to look sideways at aunty Carol. She is murmuring in agreement with Mum whilst staring vacantly at her own children. She is wearing a pair of white shorts: short shorts, white against white skin. She nods her head, and her bleached perm grazes her shoulders. Her boobs are slung low in a halterneck bikini top. Mum sometimes describes her as *mutton*.

Suddenly she turns towards me.

'Aren't you awfully hot like that, Elizabeth?' she asks.

She squints in the sunlight, wrinkling her nose, baring her teeth.

Mum turns sharply, her features compressed into a frown, her dark hair hanging over her face. She stares at me.

I am wearing cotton trousers and a T-shirt.

'There's no need for all those clothes,' Mum says irritably. She

111

turns back to aunty Carol. 'I've told her,' she says bitterly, 'but trying to get through to her is like trying to get through the Berlin Wall.' She glares briefly in my direction. '*We're very moody* these days,' she explains to aunty Carol, her voice loud and heavy with sarcasm. '*We* think *we* know best, and *we* don't care much for anyone else's opinion.'

We wish she would shut up.

'Oh dear me,' says aunty Carol. Her tone is sympathetic but otherwise devoid of expression. It is not clear whether the sympathy is intended for Mum or me.

'But you have all that to come, of course,' gloats Mum. She is delighted that her own suffering is currently unique but that aunty Carol's fate is so much worse. I follow her gaze across the terrace to the swimming pool. Jane is standing pot-bellied in the shallow end, bellowing orders across the choppy water to Alistair. Alistair is throwing water into her face. Jane is ten, Alistair is eight: they are what Mum calls 'horrid kids'.

'I'll tell you what worries her,' confides Mum, leaning periously from the chair towards aunty Carol.

Aunty Carol smiles politely.

I gaze into the distance: there is no distance; I gaze into a row of cypress trees.

'Her legs,' says Mum.

Aunty Carol shifts uncomfortably on her lounger. Perhaps she thinks that I am disfigured.

'She covers her legs because she thinks they're hairy.'

'Good Lord,' says aunty Carol. She is relieved, but uninterested.

'I cover them because I have sunburn,' I correct. I stare at Mum with narrowed eyes: this is excusable due to the bright light.

'Hairy!' continues Mum. 'Can you imagine? What a thing to worry about at her age.'

What am I supposed to worry about at my age? What does she worry about at *her* age?

'She wants to shave them,' says Mum indignantly.

'Goodness,' says aunty Carol.

'But her Dad says no.'

'Really?' Aunty Carol's attention is arrested by the mention of Dad.

'Yes,' prattles Mum. 'He has warned her: once started, never stopped.'

Aunty Carol stares blankly from the lounger.

Mum strains forward to reach her own shins and runs her hands through the oil. 'He hates it when I'm bristly.'

Aunty Carol nods slowly.

'Once shaved,' muses Mum, 'and they're never the same again.'

'I wax mine,' says aunty Carol.

Mum does not reply.

'And they are so much smoother.'

Mum is staring at the cypress trees. 'What a palaver,' she says eventually.

'Oh no,' says aunty Carol zealously, 'it's no bother at all. It's wonderful. I think she should have them waxed.'

I would have to go to the Helen of Troy Beauty Parlour in the High Street, and I have no pocket money. I have no pocket money because Mum and Dad claim that it is unnecessary; they claim that they buy me everything that I need. I remind myself with pleasure that in three-and-a-half years' time, whem I am sixteen, I will leave home. I will have a wage. I will live without them in a flat in London.

Aunty Carol interrupts my thoughts: 'Don't you want to slip into the pool? You must be very hot.' She grins at me. 'We won't look. Promise.' Her big bright teeth hang between her open lips.

'She can't,' says Mum triumphantly.

I lean out of the lounger and direct my words at aunty Carol: 'I don't want to swim today, thanks.'

'Wrong time of the month,' announces Mum.

'Let's hope your next baby is a boy,' murmurs aunty Carol. 'They're less trouble.'

'Oh no,' protests Mum, horrified, 'I want another little girl.'

'Really?'

'Oh yes. I don't like boys.'

'Really?' The note of curiosity in aunty Carol's voice has changed to a note of concern. She shifts on her lounger. 'Boys are super. My Alistair was a super baby.'

I open my eyes and peer across the terrace at Alistair. He is planning to dive-bomb Verity.

'Boys are closer to their mothers,' explains aunty Carol.

Mum closes her eyes.

'No, really,' says aunty Carol. 'My Jane, she's lovely, she's super, don't get me wrong, but she's a proper little madam. Girls have minds of their own. They're shrewd.' She slumps back onto her lounger.

'They have to be,' murmurs Mum.

'Oh yes,' agrees aunty Carol readily, 'they have to be.'

Aunty Carol tilts her face to the sun. 'Jane's a survivor. She doesn't need a lot of help from her mother.'

I suspect that there is not a lot on offer.

'I want another little girl,' mutters Mum. Sunlight settles on her eyelids. 'I've waited a long time for this one. This one will be different. Third time lucky.'

SUNDAY
23 APRIL 1989

As I hurry through the door my eyes snap shut momentarily in the glare of white walls and ceilings and floors, the hot bright haze of enforced sleeplessness. I turn from the entrance hall into the doctors' room, dropping my bag onto the floor beneath the coat rack and beginning to remove my coat. The room smells of cigarettes, curry, and the potato crisps that form a gritty paste between the cushions of the armchairs. I hang my coat on a peg and turn from the coat rack to see Ginny behind me at the end of the room. She sits at the end of the row of armchairs. I am surprised to see her because her shift finished an hour ago at eight o'clock.

She has not seen me. She is sitting forward in the low armchair; doubled, hunched, reaching towards the coffee table. On the coffee table there is a mug which she stirs, the teaspoon rattling against the china. Her head droops and the familiar auburn pony tail fans from the nape of her neck across her shoulders. I stand in the doorway for a moment. The teaspoon rattles incessantly, irregularly.

'Ginny?'

I wonder whether she has heard me; I wonder whether I should repeat myself or leave. I lay my hand on the door handle.

She raises her head and stares at me; it seems to me that she stares without recognition. My hand tightens around the door handle. I have always been uneasy with Ginny. We have never had much in common. Her auburn hair has an expensive sheen; her conversation has an expensive accent.

This morning her complexion is uncharacteristically dull. I remind myself that she is tired, that she has been working all night; but she continues to clatter the teaspoon inside the mug and it occurs to me that she may not cease unless I take it away from her. *In shock*: this use of the term is disparaged by us because shock refers to a specific physiological condition; but how else can I describe Ginny? She is shocked; she has been shocked; something has shocked her.

'Ginny, are you all right?'

The question is facile, but it breaks the spell: she breathes a long shuddering sigh, closes her agate eyes, and rests the teaspoon against the side of the mug. 'I'm tired, that's all.' The eyes remain closed.

I slide my fingertips noiselessly up and down the door handle behind me.

'But you don't want to go home?'

She shakes her head. 'No.'

I step backwards through the doorway but her eyes flick open. She stares at me and then sighs and lowers her head into her hands. 'I don't know what's the matter with me,' she mutters. I can barely hear the words; I hold my breath and step towards her. She drops her hands from her face and looks wearily at me.

I cross the room and sit beside her: 'What happened?'

She bows her head over her hands. 'At about seven thirty this morning we had a call warning us of an incoming RTA: two lads, late teens, motorcyclists, multiple injuries.' She shrugs: bike accidents are not unusual. 'So everyone was ready. And one of the lads went straight into theatre.' She glances sideways at me: 'He was blown up like a balloon,' she explains quietly, 'and he died.' She resumes the examination of her hands. 'The other one was already dead. I had to go into the ambulance to look at him.'

I murmur sympathetically.

She looks sharply at me. 'No,' she counters, 'it wasn't like that at all.'

She sighs.

'I was expecting the worst.' She glances briefly at me. 'You know. . .'

I nod.

'But it wasn't like that at all. I went out to the ambulance; and George, the driver, said to me: "I think I should warn you, doctor, that he's still warm." But I thought nothing of it.' She pauses and shrugs. 'Or perhaps I didn't know what to think.' Suddenly she turns towards me, spasmodic and pallid. 'But he was right, Beth.' Her eyes drift under the pale shining shells of her eyelids. 'I got into the ambulance, lifted the sheet, and looked down at a perfect face. He was unmarked, beautiful, still warm.' She reaches into the nape of her neck and draws the band slowly from her hair. 'I couldn't believe that he was dead.' The hair springs in a flash from her hands to her shoulders; she rakes it from her forehead with her fingers. 'It was awful,' she says. 'I can't explain why it was so much more awful than usual.'

The tannoy blurts indistinctly in the distance.

'He reminded me of my youngest brother.'

Ginny went home several minutes ago. She came into the department to say goodbye to me. 'Cheerio,' she said. She was wearing a long dark coat, her red hair nestling on her shoulders like a fox fur. She had begun walking away when Chris joined me.

'Bye bye, petal,' he called after her.

She did not reply.

He turned to me. 'What's up with Rumpelstiltskin?'

I reached towards the computer printer for the details of my first patient.

'These career women,' he began to lament behind me. 'Give them an inch and they'll take a mile.'

I lifted a folder from the desk top with a flourish.

He sighed noisily: 'Only joking. What's up with *you*?'

119

I turned towards him and grinned into his face as I walked away: 'It must be my hormones, doctor.'

Last night I telephoned my father and asked him why he had not called me during the day. His reply was as I had expected: no news. He sounded despondent so I resisted the urge to castigate him for his broken promise.

I asked him instead whether he had been to the hospital to visit my mother. Yes, he told me, twice: once during the afternoon and then again in the early evening.

I asked him whether there had been any other visitors.

'No. Verity 'phoned me this morning to say that she and Neil would drive over to the hospital after shopping this afternoon, but I had to ring her back later and tell her that your mother didn't feel like having visitors.'

Verity and Neil live together in London. They bought a house last year. I know about the legendary bedlinen: 'She has been spending money,' my mother reported disapprovingly to me when informing me of Verity's move. *Too much money*, she meant.

'And it's so unnecessary,' she lamented. 'Posh cotton bedlinen, Irish.' She stressed *posh* and *Irish*, implying incongruity. 'I said to her, if it's bedlinen you need, then there's plenty here, and you might as well take it because no one else is using it. But there's no telling Verity.'

Verity refused the offer of the flannelette sheets that had bandaged us into our beds each night and had absorbed the sweat of our dreams.

'I've always had a lot of bedlinen,' my mother told me. 'It's one of the advantages of marriage,' she added sourly, sarcastically: 'bedlinen and toasters.'

Verity and Neil are not married. They met a couple of years ago.

Verity had left home at seventeen to be an au pair in Fulham. I had carried boxes from her bedroom to the boot of the car. The boxes contained her possessions: a musical jewellery box encrusted with small white seashells; a clock radio bearing bewildering commands (timer, recall, sleep, snooze); several perfume bottles wet inside with pale liquid gold; a rag doll pyjama case, the large head rolling in a swoon. I cradled the boxes because they were disintegrating. The cardboard panels, labelled *tinned peas* and *cat food*, were hung with loose staples.

'Watch those staples,' my mother called to us from the doorstep.

When Verity and Neil bought their house, my mother sent me the brochure: the house is on an estate of new houses built at a large and distant bend of the Thames. My mother championed the local amenities: a dry ski slope; a hypermarket; and, one day, a railway line into the city. I try to picture the house. 'Two up, two down,' my mother said.

Two *what*? Are the kitchen and the bathroom included in the count? If the kitchen is not counted with the living room as one of the two rooms on the ground floor, then what is the other room? In a house so short of space, a dining room is an extravagance. Verity will have no use for a dining room: she eats from a plate on her lap in front of the television. Her meals involve no improvisation: no side dishes, salads or breads; no dipping, scraping, negotiating. They come from the freezer and the takeaway. They occupy little space. She does not entertain.

I might use a spare room as a study. Verity does not study. Her spare room will become a front room. Unlike a living room, dining room, playroom, study or kitchen, a front room is defined solely in terms of location. My mother hated the front room in my grandparents' house: 'Front rooms and Sundays,' she says sometimes, shuddering, hinting at childhood boredom and misery.

Perhaps I would use a spare room to be alone, if I lived with Neil; but, in a sense, Verity is always alone, and she is best alone in

121

company. Whenever she wanted to be alone at home she would lurk around us, withdrawn and defiant. She would sit in front of the television, the volume high. A front room cannot be a private room. A private room must be elsewhere: at the back of a house, perhaps, or the top. A private room cannot have small windows with bright brass fittings and net curtains. It cannot have a clean dun carpet from wall to wall. There must be bookshelves, but Verity does not DIY.

'End of terrace,' my mother said of Verity's house.

I try to picture the terrace, the terraces: short, low, red. I imagine the intersecting planes of the small tiled roofs. There will be tiled bunkers in the gardens, not for coal but for household waste.

Lilly was once temporarily employed by a property developer to work during the summer in a show house. She was required to create a homely atmosphere. It was suggested that she might brew coffee for prospective buyers, and bake biscuits.

She joked with me that it was her contribution to the Wages For Housework Campaign.

'Act natural,' said her employer.

This was a mistake. She was dismissed after a fortnight. 'Sex, drugs, and rock 'n' roll,' she told me; and then, more truthfully, she admitted to: 'Washing and ironing, wearing jim-jams, lying on the sofa, watching afternoon telly, playing records, eating chips, cooking curry and inviting friends.'

Ideal for first-time buyers, the brochure had assured Verity and Neil. There was mention of starter mortgages and low interest rates.

'London prices,' I commented dubiously to my mother. 'How can they afford it?'

'You forget,' she said, 'that Neil works for a bank. He has a mortgage subsidy.'

I queried the price.

'It has a garage,' she said.

✳ ✳ ✳

Ginny has left three patients waiting for Tom Grant. They have been informed that they are waiting for the Medical Senior House Officer, and that he is currently on the Coronary Care Unit.

'He's been there an hour or two,' a student nurse tells me, 'sorting someone out.'

I wonder whether he has had any sleep. He has been here since Friday morning. He will be here until tomorrow evening. Tomorrow morning is Monday morning: he will begin the working week as usual and work until the weekend, including Wednesday night. Like most of the doctors here, except the Casualty Officers, his rota is a one-in-three: he covers one night each week, and every third weekend. Doctors do not earn overtime: instead, for our compulsory extra hours we are paid a retainer at a lower rate than a cleaner.

Casualty Officers make the decision to refer patients to Senior House Officers for admissions to the wards. There are three Medical Senior House Officers *on take* on rota. Tom is my favourite. He is popular with the Casualty staff because he is helpful and accessible despite his insistence that we should not distract him with *just-a-minute-Tom-can-I-ask-you-something-Tom?* He tells us to make a decision: do we want to refer the patient, or not?

Your decision, he reminds us, not *mine*.

He explains to us that he is too busy with bona fide referrals to peek over our shoulders, to familiarise himself with every patient in Casualty, to feel confident to offer advice when he has not read the notes or done an examination.

Do you want to refer the patient? he asks us. *Use your initiative, trust your judgement, because you've got to learn sometime.*

He lectures us kindly. He told me that it is an unpleasant rite of passage for most Casualty Officers to witness the emergency readmission of the patient whom they had discharged earlier, with the diagnosis of non-cardiac chest pain.

The Coronary Care Unit is on level seven, far above the Casualty Department. When I was a House Physician, in another hospital, and my Senior House Officer was *on take*, he would surface on the wards from Casualty at irregular intervals throughout the day and night. Whenever I was not too tired, I liked the wards at night. Now, walking towards my first patient, turning from the glare of the windows into the corridor, I think of *the dead of night* and recall the hypothesis that there are more cot deaths during winter due to the longer nights: nights are dark, cold, lonely, frightening, and babies panic. In hospital, there are few dark, cold, lonely and frightening nights for staff. In Casualty, there is a risk of violence towards staff, but the nurses carry alarms. The doctors have not been provided with alarms. Perhaps it is assumed that we will provide our own, as we provide our own stethoscopes and paraphernalia to fill the pockets of our white coats; or perhaps it is assumed that we are men, that the nurses are women, and that the men can take care of themselves.

When I was a House Physician, my SHO would climb the stairs from Casualty to the wards rather than use the lifts. Sometimes the lifts were unavoidable: sometimes he was required to travel with a patient from Casualty to the Coronary Care Unit, wedging himself with the trolley between the two porters and the accompanying nurse. He would hold his breath and stare at the monitor. Between floors there was nothing: no assistance, no equipment, no space, no hope. He dreaded a death between floors.

$$* \quad * \quad *$$

Last night, I spoke to Lilly. I was asleep in bed when the telephone rang. It bleated in the kitchen whilst I rolled from under my duvet and hurried across the hallway and through the living room. I knew it was Lilly; she had said she would ring. As I reached for the 'phone I glanced up at the clock on the wall: twenty minutes to one. Lilly lisped into my ear, her voice running with alcohol. I told her what news there was because she was expecting to hear it. The kitchen glinted in the deep warm darkness. My words, fragranced with sleep, were both familiar to me but strange. Lilly said very little. There is very little to say.

Lilly and I were not friends until we were fifteen. We were at school together from the age of eleven but in different classes with different friends. I knew Lilly as the girl with short bleached hair who stood alone in the refectory at lunchtimes and urged a boycott of South African fruit. Everyone knew that she had been threatened with expulsion for displaying antivivisection posters on what the Headmaster termed *school property*. Her only interest at school was drama; the only teacher with whom she had a rapport was Mr MacKay, the Head of English and Drama. Mr MacKay took over my English class when the teacher left to have a baby, and persuaded me to join Drama Club; and so, at fifteen, Lilly and I were both involved in the school production of *A Midsummer Night's Dream*. Lilly had had a leading role in the previous production. This time she was make-up. I was Puck. Pygmy, she called me.

At dress rehearsals, slapping greasepaint onto faces, Lilly would insist loudly and repeatedly that Olivier had never shirked his nightly three-hour preparations for *Othello*. Lilly's ambition was to go to drama school, as she claimed her mother had done. The worst insult she could offer us was *amateur*; we were *a bunch of fucking amateurs*: she would scream this in the dressing room during rehearsals and Mr MacKay would call pleasantly from the stage for *a little more quiet please, Lilly*. During the final dress rehearsal she leaned towards me in the darkness of the stage curtain and asked if I had ever considered auditioning for RADA.

I arranged to stay at her house after the last-night party because it was impossible for me to return late by bus to the village. I slept on a spare mattress in her bedroom. At eleven o'clock the next morning there was a quiet knock at the door and a woman entered with a tray: on the tray was a teapot, two cups and saucers, a jug of milk and a sugar bowl. I presumed that the woman was Lilly's mother but she was not as I had imagined. She was not a Lady

Macbeth: she was golden. Below the golden head, across the white cotton shoulders, was a pastel cashmere cardigan; and on her shoes were navy blue polka dot bows. Soft and fragrant like a powder puff, she came between the beds and placed the tray on the bedside table. Then she smiled and whispered something about *sleeping beauties* before leaving without making an attempt to wake Lilly who had been vomiting noisily all night in the bathroom.

Subsequently on Saturday and Sunday mornings Lilly's mother would bring tea for two, expecting to find me asleep beneath the blankets that she left on Friday nights at the foot of the spare mattress. She thought it perfectly understandable that I should not want to return home to the village at weekends: *out there*, she called it. She told me that she liked living in town: she said that proximity to the railway station enabled her to spend an occasional evening in London at the theatre. She told me that she had once been a student at RADA for a year. For the past fifteen years she had been distributing Meals On Wheels: my mother, discovering this, began to refer to her as *Lady Bountiful*. In the early evenings she worked as a receptionist at the local doctors' surgery: lots of gossip, Lilly confirmed. I replied lightheartedly that we should avoid pregnancy tests but Lilly looked puzzled and said that her mother was *okay about things like that, and, anyway, she'd probably want to adopt the bastard*.

Lilly's father was a teacher at a school in London. He was Head of Maths. Chalk dust dropped from his tweed jackets and his holly-coloured jumpers of waxy green and berry red, but otherwise his presence at home was undetectable: he arrived home late in the evening and sat until bedtime in his study with a pile of unmarked books on the arm of his chair and a tumbler of whisky in his hand. He chewed gum, a habit acquired ten years previously when giving up smoking. He was animated only when the public examination results were published each summer; and at the end of the year when his favourite newspaper printed its annual quiz. On the day of the quiz he would follow us round the house, flapping the newspaper and demanding to know about the year's disasters and crises and scandals, expressing dismay whenever he could not obtain a satisfactory answer but writing something nevertheless in pencil against each question. At all other times he left us alone: smiling when he saw us but turning away. *Girls' talk.* Each year on my birthday and at Christmas I received a card from Lilly's mother signed *with love and best wishes from Anne and David.*

Lilly's mother, unlike mine, did not complain about periods: she never mentioned them; perhaps she did not have them. She had not had a baby since Lilly, whose christening photograph graced the hallway. My parents did not frame photographs but left them bulging from yellow wallets in a box in the cupboard beneath the stairs. I had not been christened. Lilly's parents, unlike mine, did not refer to their children as *kids.* They spoke of Lilly's elder brother Simon as *our son,* and Lilly as *our lovable daughter.* This was said sarcastically of Lilly, but indulgently, her father ruffling her silky white hair. Lilly's mother was fond of telling people that *Simon has brains but Lilly has talent.*

Simon's brains were mathematical like his father's; he was studying Maths and Economics at Reading University. I remembered him vaguely as a sixth former with long hair. Apparently he had once owned the poster of Jim Morrison that hung above Lilly's bed. Lilly's mother, attempting self-parody, called it the poster of the ascetic young gentleman; Lilly, similarly, would retort that Jim Morrison was the most gorgeous man that ever lived; whilst Simon had insisted that it's only rock and roll. His record collection extended in cardboard boxes beyond his deserted bedroom into the hallway. Lilly delved for Patti Smith records and referred so frequently and knowledgeably to '68 that I assumed Simon had been politically active at the time whereas in fact he had been nine years old.

Simon was accompanied home in the holidays by his girlfriend, Natasha. Lilly informed me one day that I would meet them both at the following weekend. I arrived on the Friday evening to find their coats on the pegs in the hallway and their shoes on the mat. Lilly led me into the kitchen to be introduced. Simon and Natasha were standing together at the window. Simon's hair was short and he had gained weight.

'Chips,' explained Lilly, guessing my thoughts and pinching his fattened cheek between her forefinger and thumb.

'Peroxide,' he replied, laughing and gently tugging her hair. 'Roots,' he added, tapping her shadowy crown.

Natasha's hair was long and dark, hanging to her waist. She wore a man's shirt over her jeans, the white cotton scallops of the shirt tail reaching towards her knees.

Simon had been living in Reading on chips and cigarettes. On his first evening at home we ate chicken casserole with runner beans and sweetcorn and new potatoes, followed by cheese and biscuits. After the meal he went into the garden to smoke. Slumping against the back door, illuminated by the kitchen window, he stabbed a cigarette between his lips. Natasha preferred valium: there was a bottle of tablets in her make-up bag in the bathroom. The tablets had been prescribed for Mrs Philippa Delaney, her mother. Also inside the make-up bag was a small pink case similar in appearance to a compact: Lilly opened it one day to reveal a diaphragm nestling soft and pale like a pearl inside a shell. We knew all about the cap: at school Mrs Pincott, the Biology teacher, had distributed a leaflet to the girls during the annual fourth form sexually segregated Social Responsibility Seminar. Years before, when I was too young to be left alone, I had sat at my mother's feet in the bathroom whenever she washed her cap with soap and water and dried it gently with a towel before dusting it with powder: thus it remained as soft and clean and pink and supple as the flesh of a young white woman is supposed to be.

Natasha slept with Simon in his bedroom. When she was not in the bedroom she was in the bathroom washing her hair or in the hallway speaking indecipherably on the telephone to foreign friends: she was a student of Modern Languages, French and German. Sometimes during the afternoons she came into the kitchen to concoct: chocolate mousse, banana fritters, oatmeal

128

cookies. Bowls lay in the sink collecting filmy water whilst she sat at the table chatting to us about her friends: B.B., R.B., Vicky, Nicki, Trixie, Ritzi, Loco, Lukey, Sammy, Seb. Occasionally during holidays she and Simon left to stay with friends; and sometimes they went to visit her brother Anthony (Ant, Anti, Ants-in-your-pants) who had moved from London to live in a community in Wales. Occasionally they stayed with her parents who were separated but living in London; her father a Professor of Economics, her mother a journalist.

'What do you think of Natasha?' Lilly asked me one day. She was lying on her bed; I was lying on the mattress. The floor between us was encrusted with empty coffee cups; the cassette player crackled Pink Floyd. Lilly raised herself, propping her chin with her hand: 'She's all right, isn't she,' she added. *All right*: the ultimate accolade.

If Simon and Natasha were absent when Lilly's parents were planning a trip away from home, Lilly's mother would feel obliged to perform a certain routine: she would ask us anxiously whether it was advisable for her to leave us alone.

'What's the problem?' Lilly would demand.

The problem, we knew, was my parents: Lilly's mother was aware that my parents did not allow me to stay at home for any length of time without them. She did not understand that this was due to my parents' concern for the size of their 'phone bill: I was *irresponsible*, I would make 'phone calls; and I would also probably forget to shut the shed door at night. Lilly's mother had only ever used the word *irresponsible* to refer to politicians.

Lilly had decided to study English. She was horrified by my intention to study Medicine. She would wrinkle her nose and then claim with pride that she had never needed a doctor, that she had never been ill. She went eventually to London University, as her father had done.

I found it hard to accept that anyone from my parents' generation had been to university: I believed that everyone had left

129

school at fifteen in the olden days, in the black-and-white past, and that universities were an invention of the late 1960s. Lilly's father, however, had been to university in London in the days of *smog*. I knew that he would have lived in *digs*: my mother often talked about *digs*, implying that I would have to live in them when I became a student. If I thought hard enough about it, I could imagine Lilly's father resting a big black bicycle against some big black railings and then climbing steep wet steps to a front door; returning to a room with limp brown curtains and a meter; his expression startled beneath an unrelenting and pitiless haircut, his neck bound by a college scarf, his ankles wiry with bicycle clips. He was hoping not to disturb the landlady. The landlady was either fat with an apron or thin with rollers in her hair.

Lilly has never lived anywhere other than London or the suburbs. She left home for university and met Harv: an ex-pat American lecturer with an estranged wife in New Jersey and a flat in Islington. His name was Jason but Lilly called him Harv. She moved into his flat after a term in a hall of residence. She occasionally returned home for a visit: *putting in an appearance*, she called it, telephoning me each time and inviting me to join her. I would arrive to find the family in the distance in the garden, encircling the rosebushes: the older couple leaning towards the flowerbed, probing amongst thorns, debating pruning; and Harv turning to smile at me in greeting. Sometimes I found them in the living room; Harv folded onto the sofa, long-limbed and awkward on subsiding cushions but nevertheless attentive and eager to participate in the courtly exchange of pleasantries. Lilly liked to pinch his cheek and exclaim that he was *real cute*. They stayed together for five years. Simon and Natasha separated not long after their graduation when Natasha went to live in Berlin with a friend, Hans, to whom Lilly would refer bitterly afterwards as *Hans Christian Andersen*, or *Handy Andy* or *Andy Pandy* for short.

$$* \quad * \quad *$$

Lilly has only once contacted me during the day from work. A couple of years ago she rang me one afternoon and asked me to meet her in the evening for a drink. There was nothing in the content or the tone of the request to imply urgency but I knew that I should comply. She was an infrequent caller at the time. It was also unusual for her to decline an invitation to my flat, and even more unusual for her to fail to invite me to Islington. Usually she was eager for visitors.

'It's all right,' she used to insist cheerfully. But it was not. It was not all right because it was not her flat; it was Harv's flat and she was a lodger there since their separation.

I was pleased to be able to avoid the flat; I was not pleased at the prospect of meeting in town. I was completing a thirty-six hour shift at the hospital and beginning another in the morning. I had been looking forward to a quiet evening; I had been looking forward to watching *Dallas*. I decided to watch *Dallas* before leaving, even though I would be late to meet Lilly. We had arranged to meet at nine o'clock: she wanted to go home after work to change her clothes and have something to eat. She was teaching in a school in Waltham Cross. Once again I would be denied an opportunity to see her as *Miss*. I could not imagine her as *Miss*. *Misdemeanour*, she used to say.

I cannot imagine anyone as *Miss*. *Miss* is a character in a sit com, young and giggly in a garter or old and hideous. Single women have a short shelf life.

The best time of your life, my mother used to tell me, laughing. And I was puzzled because I knew that she had had no experience of life as a single woman. She was nineteen when she married my father. My father used to insist that *your mother rules the roost* – but it was untrue: for all but the most unpleasant or routine decisions and duties she would insist that *we wait until your father gets home*. And so we would wait for his car to prowl beneath us into the garage, turning day into night.

My mother used to urge me *to go for what you want from life*. Her tone implied recommendation, as if she was enjoying success.

So, was this what she had wanted? Marriage to my father, and a life at home with Carrie and Verity and me?

No, she had wanted to live outside London. And in this she had succeeded. London was somewhere to leave, not somewhere to live. She cannot comprehend that people choose to live in London; she is baffled that people pay for the privilege; she is nonplussed by gentrification.

My mother used to speak to me of children in London who *never see cows*. I saw cows every day from my bedroom window: they were lumps of black and white, inert in distant fields like pieces of Lego. Children in London were *Dr Barnado* children, *Oliver Twist* children, children who wore *leg irons*. There was a collection box for them on the counter at the local chemist. Once a year we raised money for them at school by selling *Sunny Smiles*. A national charity issued us with copies of a booklet of black and white photographs of smiling children; the booklet was called *Sunny Smiles*. The children lived in *homes*. Photographs were exchanged for financial contributions, and contributors received the photograph of their choice. The photograph of the black baby remained until last in the booklet, until it was bought by a pitying adult.

A couple of years ago, walking across the hospital car park at the end of the day, contemplating meeting Lilly in the evening, it occurred to me that my mother had not protested at my decision to study medicine in London because she had been ignorant of the alternatives and dazzled by the prestige.

But she had been deeply suspicious of Lilly's choice of university. 'Why London? Why not somewhere up North with scenery?'

When I had qualified, she had expressed dismay at my decision to stay in London.

'Job!' I insisted, my irritation whistling into the telephone mouthpiece.

I had been anxious not only about my own job, the compulsory pre-registration year, but Jem's job, too. And also there was *home*:

Jem and I had been living together for a year in the one-bedroomed rented flat in Bethnal Green.

'Bethnal Green in the heart of the Docklands,' we would joke with friends. The friends would laugh appreciatively: they had been lucky enough to find flats in Archway on Highgate Hill or Finsbury Park in Islington.

How had London become valuable? The answer rattled around inside my head as I searched my flat for my purse: service industry, financial services, communications. The words belonged to the BBC, and to the A level Economics and Geography syllabuses studied by Kieran and Lilly at school. Squalor remained in these accounts but in an inner city, I had heard poverty in London described as *a cancer*. I understood that cancer in this context meant *alien, uncontrollable, unpredictable, relentless, degenerative, degrading, ugly*.

'Inaccurate,' I insisted to Kieran and Lilly whenever they used the expression, 'inappropriate, unoptimistic.'

'No imagination,' they accused. 'It's a *metaphor*,' they explained, gloating with wordpower.

My mother never used the expression *inner city* but spoke instead of *slums*; she never referred to *docklands* but to *docks*. London, for her, was still the city of the blitz.

London, for me, after my grandparents had gone, was a city of day trips.

Mum, Dad, Verity and I went into London occasionally at weekends but more often on bank holidays or during the school holidays. It was important to leave home by ten. Dad would shout this to us from the kitchen, his voice thick with marmalade. Verity and I were upstairs, choosing suitable clothes, our bedrooms ringing with Mum's suggestions. 'Cat suits today, girls, and don't forget to pack a nice warm jumper.' Mum was busy in the bathroom; but eventually she hurried into the hallway to bellow a checklist of essentials. 'Hats, coats, gloves, scarves!'

Shortly before eleven o'clock Verity and I would climb into the car and settle on the back seat, sweltering; and Mum would sink into the front passenger seat, pressing her dark hair against the head rest. At the start of the journey she would lift her bare feet onto the dashboard and begin to clip her toe nails. Then, when the nails had been clipped, she would reach into the bag of sweets on her lap.

'Save some for later,' Dad objected, glancing briefly at her fingers.

'One at a time,' she echoed, passing the sweets over her shoulder towards the back seat: 'and give the wrappers to me,' she emphasised amid the high pitched squeaks of unravelling polythene.

She liked to replace our wrappers in the bag and transfer them to a litter bin when we reached our destination.

Dad was silent throughout the journey at the controls of the car. He listened to the news programmes broadcast by local radio stations. Our local radio stations were based in London: sometimes we rolled past the headquarters, our car reflecting briefly on walls of glass and steel beneath the zig-zag of neon numerals. The headquarters towered mute above the traffic but the voices reached us, impaling themselves upon our aerial. Mum called the chat shows and 'phone-ins 'a bloody noise'. She wanted to listen to pop music. Dad replied that she had raised kids with their heads full of The Jackson Five.

Mum claims that Dad knows the streets of London *like the back of his hand*. I used to gaze at the back of his hand as he tightened his grip on the gear stick. It was a large hand, covered with dark hairs. I used to feel pity for him as the car jerked through the London traffic. I expressed sympathy for him on one occasion but Mum made efforts to convince me otherwise: 'he loves driving,' she said. He smiled, and the controls on the dashboard winked at him like the controls in a cockpit. He bought a new car every two years: *on the business*, my mother would explain to me. This explained nothing to me and probably not much more to her because she often complained of *new cars but no new shoes for the kids.*

When I was a child we had a new car, a fitted kitchen, and a villa in Spain: we were considered well off by friends and relatives and neighbours. No one understood that we had a car and a kitchen and a villa because we had nothing else: no pocket money, no hairstyles, no pet dog, no trips to the cinema *because you can wait until it comes onto the telly,* no books or records *because they're a waste of money because you never look at them twice and anyway why else do we have a library?*

Lilly used to tease me, calling me *Rich Kid.* I should have protested that her parents had monthly salaries and annual increments and sick pay and pensions; that they drank wine in the evenings and went to the theatre at weekends; that their house was old but decorated with a snow of blossom each spring, and their car was old but hilarious when it needed a bump-start in the mornings.

As far as I know, Lilly has never listened to conversations between her parents about *livelihood;* nor has she ever saved birthday and Christmas money in a piggy bank to donate to them in the future. Her parents did not face a future of hardship. They were planning early retirement in the town house close to the station; in rooms hung with photographs and books, in a garden sizzling with fruit and rattling with the remains of the tree house. My parents, on the contrary, were always talking of *running:* we've had a *good run* so far; our luck is about to *run out.*

Our new family cars were ordered only when great attention had been paid to the choice of colour: sky blue or metallic blue? There was no choice of model: my father ordered the same model each time; it was described by the brochure as stylish but reliable. This was how my father would have liked to have been described: stylish but reliable. He had learned to lament *the old days* with a smile. He had learned to tell the story of how he sold his motorbike and bought his first car on the day that I was born. I felt remorse whenever I glimpsed his hand reaching for the stylish but reliable gear stick: he had been a mechanic until I was born and I knew that he would rather build motorbikes in the backyard than order cars from brochures.

When we drove into London we came from the north, our car linking with others in a chain broken only by pedestrian crossings. The pedestrians cringed beneath dim umbrellas. The streets were noisy with the sighs of vehicles running through rainwater. We were sealed behind glass, sitting in the car, watching shoppers drifting in and out of patisseries and bakeries. The shops were warm and bright, the shelves lined with tan loaves and sparkling doughnuts. The bleached fossils of celebration cakes were on display in glass cases. I watched shoppers drifting from the patisseries and bakeries to the greengrocer to buy crackling raw leaves and calloused dun roots. During the journey we passed several Odeons, massive chalky outcrops amongst terraces of shops. A restricted choice of films was available, graded for consumption. The titles were displayed crookedly above the doors like cake decorations pressed unevenly into icing.

Eventually we reached Highgate and rolled down the hill into central London, passing the statue of Dick Whittington's cat. 'Turn again,' said my mother every time, delighted with the legend of her birthplace; and I recalled a picture book, a learn-to-read book, a brightly painted illustration of Dick Whittington with his possessions in a bundle over his shoulder. The bundle was made from a red polka dot handkerchief. I was troubled in early childhood by the thought of so few possessions: where were his toys? where were the boxes filled with cards and counters and dice, the Snap and Ludo that my mother considered good for journeys and packed for us into the back of the car?

Below Highgate, at the foot of the hill, the car slinked into Bloomsbury past the grey buildings of the hospital. The hospital gates were open but forbidding. Signposts appealed to patients and visitors but displayed unrecognisable words: oncology, urology, physiotherapy. They were long thin waxy strips piled in bundles at the gates like unlit candles. Beneath the signposts women

136

wearing caps and capes on their heads and shoulders hurried along the pavement in pairs.

'Irish,' my mother would say, indicating the nurses, frowning in pity, 'over on the boat from Ireland.'

Did we ever go to London to see the Queen? I remember black taxis circling Buckingham Palace like flies. I remember Madame Tussaud's; I remember the zoo. Often I came home from London with a litter of admission tickets in my pockets and the sensation of turnstiles against my stomach. Sometimes the spectacle was free: a lace of lights in the dark December sky above Regent Street; a dragon reeling around Trafalgar Square on Chinese New Year. There was always a treat when my father rolled the car into a parking space and took us across the street into a café where we sat at a formica table, peeling off our gloves and hats and choosing meals without greens – cheese on toast, omelette and chips – and anticipating the squeeze of scarlet sauce from sachets onto our plates.

On that evening a couple of years ago I travelled underground to meet Lilly. I went late to the station and joined a queue at the ticket office. After buying a ticket I stood on the escalator and watched the steps dribble slowly beneath me to the tunnels. The staircases were noisy with wind: an airless wind: a ghost of a wind. I stepped from the escalator and drew my coat tightly around me. My mother had hidden in underground stations during air raids. Sometimes there had been no time to reach a shelter so she had hidden at home in the cellar. 'Holding my breath,' she used to tell me; 'holding it tightly.'

Incarceration in the cellar was used as a punishment after the war until she was tall enough to reach the latch.

I walked from the stairwell onto the platform. The information board was blank. Suddenly I realised that I disliked London. Jem had left the flat and I was supposed to be looking for somewhere else to live. Rents were exorbitant. Doors were opened only after

137

a prolonged shudder of locks and bolts and chains. Sometimes I was welcomed first by a spitting entryphone: *Yes?*

No, I did not want to live in London; but where else? I glanced behind me at the map on the wall: Network South East. It bore a corporate logo. Lines extended in bold primary colours from London into Kent, Surrey, Sussex, Hampshire, Berkshire, Oxfordshire, Buckinghamshire, Bedfordshire, Hertfordshire, and Essex: Home Counties. Why *Home* Counties? They were not home to me.

I did not want to have to wade to the station in the morning through a swill of conical fast food coke cartons. I did not want to have to witness the sparring of stiletto heels on concrete, the sole street life of London. I did not want to stand at the ticket office and write another large cheque for another travel pass, glimpsing an impatient pair of hands on the other side of the window. I did not want to go into underground tunnels and hear the growl of train doors on trapped limbs.

As the train trundled through the tunnels I thought hard about why my mother's parents had stayed in London. My grandfather was Scottish. Work, my mother had insisted. Sometimes she cited the depression. My grandfather had come to London from Glasgow as a teenager. It did not occur to me to ask for my grandmother's reasons: London was my grandmother's home; a woman's place was in the home; my grandmother was a conventional woman. Wartime, however, was an exception: evacuation was advised, women and children first. My grandmother stayed amid the bombs but sent her mother away to her death in the countryside. Away with her small child, my mother.

When I was a teenager I went alone into London on Saturdays. I left home early, glancing into the kitchen on my way from my bedroom to the front door.

'I think I'll go into London today,' I'd say nonchalantly to Mum from the doorway.

The kitchen was warm with the smell of nightdresses and toast. The radio on the breakfast bar was ringing with a peal of wedding announcements. Mum and Carrie sat together at the table. Mum was probing Carrie's lips with a spoon; Carrie was rigid, resisting the spoon, suppressing a scream. I would step away before Mum could reply. I would escape. She would call out to me as I shut the front door behind me.

'Have you got enough money on you?'

When I began the habit, when I was thirteen, I was a half fare on the bus. I stopped when I was sixteen, when I found other things to do, but the bus conductors still considered me under fourteen.

At thirteen, unlike me, Lilly was a little girl. She stayed close to home on Saturdays. She went with her brother to the local tennis court in the morning; and in the afternoon she sat in an armchair, wearing an old shirt of her father's, eating everything that her mother had bought earlier in the local delicatessen, and gazing beyond the pages of a book towards the television screen. On Saturday afternoons, the television screens that were not bright with sport were black and white with ancient tap dancers. The images were multiple on screens in shop windows in London like images on the surface of a fly's eye.

Whilst Lilly had been skipping across the tennis court, a pair of rosy brown pigtails chaotic on her shoulders, I had been standing at the village bus stop waiting for a bus to take me into town; and whilst she had been strolling home with Simon, I had been leaving town on a bus bound for London.

The bus stop in town was at the bus station. The bus station was a terminus, built in the 1920s or 1930s. The driveway was a crescent and the grounds were planted with conifers and flower-beds. The quixotic monkey puzzle trees were impressive but the flowerbeds were unruly with hollyhocks and dandelions. The garage was noisy with London buses steaming under jets of water. The bus drivers were Londoners carrying packets of sandwiches. They were cheerful because this was the countryside. I went with them on their return journeys to central London.

In London, I liked to wander through the streets and squares of the West End. During the winter, the shop windows lined the pavements like lanterns; during the summer, the tall buildings cast cold shadows. I wandered the streets drinking milkshakes and eating ice cream and bars of chocolate. I liked to stay until early evening, delaying the journey back home.

1973

I am in the kitchen, heating the milk for my bedtime drink. I stare into the saucepan. I am waiting for the milk to seethe against the hot metal.

Heat the milk until it boils, Mum always tells me. *Do not boil*, warns the cocoa tin.

Mum claims that there is nothing worse than lukewarm cocoa; but the cocoa tin insists that *boiling impairs flavour*.

I glance at the clock: it is five to nine. I am supposed to be in bed by nine o'clock. Tonight I am late. I glance at the window. Darkness piles against the glass. My feet are cold: I shift my weight from one to the other. The hem of my nightie brushes against my shins.

At nine o'clock Dad will settle in front of the television in the living room to watch *The News*.

The Nudes, Mum calls it.

It lasts for twenty-five minutes; it is followed on ITV by *News At Ten*. In between the news programmes, and afterwards, there are documentaries: *Panorama*, *World In Action*, *Horizon*. Later there is *Newsnight*. Music rattles below me all night in the living room, fanfares announcing each programme. I watch *The News* on Monday nights because I arrive home from Guides after nine o'clock.

'Sit quietly,' Dad says to me, 'because I'm watching *The News.*'

Mum rolls her eyes and jabs a finger in the direction of the screen: 'News, news, news,' she complains, 'morning, noon, and night.' Then she turns to my father: 'What's changed since six o'clock?' she goads. He never replies so she turns away muttering: 'What's changed since the day I was born?'

The newsreaders wear suits. They sit at the desk and talk about rebels. Maps of foreign countries appear on the screen; and voices drizzle from distant lands into the studio. Sometimes we see a man squinting in foreign sunshine and speaking into a microphone. He does not wear a suit; it is too hot to wear a suit. His shirts are always very clean: does someone wash them for him? Or does he take a lot of clean ones with him in his suitcase? Mum says that people in foreign countries wash their clothes in rivers, beating them clean against stones. In Spain we buy washing powder and wash our clothes in the bath.

The man in the foreign sunshine seems excited when he speaks into the microphone. I wonder what he does for the rest of the day. Is he allowed home for Christmas? I wonder whether he will ever swop places with the newsreader at the desk. They are both called *John* or *Peter*; everyone on *The News* is called *John* or *Peter*.

'Thank you, John.' 'And now over to you, Peter.'

If the news is not foreign, it concerns *the government*: it concerns *policy*, or *disputes*, or *backbenchers*. There are photographs of the Prime Minister; and comments from MPs, Leaders, Spokesmen, Chairmen, and sometimes from *His Lordship* and *The Right Honourable*.

'*Right 'Orrible,*' says Mum predictably.

There is also *Mr Speaker*.

'If a woman became *Mr Speaker*,' I once asked Dad, 'would she be known as *Mrs Speaker*?'

'*Madam Speaker*, I expect,' he said.

Madam? No one is ever called *Madam*. *Madams* carry hand-

142

bags and wear support stockings. They carry smelling salts. I will never be a *Madam*.

Dad says that women's voices are too high to read *The News*. 'And their brains are too small,' adds Mum.

Initially, I thought she was serious. I looked across the room at her in surprise.

She stared back. 'I'm joking,' she informed me, without a smile.

'Well, I'm not,' said Dad.

'I know you're not,' she retorted, turning towards him; 'because you wouldn't know a joke if it stood up and slapped you in the face.'

In the mornings a newspaper is wedged in the letterbox when I come downstairs for breakfast. Dad extracts it and brings it with him into the kitchen. He buys it because it is small: 'manageable,' he says, crashing the pages together above the table.

Mum reaches over and around it with slices of toast. Eventually Dad folds it and places it on an empty chair.

'You never read a bloody word,' Mum complains, scooping it from the chair.

Dad shrugs: 'I can't concentrate in here.'

At the end of the day the newspaper is thrown into the cupboard under the stairs: silver milk bottle tops for the blind; newspapers for the Scouts. The Scouts collect on Tuesday evenings, ringing the doorbell at half past six.

'Answer that,' Mum calls to me from elsewhere in the house. 'It's only the Scouts.'

'I can't,' I call back, shutting myself in the bathroom. 'I'm in the bathroom.'

Eventually I hear her at the door, greeting Simon Denning or David Smith or Alex Renton and heeding their request for no magazines with staples please as she relinquishes the bundles.

*

Dad watches *The News* in the evenings when he is not at work. Sometimes Mum sits beside him with a library book thick and stiff inside the folds of a glossy cover. Sometimes she stands at the ironing board, thumping it with the iron; drawing the hot metal through the creases whilst glancing occasionally and briefly at the screen. When Dad is at the office she sits with me on the settee and we watch *Steptoe and Son*.

'Don't tell your father,' she says, wiping tears of laughter from her eyes; and I do not know whether she is serious.

It is almost nine o'clock. The door opens. Dad enters the kitchen and crosses to the sink. He lifts a cloth from beside the taps and wipes the table. Each stroke sweeps across the white surface of the table like the track of a sleigh in snow. He returns to the sink to rinse the cloth.

'Have you done your homework?'

'Yes.' I remove the saucepan from the heat.

'All of it?'

I spoon cocoa from the tin into my cup. 'Yes.'

He moves around the table and peers over my shoulder. 'Don't forget to rinse the saucepan, please, Elizabeth, as soon as you've finished.'

I lift the saucepan and splash some of the steaming milk into the cup. *Mix to a smooth paste*, the tin instructs.

I replace the saucepan on the stove and stir.

Repeat, says the tin.

Mum agrees that there is nothing worse than lumpy cocoa. I lift the saucepan again and pour the rest of the milk slowly into the cup. I begin stirring it. Dad walks behind me to the window and stares into the garden.

'Is the shed door shut?' he asks.

Poised to leave, my hands wrapped around my cup, I freeze. Sweet steam drifts from the dusty grey milk into my face. He has realised that I have forgotten to shut the shed door. I wish that I had hurried and left the room; I wish that I had not waited for the milk to boil. I wish that I liked instant coffee because I could be upstairs now drinking it in bed. Instead I will have to stand here whilst he shouts at me; and then I will have to walk in darkness to the shed at the end of the garden, splattering torchlight ahead of me onto the path and the bushes and trees.

I shrug, feigning nonchalance: 'I asked Verity to shut it.'

He turns from the window in a flash of irritation: 'But you didn't check.'

I didn't check: he is right. He likes to say that he is *always right*. Now he is triumphant, but this was an easy contest. He requires me to say something in my defence but there is nothing for me to say. I shrug and quietly repeat myself: 'I asked Verity.'

His eyebrows rise contemptuously. '*You asked Verity?*' He emphasises the words to ridicule them: Verity is inherently unreliable. He turns again to the window. 'Well, it's not shut,' he snaps, tiring.

'I'll shut it, then,' I snap in return; and then, to spite him, I smile cheerfully at his reflection.

The cocoa pools lukewarm in my cup, the surface tightened with a growth of creamy skin.

I wonder if I am allowed to leave the room. I reach behind me for the door handle.

A sigh spills noisily across the room towards me. 'You are so very irresponsible, Elizabeth.' He does not turn round to face me. My fingertips linger on the handle.

'You are such an irresponsible child.' The voice is still low.

I lift my hand from the handle and fold my fingers round the cup.

'The rabbit is your responsibility –' Snowy lives in a hutch in the shed '– and I shouldn't have to remind you.' He turns towards me. 'It's not too much to ask, is it?' The voice is now slightly raised; the eyes wide, the lips narrow. 'Is it too much to ask you to shut the shed door at night?' The eyes are unblinking. 'Is it?'

145

Within each pale iris the pigment is clotted like wax. 'Is it?'

I shrug: 'I asked Verity,' I whisper.

The eyes snap shut in exasperation. 'I'm not interested in Verity; I don't want to hear another word about Verity. You should have known better than to trust her. What is the *matter* with you, Elizabeth?'

Rabbits need fresh air; the nights are not cold; there is a bedroom full of warm hay inside the hutch: what is wrong with Snowy spending the occasional night under the stars?

'I should be able to *rely on you*, Elizabeth.' He turns his back on me. 'I shouldn't have to keep checking up on you. You're not a baby any more.'

I reach slowly behind me for the door handle, the cocoa skin wobbling in my cup.

'I just don't know what's the matter with you lately.' The words ebb wearily from him; I wait for them to die away. 'I just don't know.' His hands rest on the edge of the sink, large and brown on the stainless steel like lumps of dough. 'You've been no help at all around here lately.' The words are brimming with recrimination, 'You're a hindrance, a walking hindrance; I shouldn't have to keep checking up on you.' He turns to face me. 'When are you going to grow up?' It is a plea. It echoes around the kitchen. There is no answer so he turns away, glaring at the window. His eyes burn unseeing on the blackened glass.

Above him, on the wall, the clock shudders: the long hand slots into place at nine o'clock. He remains hunched at the sink. My fingers slips soundlessly behind me onto the door handle. I pause. Eventually the hand shifts again on the clockface: one minute past nine.

'Where's Mum?'

I pull the door towards me.

'Upstairs.'

The response is perfunctory.

I step backwards through the doorway. 'In bed?' I begin to close the door.

'Yes.'

✳   ✳   ✳

Lilly and I had arranged to meet on that evening a couple of years ago in the pub in Soho that we knew as *our local*: it was a long way from our respective homes but it was a convenient place in the centre of town for us to meet; it was close to the underground station where there was an intersection of the Central and Northern lines. I came into London on the Central line: the line that is not central throughout its course but red and taut nevertheless across the centre of the map. Lilly travelled on the Northern line; the meandering black line of old, deep tunnels that reaches beyond central London with few staff and trains into the wealthiest suburbs. Lilly and I were connected by two of the oldest, longest, deepest, most claustrophobic and derelict lines in London.

When I approached the pub I noticed a fringe of hanging baskets above the windows. The baskets were made of wire and planted with flowers. The wire cut into the furry underbellies of peat, soil, roots; the flowers were limp and colourless under spotlights. There had been no baskets when I last met Lilly. We had not met recently; perhaps we could no longer call the pub our local. I stood in the doorway. Although brightly lit, the pub was quiet: it was vacated at nightfall by the office workers, and neglected during the week by the locals. This had once been a reason for choosing it as a meeting place.

I felt conspicuous as I opened the door. In a corner of the room, across an expanse of brown carpet, in a yellow soup of light, Lilly was sitting alone, head bowed. She was delving into a bag on her lap, searching for something; for her travel pass, probably, which she had a habit of mislaying. She was sitting beneath a wall lamp. Her illuminated hair, uniformly white and short, resembled a small hat or short veil or perhaps even a

147

handkerchief. The bleach did not lend her an air of wanton sexuality; on the contrary, it rendered her asexual. It suggested frailty: she wore the soft, precious, unworldly hair of an elderly person or a child.

The door closed behind me. Startled, she glanced in my direction with a sharp twist of a small bright head. A smile snapped across her face.

'Hi,' I mouthed, turning to secure the door before walking across the carpet towards the smile. Lilly's stylish teeth shimmered in the low light. Her mouth is a dental paradise. Her parents are staunch believers in dental care.

'I was taken to the dentist so often when I was a child,' she used to joke, 'that I thought my mother was having an affair with him.'

Lilly is always joking: she can joke with confidence because she has a beautiful smile.

'My parents wanted to give me beautiful teeth,' she jokes, 'because there was nothing they could do about my face.'

She can joke about her face because it is faultless.

'How was *Dallas*?' she asked brightly; acknowledging my lateness, guessing my reason, anticipating my excuses.

I laughed lightly. 'Bobby and Jenna are having problems. . .' I teased.

'So what's new?' she protested, laughing with me.

'. . . And Miss Ellie is worried about Clayton. . .'

'I hate Clayton.'

'. . . and, frankly,' I finished, 'I'm worried that there may be an incident at this year's Oil Barons' Ball.' There was an incident every year at the Oil Barons' Ball.

Lilly feigned concern. 'What about Peeder?' she asked with urgency. 'Where was Peeder?' She was referring to Sue Ellen's affair with a young student, Peter, during a previous series.

I sighed exaggeratedly. 'Pull yourself together, Lilly,' I said sternly: 'Peeder has gone: boys like Peeder aren't forever, and you should know that by now, or didn't your mother tell you anything?

And women in their prime, like Sue Ellen, have more important things on their minds like *did-anyone-remember-to-buy-bin-bags -or-do-I-have-to-pick-some-up-tonight-on-my-way-home-from-aerobics?*'

She was laughing as I stepped away from her towards the bar.

'How's life, then?' I called casually behind me.

'Ever onward.'

I was already waving my purse towards the bright bottles above the bar: 'Can I get you anything?' I glanced behind me.

She was shaking her head, raising her hand from the table as if to halt me. In front of her, on the table, was a small glass of honey-coloured liquid. 'I'm all right, thanks,' she said, indicating the glass.

I ordered an orange juice for myself.

'Crisps?' I called out to Lilly. She likes crisps.

'No, thanks.' Her fingertips tapped almost soundlessly on the tabletop.

The barman placed a glass in front of me. It was filled with an orange glare. I paid and waited for my change, reaching across the bar for the ice bucket. I shovelled a dessertspoonful of ice into the glass, collected my change, and returned to the table. I sat down opposite Lilly.

Her eyes were bright but sunk into dark bruises of weariness.

'So,' I began, 'how are you?'

She wrinkled her nose and raised her glass, hiding her face. She did not say fine, thanks, and how are you? I was not fine: I had just finished a thirty-six hour shift including an hour and twenty minutes of sleep; I had to face the prospect of sleeping alone again in an empty flat in Bethnal Green and starting another thirty-six hour shift at eight o'clock in the morning.

'Work?' I ventured sympathetically: this meant *are you having a hard time at work?*

Lilly lowered the glass and shook her head, grimacing. I did not know whether the grimace was a reaction to the scotch or to the question.

'No,' she breathed finally. She placed the glass on the table. 'I'm pregnant,' she said. She said it calmly, but not quietly. Lilly never speaks quietly; and, besides, there was no one else nearby to overhear her.

'Oh,' I said. I stared into the dark eyesockets. 'Are you sure?'

'Of course I'm sure.' The voice was level but brittle with indignation. The darkened gaze traced my own circular bruises. She frowned: would-I-have-called-you-all-the-way-across-London-if-I-wasn't-sure?

'I meant,' I said hurriedly, 'have you had a test?'

I was amazed that we had never had to have this conversation before at any time during all the years that we had known each other.

'Of course I've had a test.' She spoke despairingly. Was she despairing of me or the pregnancy? She sat still, her head slightly bowed.

'Oh, Lilly,' I said suddenly, very sadly; and then I held my breath.

She shrugged. What did it mean, this soft flutter of shoulders? Was it an expression of fatalism, *it happens*? Was it helplessness? Was it *a what-does-it-matter-to-you-anyway*, thrown in my direction? Whatever it was, it was also a shudder of anger. Lilly had been betrayed by her body: she had paid attention to Mrs Pincott, our Biology teacher, during sex education classes; she had learned about *precautions*, about the small devices locked in Mrs Pincott's cupboard or glimmering on the silky white screen at the front of the classroom in the roaring beam of the slide projector. She had chosen the pill and then, several years later, heeding warnings in newspapers, she had swapped the pill for the cap. The cap, however, is only 96% effective.

Pregnancy happened to other girls: at school it happened to girls like Debbie Barnham and Mitzi Tanner and Donna Quigley. Debbie Barnham and Mitzi Tanner and their friends – Sharon, Lesley, Karen, and the others, all several years older than us – gathered in the toilets after lessons, standing in a line and frowning across the washbasins into the mirrors, smoothing their hands across their softly swollen teenage stomachs and talking loudly and cryptically about *kittens*. At lunchtime one of them might run from the dining hall in tears. Then she would reappear at the end of the day at the school gates, her friends flinging their arms round her shoulders and baying accusations at her boyfriend: 'You don't fucking care, do you, you just don't fucking care!' We were never sure whether the rumours were true: none of the girls grew bigger, none of them disappeared discreetly for a few days from school. The kitten talk and the tears continued day after day, month after month, year after year.

Everyone knew about Donna Quigley although no one had been told. She grew gross in silence. Lilly and I would see her in town on Saturdays, pushing her baby brother along the street in his pushchair, kneading her fattened stomach against the handlebar. Her mother had recently left home and gone to live in Edmonton with a nineteen-year-old man known to Donna as Uncle Barry. Her father wore vests in public and never washed his hair. Her boyfriend was at another school: another planet, as far as Lilly and I were concerned, especially since it was a Comprehensive. We watched with fascination as her skirts tightened, the folds of material cutting into her stomach.

'Surely she knows,' said Lilly in amazement; 'because even Donna Quigley's not that thick.'

Eventually, Janet Grayson, who was a friend of Tracey Grant and Gillian Potts but who walked to school in the mornings with Donna, told us that Donna was 'scared stiff of what her Dad will do if he finds out and scared stiff of what her boyfriend will do if she tries to do anything about it.' We were in the toilets, delaying departure to double History. Janet was jittery in front of a mirror, flicking her gaze towards Tracey Grant and burning the air with hairspray.

'Tell Mrs Pincott,' Lilly and I urged, surprising ourselves. 'Tell Mrs Pincott.'

'Pincott knows,' said Janet mysteriously.

Two days later, Donna Quigley disappeared from school. When she reappeared at the end of the week she was shorn to her usual size but her eyes were big and dark like gaping holes.

I tried to dismiss Donna Quigley from my thoughts. Lilly's fingertip was tracing a pattern on the table in a trickle of scotch.

'How pregnant?' I asked.

She raised her head briefly, distractedly, and frowned. 'I don't know.' The fingertip continued to slide through the scotch.

'You don't know?'

She raised her head again, abruptly, firing her tongue from the roof of her mouth. 'No, I don't know.'

Then, slowly, she unwound; shutting the blazing eyes and leaning forward onto a criss-cross of folded forearms.

'Beth,' she murmured, 'I'm sorry. I'm two weeks late.'

My mother claims to have known the exact date of my conception: the night when the diaphragm worked its magic from inside the bathroom cabinet rather than from inside her body. She claims to know the exact date of Verity's conception, too.

'You were after Bob and Sue's first wedding anniversary party,' she used to tell me. 'Verity was on All Saints.'

When I was eight years old, or nine, or ten, Mum would emerge often from the bathroom in the mornings with red eyes to announce that there would be no baby this month.

I had been told the facts of life but I did not understand the references to months; but when she said *no baby*, I knew that she was not pregnant. Unlike Verity, I did not glance furtively into the bathroom and expect to find tangible evidence of a lack of a baby. When she said *no baby this month* I assumed that she would be pregnant next month. A month is a long time during childhood; I forgot about the baby until I was reminded: *no baby this month*, month after month. After a while I began to suspect that she was doing something wrong. She was being uncharacteristically inefficient. The diaphragm stayed in the bathroom cabinet working no magic and becoming dry and brittle and cracked.

So Lilly was two weeks late. She offered no further comment. The fingertip continued to etch worry lines into the grease on the tabletop. I knew that she and Harv had been separated for several months. Their separation had followed Jem's and mine; but, unlike ours, it was unexpected. I was not sure that I knew their reasons. I had not often been at home when she telephoned me. She had spoken instead on several occasions to Jem. 'Whose decision was it?' I asked him in alarm when he told me. 'Oh, you know,' he replied with a shrug. 'No one in particular.' So it had been a case of irreconcilable differences. Yet Lilly has always been irreconcilably different from everyone she has ever known. The exception is her brother, Simon: somehow she is happily resigned to her own flesh and blood. I had mistakenly assumed that Harv, sinking so easily and so often into her parents' sofa, could be regarded as honorary flesh and blood.

I had visited their flat only once since their separation. The spare room had become Lilly's room. Her teddy bear, Barnie, lay in the spare bed. I knew when I saw Barnie that a decision had been made.

I recalled the decision as I watched Lilly's fingertip slip in circles on the tabletop between us. I tried without success to imagine Harv creeping into the spare room at night. Harv did not reverse decisions.

'He's an American,' Lilly had once remarked to me; 'and Americans do not equivocate.'

Harv had been raised to pledge allegiance every morning to a flag. He would never go back on his word.

'Who . . .? I began, almost involuntarily.

Lilly looked sharply at me, her head rising so rapidly that it almost snapped her neck. I stared back, equally astonished. I had assumed that she would not object to the question; but perhaps she was right: perhaps it was irrelevant. I remembered the playground taunt: none of your business. What was my business?

Her gaze dwindled and drifted across the room. I averted my eyes. The barman grinned and winked at me.

'I don't know,' Lilly said, speaking slowly, 'what to do.'

This meant *I don't know how to arrange an abortion*.

She turned towards me and stared. Her eyes were unseeing.

'Well . . .' I began with a shrug, 'have you spoken to your GP yet?'

'The appointment's tomorrow,' she replied dispassionately.

'Well . . .' I shrugged again: take-it-from-there.

'Beth,' she said suddenly, 'I'm sorry.' She said it very quietly; and she twisted away from me in the arc of a flinch.

I was stunned: I wanted to reach across the table to her, to reassure her, but I hesitated. It would have been a reflex action but something prevented it so that my hand tensed in my lap: she had said *I'm sorry*. Lilly never apologises: she does not recognise authority, she does not defer; she boasts that she has integrity and no sense of shame.

So was there another reason? I was troubled by her reluctance to look at me. Lilly usually *looks people in the eye*. Throughout the conversation I had been resisting an urge to coax her chin towards me with my fingertips; but suddenly I did not want to touch her. I wanted to say *what do you mean?* But *what do you mean?* does not mean *what do you mean?* It means *how dare you*, and I did not want to be disapproving; not of Lilly. I could have said *it's none of my business who you sleep with*; but *business* is contemptuous. I could have said *it's none of my business who anyone sleeps with*; not even *Jem, not now*.

I was trying to exclude the voice of my mother. *Don't come running to me when you get into trouble*.

Lilly was in trouble. Sitting across the table from me, looking away. Was she *running to me*?

'Does he know?' I asked quietly. *He*.

'No one knows,' she said without expression, without looking at me.

'No one except me. Why are you telling me?'

She turned on me, bright with anger and frustration. 'Because you're the fucking doctor, aren't you?'

1980

Kieran's car disappears noisily into the dark lane. I place my key in the lock, turn it, push open the door, and step quietly into the hallway. Light is seeping into the hallway from the kitchen. The kitchen door is ajar. I step quietly towards the stairs. I hear the rustle of a newspaper in the kitchen: my father is home. Sometimes he stays at the office until midnight; sometimes he comes home earlier but goes to bed before eleven. I hear the gentle slap of a folded newspaper against the kitchen table. I wonder whether I can climb upstairs and reach the bathroom without disturbing him.

'Ah, *Miss* Hamilton.' He has appeared suddenly in the kitchen doorway.

I place my foot on the bottom stair.

'Stay where you are.'

The light from the kitchen is shining into my face.

'What time of night do you call this?' The tone is calm but faintly threatening.

I do not know what to say. It is about half past eleven, the time that I usually come home: I could tell him this but I suspect that it is not what he wants to hear.

'Eh?' He takes a step towards me from the doorway. 'Eh? What time of night do you call this?' He is standing in shadow.

If I say I don't know it will lead to accusations of irresponsibility;

so I glance past him at the clock on the kitchen wall: 'Twenty-five past eleven.'

He sighs. 'Less of the cheek, please.' His voice is slightly raised. He and Mum complain often about *cheek* and *lip*. Why does he say please? It is an order, not a request.

He takes another step towards me and places his hand on the bannister.

'It's late,' he says emphatically.

It is late and I want to go to bed. I shift my weight onto the foot on the stair.

'Stay,' he commands quietly, leaning over me.

I resist an urge to say *pick on someone your own size*.

'What time do you have to get up tomorrow?'

He knows the answer to this question: I have had to get up at the same time every morning for the past six years; and almost every morning for the past six years he has come to the foot of the stairs at five past seven and shouted to me that *it's gone seven so you're late*.

'Seven o'clock.'

'Seven o'clock,' he confirms, suppressing his delight behind thin lips; 'and how many hours is it until seven o'clock?'

'Seven and a half.'

The delight springs into his eyes. 'And how many hours of sleep are we supposed to have each night?'

I shrug: I am weary; I want to go to bed.

'Come on, doctor,' he says excitedly, hissing sarcasm. 'How many hours?'

I shrug again. 'It depends.'

'It does *not* depend.' His eyes flare in the shadow. 'Don't give me it *depends*. How many hours?'

'Eight.' I suppose that this answer is satisfactory.

'Eight,' he repeats triumphantly; 'which leaves you half an hour short even if you go to bed straight away.'

I step onto the bottom stair.

'But you're not going to bed straight away,' he hisses, 'because you and I are going to have a little talk.'

I have learned to dread his *little talks*: they are rarely *little*, and they are rarely *talks*; they are usually orders or interrogations. I hope for orders because they are easier to ignore.

'I want to get a few things straight,' he begins. His voice is low, seething with threat.

I lean exhaustedly against the wall.

'You're not pulling your weight around here.'

I am pleasantly surprised: this is a *you're-not-pulling-your-weight* talk; and I am used to *you're-not-pulling-your-weight* talks. Relieved, revived, I straighten against the wall.

He continues to talk at me.

'. . . waltzing in and out as you please.'

I look down at my shoes and wait for silence.

'. . . and it's *not on.*'

Suddenly my wish is granted: silence.

'Do you hear me?'

I raise my head: a cue for him to complete the tirade. His eyes glare at me. I look away, marvelling at the waste of energy.

'Elizabeth, we do not exist solely for your convenience. Do you understand?'

I shift my position on the stair.

'So I want to see a little more consideration. You're using this house like a hotel.'

This is a phrase favoured by my mother: *You use this house like a hotel.* She also likes to say: *You treat me like a servant.*

'It's not a hotel,' he says, 'it's a home; and a home requires co-operation and consideration.'

Co-operation and *consideration* are the key words tonight.

I cannot resist a rejoinder: 'I thought it wasn't *my* house.' I fix him with a resentful stare. I hope to remind him of his frequent suggestion that my presence is arbitrary and unwelcome: not in *my* house, he says of *my* clothes, music, make-up, friends; *you can do what you like in your own house, when you have one, but not in mine.*

'I said *home*, not *house*,' he snaps; 'but too right it's not your

158

house; but you don't pay rent either; and until you do, you're a guest and you'll abide by the rules.'

The prospect of paying money to live here is repulsive. I look longingly up the stairs, anticipating the oblivion of sleep.

'I want you in at a reasonable hour every night.'

I turn towards him, surprised. He has never before raised the issue of a curfew with me. Verity, on the contrary, has not been allowed to leave home unaccompanied in the evenings since she was found smoking in the churchyard after Guides last year.

He sighs heavily. 'I don't get it, Elizabeth.' He shrugs, lifting his hands upwards and outwards, feigning despair. 'What's the big idea? One minute you want to go to university to study medicine, and the next you're out all night every night instead of doing your homework.'

This is unfair. 'It's not all hours,' I growl, 'and it's not instead of doing my homework. I go out after I've done my homework.' I frown at him, offended. 'And, besides,' I add, 'I can't sleep unless I've relaxed.'

I am pleased with this excuse: last Sunday, when I had refused to participate in the family visit to aunty Dorothy and uncle Jack, when I had pleaded homework as usual, he had shouted at me that all work and no play makes Jill a dull girl.

His hand rises from the bannister and hovers menacingly before dropping without a sound. 'There is nothing relaxing about charging around town in your boyfriend's car.'

I have not been charging around town in my boyfriend's car; I have been having sex in it.

'This *Kieran* . . .' he spits the name, and recoils. He pauses. 'Things are getting too heavy.'

I stare hard at my shoes.

'I don't like his influence on you.'

I hold my breath.

'So I'm warning you: cool it.'

How embarrassing: I have a father who says *cool it*; I have a father who speaks like a character in a *Shaft* film. He saw the *Shaft* films with Mum in the 1970s. They went to the cinema on Friday evenings whilst Verity and I stayed at home with a babysitter. The babysitter was Sarah Crumpton, whose elder sister Dinah was Head Girl of a local secondary school and a member of the National Youth Theatre. Sarah wanted to be an actress. She would search through our record collection for the soundtrack of *The Graduate* and insist to me that Mum looked like Ali McGraw in *Love Story*.

Dad lowers his face close to mine. 'Okay?'

I cannot say *yes, okay*: it would not be credible.

This occurs to him belatedly. He straightens and clears his throat noisily. 'I want you home by eleven o'clock on weekdays.'

He clears his throat again, and relaxes against the bannister.

I frown. 'But . . .'

'No *buts*.'

The *but* was a red herring; I am unconcerned by the new rule: I can have sex before eleven o'clock.

'And I want to see you around here more often.'

This is not true.

'I want to see you helping your mother more often.'

'Okay,' I say wearily, confident that we have reached the end of the *you're-not-pulling-your-weight* talk.

'No, dammit, Elizabeth,' he barks, 'it is not *okay*.'

I regard him in horror: *Dammit?* Suddenly he is speaking like a character from *The Winthrop Boy*.

He sighs. 'Your mother has a lot on her plate at the moment. You should realise that.' He drops his hand from the bannister. 'It's not easy to have a toddler around the place.' He shrugs. 'It's not easy for her.' He steps backwards into shadow.

'You know what she's like.'

I stare at him.

He raises his eyes to mine. 'So,' he says brightly, 'let's have a little more consideration, shall we?'

'What about Verity?' As soon as I speak, I regret it: I know that I should not mention Verity, although I do not know why. 'Verity,' I say hurriedly, 'does nothing around the house.'

He turns away from me. 'Let's leave Verity out of this, shall we?'

The notes at Reception tell me that my next patient is a twenty-two-year old woman with right iliac fossa pain. The pain may be indicative of appendicitis or an ectopic pregnancy, or possibly pelvic inflammatory disease or a urinary tract infection. Pain on the right side of the abdomen is perhaps more indicative of appendicitis or an ectopic pregnancy. It is important not to dismiss too early the possibility of an ectopic pregnancy. I have known it overlooked by GPs who refer women to hospital with right iliac fossa pain, query appendicitis. My next patient has not been referred by a GP but nevertheless she has been placed in an ordinary cubicle by a nurse rather than in one of the rooms suitable for a gynaecological examination. The nurse has recorded temperature, pulse, and blood pressure. I glance over the notes. Temperature, 37.2: high, but not too high; and not, in my opinion, suggestive of an infection or appendicitis. The pulse is recorded as 90: fast, but not too fast. She might be bleeding from a fallopian tube, or she might not: the pulse in this case offers me no clue; and, anyway, a pulse tends to race as soon as someone reaches for it. There are no clues either from the blood pressure: 110 over 70; not uncommon, not necessarily a cause for alarm.

I stand outside the cubicle and gently part the curtains. Inside, the patient stares at me. She is lying on the trolley, propped against the pillows. She is wearing a hospital gown. One of the ties of the gown dangles from her shoulder in her light brown hair. Her face is pale, but lots of people in hospital are pale; lots of people in Britain are pale. Her mouth is stiff, suspended by lines. The lines are not smile lines. She lies rigidly against the pillows, her hands resting lightly on her abdomen.

'Are you the doctor?' she asks.

'Yes.' I step into the cubicle and turn away from her to straighten the curtains behind me. Usually I say *Hello, I'm Dr*

Hamilton as soon as I step into the cubicle. I straighten the curtains and turn back towards her. 'Yes, I'm Dr Hamilton. Hello.'

'Oh,' she says, without expression. 'Hello.'

I move to her bedside. I am waiting for her to say *you don't look old enough to be a doctor* meaning *you don't look tall enough to be a doctor* or *you don't look male enough to be a doctor*.

'Good,' she says quietly.

'Have you been waiting long?' I lay my fingertips lightly on her wrist: the temperature of her skin feels normal; her pulse ticks regularly.

Her gaze sweeps upwards to my face; she seems surprised: 'No.' There is the hint of a question in her voice. She frowns and drops her gaze. 'Well, maybe; I don't know.'

I pretend to tease her: 'You don't *know*?' Either she does not know how long she has been here; or she does not know what constitutes a long wait in Casualty.

She smiles faintly. 'My sister has gone off for a cup of tea. So she must think we've been here ages. I don't want a cup of tea but that's hardly surprising, is it? I feel too sick to face a cup of tea.'

I remove my fingertips from her wrist and glance down at my notes. 'Clare Tomkins?' I look to her for confirmation. She does not deny it. She stares at me. Apparently I have stated the obvious. She is waiting for me to continue. I drop the notes behind me onto a chair. 'You told the nurse about a pain on your right side?'

She closes her eyes. 'I was hoping that it might go away.' She opens her eyes again. 'I was hoping that it might settle down; but no.' She grimaces, and focuses on my shoes.

'How long have you had this pain?'

'Ages. Last night it was worse and I couldn't sleep.' She speaks slowly and quietly. 'So first thing this morning I went round to my sister's house and got her to come down here with me.' She pauses, and sighs. 'I was hoping that it might go away but it hasn't and I just can't stand it any more.' She raises her gaze again. 'I

162

didn't think there was any point calling my doctor,' she explains, 'because he'd take ages to come; and he'd just send me here in the end, wouldn't he?'

I decide not to explain to her that she would not have had to wait in Casualty to see me, that she could have been referred directly by her GP to the gynaes or surgeons.

I still know nothing about the origins of the pain. 'So the pain started . . .?'

She frowns, staring at her feet, concentrating: 'The day before yesterday?' She shrugs slightly and releases her gaze. 'I don't suppose I noticed it for a while, but it's unmistakable now.' Her eyes, fixing on mine, are unflinching. 'It's appendicitis, isn't it?'

'I don't know yet.' I still know nothing about the pain. 'Has the pain moved at all during the last few days?'

'No,' she replies, 'it has been digging away down here, right down here, in my appendix.' Her hands move gently apart on her abdomen to reveal the area of pain.

So, unlike a typical case of appendicitis, there has been no pattern of pain experienced initially in the umbilical region.

'It has been driving me mad,' she adds as she joins her hands protectively again. 'And now I can't stand up straight or walk properly.'

'So it has been getting worse?'

'Yes,' she confirms eagerly, 'it started as a grumble.'

People often refer to chronic appendicitis as a grumbling appendix: I remind myself that she believes she has appendicitis.

'I didn't want to think about an operation,' she adds wistfully, 'I didn't want to come into hospital. I was hoping that it might go away if I didn't think about it.' She sighs. 'Sometimes it does, doesn't it? If you eat fibre.'

Briefly I imagine the curative properties of All-Bran; I imagine patients spoon-fed in ambulances. I remember that my mother had a copy of *The F-Plan Diet*: It had been loaned to her by aunty Gladys and kept on the bookshelf in the living room between *The Readers' Digest Book of Pyramids* and *The Private Eye Book of Boobs*. She was delighted to discover that she no longer had to peel carrots and shred cabbage but could serve us beans on toast instead. Verity's favourite foods at the time were bath buns because of the crust of sugar, scones because of the butter, and Battenburg cake because of the marzipan. She refused to eat any vegetables other than parsnips. My mother claimed that parsnips didn't count: they were not green and leafy. Carrie, unlike my mother, eats fruit: she chooses fruit that she can peel whilst watching television, her fingers tapping a dull rhythm on long silky bananas and soft satsumas.

I return my attention to the patient. 'Try not to worry,' I tell her. 'Have you been sick?'

'I *feel* sick.' She clamps her eyelids down over her eyes. 'If I try to walk I feel sick: my legs go shaky and I feel dizzy and sick.' The eyelids lift once again; the surface of each eye is dry and sore. 'My sister says I don't look well; she says I'm pale.'

'How has your appetite been?'

'Fine,' she replies bitterly, 'until this.'

'When did you last eat anything?'

'I cooked tea last night, but I didn't eat it; or only a mouthful or two.'

'A mouthful or two?'

'It was kidney; I'm not keen on kidney; I had a mouthful or two of potato.'

My mother used to claim to be *not keen on kidney* but she cooked it frequently, usually with liver. I remember the texture of the kidney, too smooth to chew; and I remember the sight of the liver as it was taken from the bag and laced with her fingers before being dropped onto the chopping board. It was served with vegetables and potato; everything matted with gravy. Sometimes she splashed milk into the saucepan of cooked potatoes and flapped a wooden spoon inside it so that the potato would soften and rise like sap in the holes in the masher.

The patient's revulsion at kidney is understandable; it tells me little about her appetite.

'And before that?' I ask her. 'Before tea?'

'No, nothing, except a sandwich mid-morning.'

No, nothing. 'That's unusual? You usually eat more during the day than a sandwich mid-morning?'

She shrugs; tired, perplexed, irritated. I resolve to make the questions easier to answer. 'No lunch yesterday?'

'No time: I would have been late fetching my eldest from school.'

I refrain from asking about *the eldest*, from asking *which school?* On this occasion I shall sacrifice showing an interest. I shall miss hearing about the merits of St Mary's, or West Road, or Bishop's Wood, or any of the other schools that have been described to me by parents since I began working here. The Headmaster of St Mary's was recently described to me by a patient as an A Grade Psycho.

'Do you usually eat breakfast?'

'Yes.'

'But no breakfast yesterday?'

'No.'

'And the day before yesterday?' I look closely at her, and illuminate her face with my smile. 'Can you remember?'

She lowers her head. 'I've been a bit off my food recently.'

'But you've managed to eat a little something each day?'

'Yes.' The answer is grudging.

'But not in the mornings.'

She does not reply.

'And your bowels?' I finish. 'How are your bowels?'

'Normal.'

I change the subject: 'What did you do yesterday?' My tone is cheerful, interested, enthusiastic; I need to regain her attention and co-operation, I need to know whether she has been unwell for some time. The onset of appendicitis is usually sudden.

She raises her head. 'Not much,' she replies mildly. 'Got the kids up, took the eldest to school, came back home, that sort of thing.'

'And what would you usually do?'

She laughs faintly. 'Not much more.' The smile flutters and fades. It occurs to me that it must have been the same for my mother when she was at home with Verity and me: each day much like the next. 'But I slept for a while yesterday morning when I came home, and that's not normal.' She shrugs; perplexed, apologetic. 'I think the pain was starting to get me down.' She glances at me. 'Because it does, after a while, doesn't it.'

It has been a long night for this woman: it has been a long weekend: today will be a long day for both of us, in different ways. I remind myself that there was no sudden onset of pain, no pain in the umbilicus, no fever, no vomiting, no constipation: none of the symptoms associated with appendicitis.

'Have you ever had this pain before?'

'No. But my sister has. She had her appendix out a couple of years ago, and two of my brothers lost theirs when they were kids; but not me, no, I've never had any trouble.'

I must eliminate the possibility of a urinary tract infection: 'Are you having any burning or stinging sensation when you pass water?'

She looks puzzled. 'No.'

'How are your periods?' I ask her. 'Are they regular?'

'Fairly,' she answers happily.

'Are they heavy?'

'No.'

'And when was your last one?' I am interested in the last one: the last one holds the clues.

'At the beginning of the month,' she tells me confidently; and then she pauses. 'It started on the second, the third, I don't know.' She frowns.

'So you're due . . .' I shrug '. . . when? at the end of the week?'

She is staring at me. Pigment seems to bleed from her eyes into her skin: eye colour refers to irises, not sockets; but she has blue irises and bluer sockets. She has offered no response to my question, so once again I conclude that I have stated the obvious.

'How was this last period?' I ask her. 'Lighter than usual? Heavier? More pain than usual?'

'No.' The answers are coming now in short breaths.

'Heavier?'

'No. Lighter.'

I raise my eyebrows.

She barely opens her mouth when she explains: 'It took a while to get started.'

Hence the confusion over the date.

'And when it finally got started,' I encourage quietly, 'was it a normal period?'

'Yes.' Her eyelids drift down over her increasingly colourless eyes.

'For how long?' I insist, leaning towards her. 'For how many days did you have a normal period?'

'A day or so.' The eyes remain closed.

'And is that normal?' I persist gently. 'Is it normal for you to have a period lasting a day or two?'

'No.'

I decide to change the subject. I have the information that I need.

'Have you any vaginal discharge?' I start anew.

'No. Yes.' The words drift from her mouth with equal emphasis. Her face is eyeless, expressionless.

'What sort of discharge?'

'Normal.'

Ask a silly question, my mother used to say: the patient has a vaginal discharge because all young women have a vaginal discharge. I did not, however, *get a silly answer*. She has a normal discharge, not abnormal. I do not have to ask, as the textbooks suggest, whether the discharge has an offensive odour. She regards the discharge as normal; and I can check it later, if I wish, when I take a swab. The swab should eliminate the possibility of a pelvic infection.

'And bleeding?'

'No,' she says, dismissing the question as she dismissed all others. Not yet.

Now I have to ask her whether she could be pregnant. This

167

question is often asked in a hushed voice behind a curtain, the answer hidden from parents or partners. 'Is there any chance that you could be pregnant?'

Suddenly, her eyes are open wide. 'Oh God, no,' she says, horrified. 'No way.'

'So,' I shrug helplessly, smiling apologetically. 'You've not had sex recently?' I do not like to ask this, but I need to know why she is so sure. I need to know if she *is* sure.

'Well, yes,' she replies unsurely. 'But,' she continues with resolve, 'I'm not pregnant.'

'What form of contraception do you use?'

'The cap, but *carefully*.' She is suddenly animated, hauling herself against the pillows. 'I never make mistakes.' She smiles wanly: 'One mistake was enough.'

'So you've been pregnant?' *The kids* might have referred to step-children or adopted children, or foster children.

'I was pregnant at seventeen.' She settles against the pillows, apparently eager to tell her tale. 'I had to get married.' She pronounces these words with disdain; but she smiles. Then the smile sinks, and the corners of her mouth tug at the facial lines. 'And I had another one at the beginning of last year, last January.' She shrugs, resigned. 'She's fifteen months now. But that's the last; I don't want any more.' Her head drifts deeper into the pillow. 'I didn't really want another one after my first but you can't have just one, can you.' My reflection sticks to the bright surface of each eye. 'If you've got one, you might as well have another; in for a penny, in for a pound. And besides,' she says, 'my husband wanted another one. He'd have six if he could; but, then, he would, wouldn't he?'

We both smile.

'Have you ever had any other pregnancies?' I venture. 'Any miscarriages or anything?' *Anything* means *abortion*; I should have said abortion.

'No.' She pauses. 'And I love my kids, it's just that I don't want any more.'

168

I relax against the trolley. 'Have you ever considered the pill?'

She smiles kindly at me. 'Yes, of course, I've tried it, but it doesn't suit me. The cap was okay between kids because as soon as I decided to get pregnant I could do it straight away: no waiting for hormones to sort themselves out.'

I am interested: 'Why didn't the pill suit you?'

'Headaches,' she replies; then she sighs. 'I suppose I should be thinking about what to do now that I'm back to normal after the baby.' Her teeth rest for a moment on her lower lip. 'What do you suggest?'

I laugh bashfully. 'I suggest that you talk to your GP about it, or the family planning clinic: it's not really my area.' It occurs to me that I may have been abrupt. 'Is that okay?' I enquire quickly.

'Yes, yes,' she says dreamily.

I have to examine her.

'I wanted a decent gap between kids,' she says, 'and some people reckon it's best to get them over with, don't they; but not me.' She chews briefly on her lip. 'But neither did I want to be looking after kids for the rest of my life.'

'It's difficult,' I agree.

'A three-year gap seemed about right,' she continues, 'but, in the end, I didn't have an easy time: not an easy pregnancy, not an easy birth, not an easy first couple of months. I hadn't had an easy time the first time, but everyone said it would get easier. But it's not true, is it; it's not necessarily true: it wasn't easier for me, it was worse.'

'That's awful,' I mutter sympathetically.

She sighs. 'I must be getting old.'

I smile. 'You've plenty of years left in you yet.'

I smooth a strand of hair from her forehead. 'So, how are you feeling now?'

'Tired.'

'I'm going to feel your tummy now,' I tell her gently, 'so, if you could just lie down for me . . .'

She shifts expertly across the trolley, I lower the backrest and remove the pillows.

'. . . and if you could just lift your gown. . .'

She shudders as she draws the cotton across her skin. 'I've always dreaded something like this.'

I smile reassuringly. 'Something like what?'

'Appendicitis.'

My hands are raised. They are small, white, unadorned. Unlike my patient, I do not wear a wedding ring. I do not have any rings: no signet rings, dress rings, engagement rings, or eternity rings. My hands are not sparkly with sapphires or bloody with rubies. Unlike my mother, my left hand is not milky with opals. My mother's engagement ring has three opals: *small opals*, she says, *because we were poor*. The small opals nestle close to the wedding ring. Both rings are held in place by a *keeper ring* which once belonged to Nana. It is red gold, smokier in colour than my mother's yellow wedding ring. My mother has another ring of Nana's which she rarely wears. She keeps it in a small leather box. The leather jaws snap shut on it with startling ferocity. It is platinum, and embedded with diamond chips. My mother once explained to me that platinum is more valuable than gold: to me, as a child, this was unimaginably valuable; and it did not concern me that the diamonds were chips. My grandfather told me that gems and precious metals were found in the ground. It seemed to me that lucky fingers might be dipped into the soil and reappear sticky with riches. *Precious stone* meant *magic stone*. Rings appeared on hands to signify love and marriage, celebration and solemnity, loss and gain. Dress ring was a contradiction in terms: rings were gifts and heirlooms, not decorations. I never wanted a dress ring; I wanted my hands to be heavy with mystery; I wanted Nana's ring.

I nod towards my hands. 'They're probably cold.'

She smiles briefly; and then watches anxiously as my hands descend towards her.

'What frightens you most about appendicitis?'

She flinches when my hands drop like feathers onto her skin. 'Hospitals,' she replies.

'Have you been in hospital before?'

My hand creeps across her abdomen, applying pressure at regular intervals. She gasps and winces, signifying discomfort and registering mild protest. 'Yes, I had both babies in hospital.'

I pass my hand over the liver and spleen. There is no hardness or swelling. I slide my hand towards her lower abdomen. She cranes to follow my movements. Her abdominal muscles tighten.

'Try to relax,' I remind her calmly.

Her head drops back onto the trolley.

'Have you ever spent any other time in hospital?'

'No.'

My fingers reach MacBurney's point. 'You've always been fit and healthy?'

'Yes.'

I am pressing on MacBurney's point with my fingertips; she is giving no response. 'Any tenderness here?'

She frowns. 'A bit.'

I increase the pressure. She maintains her disgruntled silence. In most cases of acute appendicitis the patient finds it intolerable when pressure is applied here; and more intolerable when the pressure is suddenly relieved. I lift my fingers, and her skin rises like fresh dough. 'Does that hurt?'

'A bit,' she replies, unconcerned. 'I dread hospital because I'd have to leave the kids; I feel that I can't leave the kids.'

I am convinced that she does not have appendicitis.

'Where are they now?' I ask her.

'At home, with my husband.'

It is not yet ten o'clock. The sea, in the distance, is not yet colonised by windsurfers and powerboats.

Sunday, for me, means *leisure*: a young couple in towelling bathrobes pouring fresh coffee from a pot; a breakfast table decorated with carnations and newspapers.

I work, usually, on Sundays, and have done so for the past two years; I am no longer part of a couple; I do not own a towelling bathrobe or a breakfast table. When did leisure cease to mean kites flying in the park and begin to mean commuters at home with central heating and percolators? *Sunday*, for my mother, means *Sunday lunch*: baking, roasting, basting, carving, steaming, slicing, dicing, draining, serving. She does not dislike preparing the lunch on Sunday; especially, she claims, since she has been able to afford leaner meat. She likes the warmth and solitude of the kitchen. When she was a child, however, *Sunday* meant *Sabbath*; and *Sabbath* meant *silence*, and *best behaviour* and *Sunday best* in church, at the lunch table, in the parlour. My mother hates Sundays. 'They remind me of my childhood,' she says.

The waiting room is strewn with newspapers that have been ransacked and abandoned. The subjects of the headlines gawp vacantly from photographs. I feel no urge this morning to read about them; I have no interest this morning in *Exodus Of Refugees*, or in *Police Commissioner Speaks*, or in *Tanya, 8, Takes The Biscuit*. I wonder whether I will ever have any interest in them again.

My ideal Sunday used to begin with a trip to the newsagents. I would dress in a track suit – my clothes most akin to pyjamas – and go to the newsagents before I did anything else; before I brushed my teeth or combed my hair or filled the kettle to make tea.

'Not the papers,' Jem would mutter sleepily as I rolled away from him into the cold air of the bedroom; 'not the bloody papers.'

I left the flat on Sunday mornings on a pilgrimage to the newsagents. I joined other local residents in an ill-formed but respectful queue. We graciously avoided scrutinising each other's dishevelled hair. We shuffled our feet to aid circulation but otherwise remained silent in acknowledgement of the power of our common obsession. Newspapers were trawled in armfuls from the counter. Many people took two or three. In those days, as a student, I could afford only one.

I would have preferred to stay in bed on Sunday mornings, I would have preferred Jem to buy the newspaper; but Jem disapproved of Sunday newspapers. He resented the intrusion on Sunday mornings. Furthermore, he resented the illusion of a majority of people owning homes and second homes and several cars and enjoying regular holidays and weekly trips to the West End. He resented the depiction of the others, people captured in black and white in the colour supplement, people populating high rise blocks: *poor people*. He also resented the implication, in the glossy close-up photographs of Christian Barnard's bloodied but sterile hands, that the world's problems could be solved by the application of technology.

When I was a child I loved the photographs, the shininess of inks; and I loved the softness of the newsprint, the thousands and thousands of words. The pages absorbed the steam drifting from the pans of sprouts and swede in the kitchen and muffled the culinary clatter mingling with the protestations from the television and stereo in the living room. One Sunday, expecting to read as usual about walks along the banks of the Thames and Woody Allen's exercusions into the Manhattan psyche, I discovered slaughter: death squads in Latin America. In front of me on the television screen *The Waltons* were triumphing over adversity in the Blue Ridge Mountains, chopping logs all day and eating pumpkin pie in the evenings; but in my hands headless bodies were spinning downstream through Latin America.

Jem disliked Sunday newspapers for the same reason that I liked them: the journalists were free from the constraint of reporting daily news. For a while, when I was a teenager, I wanted to be a Sunday journalist. I wanted to stop the bodies disappearing downstream. Mum was scathing: journalists were a *nasty breed*, she said; drinking, smoking, *making a living from other people's misery*. Everyone was *a breed*, according to my mother: doctors were *an arrogant breed*.

173

My father, however, was impressed: *journalists travel*, he said. Yes, I thought; but to countries with death squads.

It is not yet ten o'clock. I wish I wasn't here. I wish I was somewhere else. I wish I was nowhere. Time passes slowly here. Yet it passes. Already it is Sunday, and soon it will be Monday. Already it is the end of April, and soon it will be May, June, summer, autumn. Time flies not when I'm enjoying myself but simply when I want it to stand still. It is quiet here today: contrary to expectation, as ever; contrary to preference, too, because the staff are bored. I wonder whether I should *keep busy* or *try to relax*. I do not know which I would prefer; I forget which I would usually prefer. Suddenly I remember nothing about life before Friday: suddenly it seems that I have never been without this feeling of dread.

I am waiting for the results of Clare Tomkins' tests. They will be available in about half an hour. In the meantime there are other patients for me to see: the details snake towards me from the computer printer. I left Clare Tomkins in a side room. She is increasingly listless and uninterested in her sister's growing collection of newspapers and cigarettes and coins for the 'phone; but she is as adamant as ever that she is not pregnant. After a rectal examination, which did not support a diagnosis of appendicitis, I explained to her that I would have to do a vaginal examination; and I moved her, as departmental policy dictates, from the cubicle to a side room to allow greater privacy. 'I'd know if I was pregnant,' she said to me as I closed the door behind us. 'I'd know, wouldn't I, doctor, because you just know things like that, don't you?'

It is a common complaint that doctors do not listen to patients, that medicine takes no account of patients' sensibilities. Patients, however, are not the only ones with intuition. I am convinced that Clare Tomkins is pregnant although the evidence is as yet undetectable in a test tube at the lab. Doctors do not dismiss intuition but reject the notion that it is uninformed and unskilled; doctors, like everyone else, learn by looking and listening whilst learning to look and listen. *Practice makes perfect*. I have heard it offered as a justification of our long working hours that we learn

174

from experience and there is a lot to learn. *Life is short, art is long*.

I have looked at Clare Tomkins and seen pain, pallor and dehydration. I have listened to her and heard about an unwanted first pregnancy, a begrudged second one, and a life thereafter with a husband and *kids* who remained nameless throughout our conversation. She is convinced that she is not pregnant and the strength of her conviction is impressive; but it derives solely from a reluctance to consider the evidence to the contrary.

'He tries,' she said of her husband as we prepared for the vaginal examination. 'He tries: he likes to think that he can manage; and of course he can manage; he can manage for a day or two. But it's not the same, is it. He's out of the house every day at eight and not back again until seven and he thinks it's all roses at home; but it's not, is it; it's not.'

'No,' I said, checking the equipment on the tray, 'it's not. Could your sister perhaps look after your children for a while?'

'No,' she replied resolutely. 'No: it wouldn't be fair. She's got three of her own. I can't go around dumping my kids on anyone else. It's not fair. They'll have to stay at home with their Dad.' She turned her head to watch me at the tray. 'But my sister's very good with the kids, of course, she offers to look after them; but they're not easy kids.'

'No?' I pushed my fingers into a plastic glove.

'The little one can't do much for herself yet. She's had some problems: she was very small when she was born; she's chesty; she doesn't settle well on her own at night. Leave her, my husband says when she's making a fuss: but you can't just leave her, can you.' She sighed unhappily. 'And the other one has always been difficult at night: bad dreams.'

After the examination I rang the Gynae SHO.

Adrian Winterson is on call this weekend. *Dr Bow Tie*, Kelly calls him; but not to his face.

I have always avoided calling him anything to his face. The

bow ties are a recent affectation; I have known him for years because we were at medical school together. His parents, unlike mine, did not bring sandwiches with them on graduation day; his parents, like most, took him out for a meal. My parents have never taken me out for a meal apart from fast food or something similarly expedient. His parents are doctors. They bought him a car when he qualified. It is parked in the hospital car park outside his hospital flat.

Adrian Winterson resented my call. Some doctors cope with the *on call* system by being rude and unhelpful in the hope that they will rarely be disturbed. Adrian Winterson adopts this strategy, but it usually fails to unsettle me. Today, in the absence of test results, he was predictably sceptical of my diagnosis. He was predictably gratified when I admitted that, during the vaginal examination, I did not feel *a mass*. Eventually, despondently, after relating all the details, I decided to inform him that she didn't *feel pregnant*.

'So what?' he said dismissively. 'I spend most Saturday nights claiming that I don't feel pissed but I usually am.'

I said nothing.

'OK,' he relented suddenly, 'I'll come down and have a look at her.'

I replaced the receiver and came to reception to stare at the list of patients who are waiting for treatment. Behind me in the waiting room a man and woman are arguing. I cannot hear the words but the voices rise and fall: hushed, intimate, but noisy with recrimination. Each exchange is a challenge. Suddenly the man is silent. The woman continues, rattling grudges. She wields opposition: you this, you that; and I said this, I did that, it's not my fault. He remains silent. Eventually she is silent too.

I stare at a packet of crisps lying opened on the reception desk: *prawn cocktail flavour*. The smell is familiar: I remember it from school trips to the local swimming pool. After swimming, my classmates and I would gather at the vending machine in the entrance hall and take turns to stand on tiptoe and slip a coin

176

into the appropriate slot. We would gaze together through the bright glass at the bags of crisps dropping like prizes from hooks. Our favourites, the bags labelled *prawn cocktail flavour*, were filled with gilt flakes and pink dust: in our eager hands they burst open like ripe fruit. When we left the entrance hall and walked across the tarmac towards the school bus our lips and tongues and fingertips were drowned in a salty pink quicksand of flavouring. At the time I had never tasted a prawn cocktail: and later, when I did, it seemed to me that it was concocted to taste like prawn cocktail flavoured crisps. Even now I am confused. What makes prawn cocktail flavour? The prawns? Or the cocktail? What is the cocktail? Is the cocktail flavoured by the prawns, or are the prawns flavoured by the cocktail?

I feel sick but I know that I am hungry: my stomach is empty, burning, tightening, yearning for food. I have not eaten properly for days: on Friday night I ate a few mouthfuls of the lasagne before pushing the sticky vegetable sauce and pale flaps of pasta across my plate into the bin. Last night I ate toast. This morning, as usual, I had no breakfast.

The receptionist sees me staring at the crisps. 'Want one?' She smiles pleasantly and leans across the desk to rattle the packet.

Pink dust drifts in a thin cloud towards me.

'No thanks.'

'Sure?' She peers at me with concern.

'Sure.'

Suddenly Vivien is beside me, spinning past me, steadying herself with a light touch to my arm.

'God, you look awful,' she says cheerfully, her face close to mine.

'Thanks,' I reply sarcastically.

'No, really,' she continues happily. 'Are you okay?'

'Yes.'

She accepts this happily, too. 'Good.' Perhaps she assumes that I had a late night last night; perhaps she is unconcerned; certainly she is hurried: she is tugging at my sleeve.

'Come on,' she urges, 'I've got something to show you.'

I allow myself to be tugged away from the desk. 'What?'

She releases my arm and skips ahead of me across the tiles.

'Vivien . . .' I call unsurely behind her. '*What?*'

The computer printer at the desk is littered with details of patients.

Vivien turns briefly and smiles. 'Come and see.'

She turns away from me and proceeds through the doors into the corridor. She is shorter than me but I had not noticed this until she bobbed beside me. I wonder whether she is regarded as *petite*: somehow, despite her slenderness, I doubt it. Similarly, she is an unlikely *tomboy*. Nor is she cast in the role of *jester*. Nor is she *small and frail* or *small and fierce*. She is none of these things. Unlike me, she is not mistaken for a nurse. I have noticed that she is adept at moving with ease amongst beds and trolleys. As she steps lightly ahead of me, the hem of her white coat bouncing against her ankles, I conclude that it is not that we are too short but that our white coats are too long.

I follow her into the corridor. 'Vivien,' I call, hurrying behind her, 'I've just spoken to Dr Bow Tie.' I know that this will amuse her.

Predictably, she squeals. 'He'll charge you for his time,' she shouts to me over her shoulder.

We turn the corner together and run into Chris. He is examining an X-ray. He turns towards us, bemused: 'Dr Bow Tie?'

'Adrian Winterson,' replies Vivien guilelessly.

'*Dr Bow Tie?*'

'Yes.' Vivien stares at him. 'Haven't you noticed?'

He opens his mouth to reply but closes it again: he cannot dispute the validity of the observation because it is indisputable; but he is perturbed by the irreverence. He regards us with suspicion. Perhaps he is troubled by a sense of loyalty to Dr Bow Tie; perhaps he is pondering his own vulnerability and wondering whether he too has a nickname.

I turn rapidly to the X-ray. 'What's that?' I exclaim. The ghost of a long object shines inside a shadowy rectum.

'It's what I've brought you to see,' Vivien replies with satisfaction, stepping back and gazing with interest at the flickering screen.

'What does it look like?' Chris asks me sarcastically.

I peer closely at the X-ray. The object is eight or nine inches long.

'Twenty-year-old-male,' Chris informs us. 'Says he inserted it himself on Friday night and then couldn't get it out again.'

'How embarrassing,' I mutter.

Vivien, engrossed in the image, murmurs quietly in agreement.

Chris folds his arms and shakes his head, laughing dismissively.

'Well, it is,' I insist. 'I mean, what do you say?'

'Yes,' Vivien agrees, rounding on him, 'what do you say?'

Chris shrugs. 'Well, I don't know.'

Vivien and I exchange glances.

'What did *he* say?' she enquires with interest.

He shrugs again.

Chris sighs. 'He just said that it's something he likes to do sometimes.' He continues to feign a lack of interest.

Vivien turns to me. 'At least it's not the fruit bowl syndrome.'

'Fruit bowl?' Chris, excluded, becomes irritated.

'The apocryphal woman,' I explain patiently to him, 'who came into the department with an apple stuck inside her: she said that she'd been jumping over a fruit bowl when she slipped and fell onto it.'

Chris's gaze flicks between us. He smiles unsurely.

I return to the X-ray. 'So,' I ask Chris, 'have you got it out yet?'

'No,' he says, matter-of-fact; 'I've called the surgeons.'

I look at him with surprise. 'Really?' I look back at the X-ray. 'What goes up must come down, Chris.' I turn to him and realise instantly that I have offended him.

His face is rigid. 'Perhaps you are adept at crawling up rectums, Beth,' he comments, 'but I'm not.'

Confronted by his defiant gaze, a gaze usually amiable or amiable enough, I would like to reply; but Vivien interrupts us, oblivious to our exchange. She has been studying the X-ray; now she turns brightly to Chris. 'Is he gay?' she asks.

'No,' he replies, barely distracted.

'How do you know?' I rejoin.

Chris sighs heavily, wearily. '*Beth*,' he emphasises, 'he's not gay.'

My smile is bitter with irritation. 'So you say; but how do you know?'

'I *asked* him.'

'You *asked* him?

'Yes.' The reply is saturated with exasperation.

'Why?'

His eyes narrow.

'Why did you ask him?' I repeat. 'Why is it relevant?'

His front teeth sink briefly into his lower lip. 'Of course it's relevant,' he falters.

'Why?'

He is uncomprehending. 'Everything's relevant.' The statement is convincing; but it enables him to conclude that he has a right to know everything about a patient. A doctor cannot know everything about a patient: any assumption to the contrary results in misunderstanding and distrust. A doctor does not have a *right* to know *anything* about a patient: I reach this conclusion with surprising passion.

Vivien shrugs. 'She's right, I suppose,' she says to Chris: 'It's not relevant.'

'Yes, it is,' he snaps.

'No, it isn't.'

'Yes, it is.'

'Why?' She challenges him, chin jutting.

There is a pause. 'Look,' says Chris eventually, his tone conciliatory, 'don't get me wrong, I don't *mind* if he's gay. . .'

Vivien laughs derisively, tossing her head. 'You *don't mind*?'

Chris is embarrassed. He opens his mouth to reply.

Vivien anticipates him. 'Don't give me any of that some-of-my-best-friends-are-gay crap.' She turns abruptly and walks away.

I watch her sauntering along the corridor. I watch the hem of her white coat lapping at her ankles. Tomorrow we will not be here; tomorrow we are off duty. I wonder what she is planning to do tomorrow. Both she and Chris live in the hospital. I wonder what they do when cast adrift in the hospital on a weekday without work. At least I can go home; but at home I am reminded nonetheless of illness; weekdays at home remind me of childhood illness. My childhood illnesses were mild and I could lie undisturbed on the sofa in the living room and watch the early morning chill melting on the windows when the twin tub began to bubble in the kitchen. I could listen to the distant rattle of the kitchen radio – *hits, requests, golden oldies* – and look forward to a bowl of tomato soup for lunch. During the afternoon there was a black and white film on television, described in the newspaper as a *matinee*. My mother invariably recognised the film or the cast. 'From my childhood,' she wouild say, pausing at the door and gazing at the screen, at the women with pencilled eyebrows; 'and what a load of old rubbish,' she would conclude, smiling as she backed away.

Vivien disappears from view. In September we will both be gone; our six-month contracts end on the last day of August. No one is a Casualty Officer here for more than six months; no one returns unless temporarily as a locum. Medicine in Casualty is band-aid medicine; it is useful experience. It is useful experience at the beginning of a career in medicine: an initiation rite. After six months in Casualty there is nothing more to learn about the job and nothing more to be: Casualty Officers have a limited role and no career structure. There are rarely senior posts in Accident and Emergency. In this department there is no registrar or senior registrar. There is a consultant because the hospital is large and the management relatively progressive.

Vivien, like many newly qualified doctors, wants to be a GP. She is luckier than most because she has a place on a GP training scheme. The required periods of training have been organised for her in local hospitals: six months each of Casualty, paediatrics, obstetrics and gynaecology, and geriatrics. I do not have a job to start in September. I do not want to be a GP. I want a career in hospital medicine. I should begin to enquire and apply, to arrange visits and attend interviews; and I should prepare to do so again within the next year or so because all posts, apart from consultant posts, are temporary. All posts, apart from consultant posts, are training posts; so I should prepare to move again because a willingness to seek the best training is regarded as evidence of commitment. There is no promotion without commitment; there is no consultant post without promotion; and without a consultant post there is no end to apprenticeship.

I envy Vivien because she can work in a health centre cosy with posters and receptionists; she can choose her colleagues; she can employ a deputising service to attend to her patients during the night and at weekends. But I do not envy a workload of coughs and colds and problems euphemistically known as social. My father used to talk of the easy option: sometimes he was scathing, and sometimes respectful. Training to be a GP is the easy option: I wonder whether my father would be scathing or respectful of my decision. He used to accuse me of 'making things difficult' for myself.

Vivien is gone. Chris has sunk into silence. I step alone into the corridor, wondering whether any of us will ever be friends. I recall my conversation last night with Lilly: if it is so difficult for an old friend to know what to say to me, how would it be for a new friend? There might be no new friends for a while. There was once little enough time to make friends, but now there might be even less; there was once four and a half months, but now I might be leaving even sooner.

I glimpse Chris as I step away. He is gazing into the corridor, dismayed at Vivien's absence; and now he turns to me. His expression is forlorn.

His eyes meet mine: *What did I say?*

I hesitate.

What did I do?

Reluctantly, I sympathise. 'Oh dear,' I concede, whispering gravely, 'you're not doing very well today, are you?'

Suddenly we are smiling at each other, teasing a smile onto each other's face. Who began this smiling? Me, probably: women smile with the gentlest of prompts because they are eager to please.

'Would you like a cup of coffee?' he asks me.

I would love a cup of coffee. 'Yes,' I tell him thankfully, 'yes, please, I'd love one.'

He turns instantly and reaches into a passing group of nurses. 'Alicia,' he says to one of them, placing his hand on her arm, 'can you bring us two cups of coffee, please?'

I regard him with horror: 'Chris!'

He looks at me, surprised, requesting an explanation.

I find myself incapable of explaining. 'I'll make it myself,' I say pointedly.

Alicia looks vaguely offended. I smile kindly at her. Then I turn away, glancing at Chris and muttering incredulously: 'Strangely enough, some of my best friends are men.'

I leave the cubicle, shut the door behind me, and lean against the wall.

'I can't examine the patient unless she's undressed,' I told the nurse; an agency nurse.

I hesitate outside the cubicle. Inside, the nurse is peeling layers of clothing from the elderly woman, flinching at fleas, avoiding a puddle of urine on the floor. I reach for the door handle but recoil. I will go and see whether the results of Clare Tomkins's tests have arrived.

Clare Tomkins is twenty-two-years old. She is Mrs Tomkins. She will remain Mrs Tomkins throughout her life, in spite of divorce or bereavement, unless she chooses otherwise. She has joined the ranks of married women; she has gained a status never to be relinquished: *title*, Mrs. When I was younger, it never crossed my mind that I would not marry: a husband and children were the essential building blocks of a life.

With my schoolfriends, I speculated on the nature of husbands and children: the relative age of the husband (a year or two older than me, ideally); the number, sex, sequence and names of the children, the importance of their schooling and hobbies. It seemed sensible to become engaged at eighteen, after leaving school and finding a job, and to stay engaged for a couple of years. An engagement should not be too short (my schoolfriends could all cite disasters) nor too long: the six year engagement of my mother's schoolfriend aunty Jane to uncle Brian had resulted in a unhappy marriage. An engagement should allow time for the couple to get to know each other properly and to raise a deposit for a flat. Eighteen was a good age *to get engaged*, and two years of engagement was *about right*: these were the words of advice offered to me by my mother and grandmother.

I expected to marry at twenty or twenty-one and have my first baby at twenty-two or twenty-three. I would have been following the example set by my mother: *not too young*.

By the time I was eighteen, I hoped to marry sometime after qualification. Gradually my aspirations have been worn away and replaced by others; and now I am twenty-five, unmarried, childless, but still young. It was the same with sex: initially, as a child, I expected sex after marriage; then, at thirteen, I decided that it would be acceptable to sleep with my fiancé; at fourteen, I was impressed by the notion of true love, regardless of status; later, I settled for friendship and trust. Now, without husband or fiancé or love or trust, I sleep alone.

I was planning to be a ballerina, a swimmer or a skater: someone graceful but strong; someone excelling; someone with long hair tied into a bun. Then came puberty and O levels. I excelled at O levels.

'Medicine,' suggested Mrs Pincott.

I had already decided to study medicine; but whilst I knew that nurses wore long hair tied into buns, I had not seen any lady

184

doctors other than Dr Miller and Dr Arnham. Dr Miller was a locum at the local health centre. She was described to my mother by the receptionist as 'a young mum, marvellous for women's problems'. Dr Arnham was nearing retirement. She loomed large in tweed and sipped coffee throughout consultations. Her two children were at university.

'Nice children,' said my mother approvingly, quoting the receptionist.

I straighten against the wall and turn to the corridor to see Chris striding towards me, holding out a piece of paper. The corners of the hem of his white coat are lifting around his knees like tiny wings. He is staring at me, forehead contracting, mouth open. I step towards him, my hand rising. I want to say: *I know*, but he is already speaking: 'There's a woman here, pregnant, with a haemoglobin of five.' He holds the piece of paper towards me, horrified.

I know, I know. 'I know.'

His eyebrows spring up his forehead.

'No,' I explain rapidly as I pass him, 'I mean, I was waiting for confirmation.'

The piece of paper is now in my hand: Clare Tomkins's test results.

I step away from him across the tiles, and I am smiling. My diagnosis was correct: ectopic pregnancy. Art is long, but I am learning. Chris is staring at me. I want to explain that Clare Tomkins is dying but that she will not die; that she will have a long night, longer than mine, that she will have to stay here in the hospital when I have gone, but she will live.

I smile. 'I'm going to get her ready for surgery,' I call over my shoulder as I turn and hurry away.

I am at home at last. I step into the hallway and close the door behind me. I do not have to leave again for two days. Walking from the hallway to the living room, I realise that I am treading lightly. There is nothing to disturb but silence; yet silence is so easily disturbed. I walk the familiar route around the living room, switching on the lamps. The kitchen is dark. The ivory telephone glows in the darkness like a heap of small smooth bones. It crouches, ready to surprise; naked and brutal without the answering machine. For the first time in two years I regret giving the answering machine to Jem. Tonight I want to screen my calls so that I can neglect to answer some and prepare myself before answering others. Tonight I want to be able to ease the callers painlessly beneath my skin.

I step into the kitchen and look at the clock: 9.42. I have not eaten for a long time. I shudder with hunger. All my muscles are tense; the muscles around my eyes are tense. I reach for the spotlight. Next to the black plastic lead lies the telephone wire. I follow it with my fingertips to the plug. I pinch the pin and ease it from the socket so that my contact with the world is temporarily suspended. The pin lies on the work-top. I will re-insert it later, when I am ready.

I am going to make some soup. I will eat the cheese, hummus and pitta bread that I bought at the shop, but first I am going to make soup. Soup is a starter.

'Starters are unnecessary,' says my mother. She is wrong.

The raw materials are in the vegetable rack: I reach beneath the worktop and pull it towards me. The tiny wheels slide across the tiles in a coquettish dance. The wire baskets contain two potatoes, two onions, a leek and a bundle of carrots. I feel like a survivalist. I lift them from the beds of newspaper and lay them on the worktop. Unlike my mother, I do not cover the worktop with newspaper: a worktop is for work. I take the potatoes and carrots to the sink and scrub them in a stream of water; I do not peel them. Then I chop them on a chopping board with one of the landlady's formidably sharp knives and throw them into a saucepan of water. I do not add salt.

186

'Just a pinch,' my mother used to say, reaching for the pot of salt.

'No, please,' I'd repeat, 'not for me.'

She would slam the pot onto the work surface and turn to me, hands on hips: 'How am I supposed to ensure that the same saucepan contains a pinch of salt for us and none for you?'

We argued similarly about garlic: I wanted garlic but she decreed 'not in my kitchen'. Pepper was the only spice permitted in her kitchen.

I peer into my spice cupboard and take a clove of garlic and a piece of ginger from the shelf. Then I search among the jars for cinnamon, ground cumin, ground coriander, chilli powder. Lining the jars next to the cooker, I close one cupboard and turn to another for a tin of tomatoes and a packet of red lentils. The packet of lentils sags in my hand and spills a rich red sand into the saucepan. I place the lid on the saucepan, lower the flame, and decide to telephone my father.

'Hi, Carrie, it's me.' I panic momentarily that she will mistake me for Verity.

'Hi, Whizz!' Whizz is her nickname for me: Lizzy, Whizzy, Whizz. She has no nickname for Verity.

'How's life?' I begin breezily.

'Oh . . .' she affects adults weariness '. . . so-so.'

'So-so?' I smirk briefly to myself before continuing. 'Have you been to see Mum this evening?'

'Yes.' She pauses. She has retained a child-like telephone manner: listening in awe, awaiting direct questions, replying briefly and shyly.

'Yes?' I prompt. 'And how was she?'

'Fine.'

'And did my flowers arrive?'

'Yes,' she says. 'And they're lovely, Whizz; really, really lovely; the best on the ward.'

'Oh. Good.'

*

Carrie mutters: 'Hang on a minute.' There is a muffled squeak in the receiver.

'What, Carrie?' I enquire mildly. 'What are you doing?'

'Painting my nails.'

I picture the receiver slung between her chin and shoulder, her hands free; I picture the close attention paid to the brush on her nail. Carrie has learned the habit from Mum.

'Yuk,' I comment cheerfully.

'Yuk yourself,' she replies, unconcerned. Then she sighs. 'Are you coming home? Please? Whizz?'

'Well,' I soothe. 'Well, I might. It depends.' I am panicking again.

'Oh good,' she says, easily satisfied. 'I'm going into London next Saturday.'

No, you're not, I think. *Going into London* means *going into London with Mummy*. At thirteen, Carrie still goes nowhere alone.

'What for?'

'Shopping: clothes; summer clothes.'

Summer? 'Is it summer already?' I turn involuntarily to the window. The sky is taut with rain.

She sighs again. 'You're kidding, aren't you, Whizz? It's roasting.'

This is an exaggeration. She wants new clothes.

'Jem called me yesterday,' she says cheerfully.

I am surprised. 'Oh?' I remind myself that he rings her sometimes; on her birthday, usually.

'He wanted to know if I wanted to go over there this weekend; to go shopping and play with their baby and everything.'

Their baby: I do not bother to point out to Carrie that Alice is not *their* baby. Alice is Diane's baby. Carrie knows this; it was a slip of the tongue.

'And you didn't go?'

'No.'

'Why not?'

'Work.'

'Work?'

'Homework.'

Homework? Carrie? 'Homework?'

'Yes, you know,' she says impatiently. 'Geography project. It has to be finished by tomorrow and we've had three weeks but I didn't start until Saturday afternoon.'

This is typical of Carrie.

'Geography's crappy,' she says.

'Crappy?' I laugh. 'Who says?' I know the answer.

'*Everyone.*'

Everyone: her friends; Anna, Sharon, Nicci, Tania, Clare. I imagine the chorus: *Geography's crappy*.

'Don't you think so?' she asks me. 'Didn't you hate Geography?'

I never studied Geography. Lilly and Kieran studied Geography. It revealed to them the patterns of social life on the globe: the migrations of peoples, the histories of settlements. They talked together about the rise and fall of heavy industry in South Wales, the swelling of Lima and Manila. They studied Geography with History, Economics, English, Languages: subjects providing topics for conversation in the sixth form common room after lessons. They were options, chosen by them at fourteen and sixteen.

I had no choice: if I wanted to study medicine, Geography and the humanities would have to be sacrificed in favour of science. I studied Biology, Chemistry, Physics: subjects that did not provide topics or classmates for conversation. Most of my classmates were boys hoping to become engineers. There was one girl, Annabel Laughton, who wanted to become a vet; but she failed the lower sixth exams and opted for osteopathy instead.

'What did you do today?' Lilly would shout to me across the sixth form common room when I returned from a session in the labs. 'Did you discuss the changing role of the test tube in modern Western society?'

189

I would be standing at my locker, plastering my hands with lotion. I hated Biology because it made my hands smell of formaldehyde.

Carrie wants to be a lawyer. A *lawyer*: a feature common to the American television shows which she likes to watch.

'She wants to be a DA,' my mother said to me last year on the telephone, a note of uncertainty in her voice.

'Say it fast enough,' I replied lightly, 'and it sounds like BA.'

My mother is familiar with BAs: the children of several of her friends have BAs. Lilly has a BA. 'Bachelor of Arts,' my mother used to say, wrinkling her nose with disapproval at Bachelor. I am entitled to write MB BS after my name: Bachelor of Medicine, Bachelor of Surgery.

'Carrie,' I ask, 'is Dad home?'

'No,' she replies, 'he's gone to Bob Thompson's for half an hour.'

Bob Thompson is a business associate. I imagine my father at the door telling Carrie very clearly that he is going to Bob Thompson's for half an hour: how long ago?

'And you're on your own?'

'Yes?' She is indignant: she is thirteen; there is no reason for me to be concerned.

'And are you ready for school in the morning?'

'Yes?' The same tone.

I change the subject: 'Anything happening this week?'

'We're going sailing on Thursday,' she says brightly. We: Anna, Sharon, Nicci, Tania, Clare?

'Who?'

'My class?'

'Your class?'

'Yes, for PE.'

When I was at school, PE was confined to the school gym or the school field. The field was too hot during summer, too cold during winter, and always too public. The gym was preferable. The most popular indoor activity was badminton, due to the possibility of losing the shuttlecock in the rafters. The least popular activity was the horse: leaping over something that looked nothing like a horse and listening to Mrs Hammond, the PE teacher, shouting, 'Watch you don't split your difference.' Mrs Hammond was forever under suspicion of pregnancy because she was married and childless, and because she stood on the sidelines during lessons in a baggy track suit.

'On Friday, Verity and Neil are coming over for tea.' Carrie says it happily.

'Oh.' I try to sound interested.

Carrie thinks badly of no one. She forgets rather than forgives. It distresses her that Verity is so disliked.

She can't help it, she said once in Verity's defence.

Can't help what? I demanded gleefully.

Now I shudder: Verity and Neil. Neil is inoffensive. Recently Verity told my mother that they have decided to get engaged at Christmas. What does this mean? Does it mean that they have decided to decide to get married? Or does it mean that there will be a party? Verity would enjoy the presents, but not the party. She has been more insular than ever since she met Neil; more tightly wrapped than ever in her shiny pink skin. I remember the expression SWALK, Sealed With A Loving Kiss. Verity has been shrink-wrapped with a kiss. Yet she is somehow unavoidable like the sun burning in the distance in a cold and empty sky. Neil is insignificant. He is an accessory with a credit card and a car.

'Carrie,' I say, 'I'd better go. Will you tell Dad that I called?'

'Yes.' She is monosyllabic again; perhaps she is peering at her nails.

'Carrie?'

Silence.

'Will you?'

She sighs with mock weariness. 'Yes.'

'And ask him to call me if there's any news?'

Another sigh. 'Yes.'

191

'Okay, then. Bye.'
'Bye, Whizz. Bye for now.'

As I replace the receiver, I remember a time before Carrie was born, a long time ago. We were in Spain, Mum, Verity, and me; sitting at a table in the local bar, in the early evening, after our daily shopping trip. Our bags were slumped at our feet, long loaves nosing floor tiles. The speckled formica surface of the table had been wiped clean by Consuela when we arrived. It was still damp beneath the latest edition of *The Costa Blanca Weekly Gazette*. We had been given *The Gazette* earlier in the day by a neighbour.

'Like gold dust,' the neighbour had informed us, handing it through the car window when she returned from a trip to the coastal resort.

The headline was *No To Nudists*.

Consuela was at the far end of the room, wiping tables, talking over her shoulder at someone in the kitchen. The bar was empty of customers. The bright oil-scented air rang with the tinny tones of the television on the wall. Mum and Verity were staring at the screen. Mum was stirring a cup of coffee, the teaspoon dragging a ball of milky froth around the surface. Verity was sitting behind a long glass of silky black coke. My fingers were frozen to a glass of Fanta Naranja. On the screen, sperm were wriggling towards a spinning ovum. The tone of the incomprehensible narrative was educational.

We were inadvertently watching a Spanish version of *My Body, Your Body*. I had watched *My Body, Your Body* at primary school: there had been eight programmes, culminating in the swimming pool scene. My fingers tightened around my glass of Fanta. I hoped that we would not have to see a Spanish version of the swimming pool scene: girls and boys clambering in and out of a swimming pool, the camera leering at their naked bodies. I had wondered whether they had dedicated their bodies to science, or whether they had been paid, and how much. I looked around the room for Consuela. She was behind the bar, oblivious, wiping and chatting. Usually in the early evenings the television programmes were about wildlife.

Verity was rising slowly in her seat, peering over the glass of coke. She was following the progress of the sperm, eager to see which of them would succeed in fertilising the egg. Mum continued to stare blankly at the screen, the teaspoon twisting aimlessly in her cup. Then she frowned, and closed her eyes. The teaspoon continued to ring monotonously against the cup. A few tears fell silently from the tips of her eyelashes into the spinning frothless coffee.

$$* \quad * \quad *$$

I am sitting on the sofa, too tired to go to bed. I am listening to Greig's piano concerto in A minor. A recording which, once upon a time, played in the evenings in my grandparents' front room. A piece with a beginning, middle, and end. I have been wondering why I contacted Lilly on Saturday, rather than anyone else. It must have been a reflex action: Lilly is my oldest friend. I could not have reached Harriet: she was away for the weekend. Harriet is a newer friend. I have known her for two years.

I met Harriet at a Christmas party in the anaesthetics department of the hospital where I began my first house job. She came with Ian; her boyfriend, my immediate superior.

'Meet Harriet,' he urged, appearing in front of me from a crowd, pulling me behind him across the room.

She was alone at the buffet table, reaching absently into a tupperware bowl and sucking hula hoops from the tips of her fingers. All around her people were circulating; flapping paper plates pungent with stilton and noisy with pieces of carrot and celery. They were wearing white coats: the men garlanded with tinsel; the women decorated as usual with bows in their hair and on their shoes. She was not wearing a white coat. Her clothes were casual but expensive, made from materials designed to withstand the elements: canvas, denim, wool, linen.

Sometimes I tease her that she is *the-kind-of-girl-you-can-take-to-dinner-with-the-consultant*. This is hardly surprising: she has had a lifetime of practice; her father is a consultant urologist. Thus she takes Ian to dinner with a consultant, and not vice versa. Ian is still a doctor but no longer my superior; still working in a hospital in London, still failing exams, still talking endlessly about leaving a career in medicine to become a sheep farmer in Wales.

Harriet was once a student nurse. After qualifying, she left nursing to study for a degree in Social Science. I once asked her why she had chosen to train as a nurse. She shrugged; and then she laughed and said that if she had not been a nurse she would not have met Ian and if she had not met Ian then she would not have met me. She asked me why I had chosen to be a doctor and I said, 'You have to do something and it beats typing.'

'Or nursing,' she said.

Or nursing.

Before nursing, she was a schoolgirl in Shropshire. On her desk there is a photograph of schoolgirls seated in rows; hands resting in bottle green laps, faces shadowed by bottle green hats. Harriet pointed out to me that the hats were secured by elastic under the chin: 'To keep our mouths shut.'

Unlike me, Harriet was educated *privately*, at a *public* school.

The schoolgirls undertook Community Service on Wednesday afternoons.

'Community Service?' I wondered aloud when she told me. 'It makes it sound as if you were delinquents.'

'We were,' she agreed enthusiastically, 'we were.'

Cookery on Mondays, Games on Tuesdays, Community on Wednesdays, God on Thursdays, and Macrame on Fridays: eventually she admitted that she was joking about the macrame.

'It was a good school,' she said, 'and good schools are the worst.'

After speaking to Carrie, I rang Harriet. For a while the ringing tone rattled in my ear. Harriet answers the 'phone at work as 'Harriet Creighton', without an upward inflection: a statement of fact. She works for an international health charity: she has been very successful; her promotion during the past two years has been rapid.

'I sell ideas,' she says whenever explaining her job; 'and it's a competitive business.'

Often she is unavailable and I speak instead to an assistant. Harriet has two assistants: one secretarial, one research; Lucy and Barbara. They sing into the telephone: 'Harriet Creighton is not available; perhaps I can help?'

'It's Beth,' I admit.

'Oh.' Initially they are disappointed; and then friendly. 'Hang on a second, yes, she's free.'

At home she answers with, 'Hello?'

'Hello?'

'Harriet . . .'

'Beth!' Her tone was similar to the tone adopted by an adult towards a small child: fond but puzzled; what-have-we-here? 'Beth, I called you about an hour ago but there was no answer.'

'I wasn't home from work,' I said dismissively. 'What time did you get home?'

She was equally dismissive: 'About eight.'

'Tired?'

'Mmmm; ready for bed.'

I pictured the paisley pyjamas and bunny rabbit slippers.

She and Ian have been to Wales for the weekend.

'Oh God, Beth,' she said, 'why are men like this? Every time Ian laid eyes on a hillside he had to go and conquer it.'

I laughed. 'Isn't it something to do with territory?'

'No.' She sounded puzzled. 'That's urination; this was climbing.' She sighed. 'Or attempted climbing: he's so unfit that he knackered himself and I had to do all the driving.'

She told me that he had gone out as soon as they arrived home. 'At half past eight he said, "I said we'd go over and have a drink with Marty and the boys" and I said, "They're your friends, you go." A girl's gotta do what a girl's gotta do and I'm going to henna my hair tonight.'

'You're henna-ing your hair?' I modify the image of pyjamas and slippers, adding a plastic hood sticky with slops of henna.

'No,' she sighed, 'I couldn't be bothered. You can help me with it when you come. You can have the leftovers, if you like. We can have a henna party.'

I knew that she had been planning to visit her parents in Shropshire this afternoon, so I asked about the family.

Anyone would think that you don't have one of your own, she exclaims sometimes.

She has never met my family. She confuses the name Verity with Constance, Prudence, Faith, Hope and Charity.

Hardly, I say.

She told me that her parents were well, and then she talked about her sister Judith, and Judith's children: Lara, Laura, Lana, Tamsin, Tamara, Cora, Caitlin, Katie?

'How's Tamsin?' I was guessing that it is Tasmin who has had meningitis.

'Oh, she's fine, she's fine,' said Harriet; 'Judith still worries a bit; but she would, wouldn't she.'

I remembered a little girl, aged five or six, in Harriet's parents' firelit living room: *Come here, darling, and say hello to Beth*. She was prissy in a kilt and black patent leather party shoes. Her long flaxen hair was tucked behind an Alice band: Tamsin or Lara?

Harriet is the baby of the family not only because she is eight years younger than her twin brother and sister but because she is unmarried and owns a sports car. Matthew and Judith are members of the older generation: Matthew is a psychiatrist; Judith was a dancer but retired when she married Richard. It is difficul for me to imagine Judith in any other dance than a belly dance: she is tubby beneath teased angora jumpers and highlighted hair; she has a smoke-saturated laugh. She is ten years younger than her husband. Her husband, Richard, is a businessman. Judith is his second wife.

Did your parents mind? I asked Harriet when she told me the tale of the affair and divorce. Harriet laughed and said that they were relieved that he was not a doctor.

Judith runs a business from home: a soft toy manufacturing company, *Soft Options*. Home is a large house in Buckinghamshire.

Big Bucks, says Harriet.

'I had an argument with my father about the car.' Harriet sighed. She is always having an argument with her father about the car. He thinks that she should sell it and buy *something sensible*.

'Harriet,' I said suddenly, 'I'm off work tomorrow and Tuesday.'

'Oh good,' she replied happily, tolerating the change of subject. 'I'm in Birmingham tomorrow; but come up on Tuesday. Fetch me from the office at five and we'll go shopping or something.'

'You're in Brussels on Tuesday.'

There was a pause. 'Really?' There was the sound of pages turning rapidly beneath her fingers. 'Ahhhh,' she said eventually, knowingly, 'but I'll be back in London by six.' The cover of the diary thudded back onto the pages. 'Come anyway. Get something nice for tea from M&S. I'll leave the key out.'

Out means under the flowerpot at the foot of the steps.

'Beth?' she asked, towards the end of the conversation, 'are you all right?' Her tone was anxious.

I tried to sound puzzled: 'Yes?'

I will tell her everything on Tuesday.

MONDAY
24 APRIL 1989

At work I am often tired, and always anxious, and sometimes despondent, but rarely distressed. At home it is usual for me to be distressed. Somehow it is easier for me to be a doctor than a daughter. Last night, by the time that I said goodnight to Harriet, I was aware that I have been worrying about my mother for as long as I can remember.

It is Monday morning. I am lying in bed whilst others are leaving home for work. I have been awake since half past seven, listening to the couple downstairs: the periodic flushing of water into pipes; the constant drone of the radio; and, now, the pressing of the front door into its frame. Their footsteps bump on the carpet on the stairs and fade until there is silence. I raise my head from the pillows and look at the clock: twenty to nine. I drop back onto the pillows but twist into a different position beneath the duvet, dragging cooler cotton onto my skin. Sunlight glows all around me on the walls.

It will not be long now until I know more about the fate of my mother. This morning she will have a laparoscopy: A telescope, my father said when he returned my call last night, a tiny telescope through the tummy button. I do not know whether he was translating for his own benefit or mine. At lunchtime, he said, you can call the hospital for news. I do not want to call the hospital: I do not want to speak to the house person or the ward sister, I do not want to be a relative.

I wonder how my mother is feeling this morning. I remember when she booked an appointment for Verity to see a dentist about a recurrent wisdom tooth infection. Verity hates dentists more than anything else. On the morning of the appointment Verity was sitting opposite me at the kitchen table, listlessly fingering a slice of cold sticky toast.

'What if I have it taken out?' she was murmuring in despair.

My mother was buttering another slice of toast. 'Que sera, sera,' she replied.

Verity scowled at her: 'What does that mean?'

My mother sighed, because Verity was studying Spanish at school: 'It means what will be, will be.' Then, in a fluttering falsetto, she began to sing: 'Que sera, sera, whatever will be, will be.'

My father peeked from behind his newspaper and delighted us by rolling his eyes and exclaiming, 'Hardly Doris Day, eh?'

Last night my father said *it all depends*.

He believes that all the possibilities for the future are present this morning in the small bright lens of the endoscope.

'That's right, isn't it,' he said last night. 'Everything depends on tomorrow, that's what the doctor said.'

The doctor.

I am a doctor and perhaps I should have said yes; but I am a daughter and I wanted to say no. In the end, I said nothing. He did not notice that I said nothing. He has learned to accept silence from me. I wanted to say that, for me, everything has already changed; I wanted to say that I do not need a lens, I do not need to be a doctor, to know about my mother. Everything is changed for me this morning not because I can see the future; but because, last night, I saw the past. Last night, when I said goodnight to Harriet, I started to think: I have been lying here and thinking, like a doctor, that it is important to remember the details. Throughout the weekend, the details have been falling distantly around me like shooting stars. I had not forgotten, but nor had I remembered.

I raise myself from the pillows. The window is blazing beneath the thin curtains: maybe Carrie is right, maybe it is roasting. I do not have a sea view, not even a sea view involving contortions on the window sill; but I see the sea each day in the distance from the windows of the hospital and it is soundless, motionless, often indistinguishable from the sky. Last night, when I saw it from the bus, I was surprised by the fluorescence of the white horses; as sinister as flowers in darkness. This morning I shall walk to the shore. I do not want to wait here alone until lunchtime.

I shut the door and step from the porch onto the path. My eyes shut involuntarily against the sunlight that bursts from the sky onto the white walls of the house across the road. Re-opening them cautiously, lowering my gaze, I walk down the path and around the pile of rubbish bags at the gate. The plastic glows darkly like hide. I open the gate and step from the path to the pavement. A breeze slaps across my face, and a cold tear strokes my cheek. I raise my hand to wipe it away but it has already dried. I look at the sky, raising my head and tottering briefly on the pavement. The sky is polished, unmarked by cloud.

At nine o'clock the High Street is already empty of workers and busy with shoppers: it is a street of women and children. The children are everywhere in pushchairs, passive beneath plastic canopies, silent beneath layers of clothing tied with zips and toggles and laces; not yet hungry and tired. The women move slowly and noisily with them along the pavement. Older women, without children, are sprightly in headscarves and short boots. Occasionally there are young men in grey suits standing impatiently on the kerb, holding slim folders or newspapers under their arms, waiting for opportunities to dart across the road towards parked cars, to drive away: company cars, central locking.

It is a street without patients. I look around me and see no illness, although I know that it is here: I know that everyone has a medical history, transcribed in biro or felt tip pen by doctors onto colour coded cards, and stored somewhere in unsent envelopes; and I know that everyone has a medical future. I have always known that my mother went into hospital when I was a child, but, until last night, I remembered only the birth of Carrie; but then, suddenly, last night, I began to remember everything else.

In the distance, beyond the High Street, I can see the sea. *I can see the sea*: a childhood refrain sung in the car before disembarking briefly to peer across the beach in the drizzle. Even on holiday in Spain the sea was distant. Now I cross the High Street and walk towards it. *The deep blue sea*: the blue is deep, not the sea. The sky is a pale minty blue by comparison. I can see the sea but I cannot hear it. My neighbour told me that it can be heard in town on Christmas Day, noisy in streets empty of traffic. I turn from the High Street into the lanes. The lanes are always blocked by traffic. Ahead of me there are two large vans: one marked *Bread and Pastries*; the other, *Laundry*. The laundry van is making a delivery at the back of a hotel. Wicker laundry baskets, dropped by two men from the back of the van, thump onto the cobbles: wicker laundry baskets, real laundry baskets, props in a farce. The bread and pastries van is reversing into a space between parked cars. The spectacle is watched by two men standing beside a small van bearing a lattice of ladders. Chamois leathers hang limp in their hands: window cleaners. One of the window cleaners is wearing a hoop earring, like a pirate.

The driver of the bread and pastries van is leaning in and out of the cabin like a jack-in-the-box. Suddenly the wheels push against the kerb and the van shudders. A motorbike hovers at the bumper, the engine spitting with impatience, the rider inanimate in helmet and leathers. The van slots into the space and the motorbike passes. The driver disembarks from the van, grabs a clipboard from the dashboard, and slams the door. He strides along the pavement in his short white coat and turns in front of me into the doorway of Joe's. The large windows of the café are hazy with steam. The door is open. Two young women stand on the doorstep, talking loudly to the driver, supervising the delivery, smoothing their hands against their calico aprons and running their fingers through their hair.

'I'll be in Joe's for coffee tomorrow morning,' Chris said to me when we left work last night. 'Half ten. Come along.'

'Maybe,' I said.

Maybe. Later.

I walk to the end of the lane and onto the seafront. Hotels claim exclusive views of the main attraction. Sunlight splashes from the water and washes over them so that they glow like cliffs. A few people, solitary or in couples, stand beneath them and stare out to sea. I walk down the steps from the road and across the tarmac onto the pebbles. My mother hates pebbles. 'What's the point of pebbles?' she used to complain. She considered sand to be fun. I have never liked sand. It buries itself inside things. Whenever I went to a beach with my mother, it was a sandy beach. This is not a sandy beach. The pebbles roll beneath my soles. I can hear nothing but the sea. I glance behind me: crowning the bank of shingle are the familiar seafront buildings, the long row of stiff white Victoriana. The seafront traffic is now invisible and inaudible. Close to me, the waves tumble unevenly towards the shore, blown in different directions by the breeze. They snow onto the beach, the undertow drowning with screams on the stones beneath them. The toes of my shoes are wet and shiny.

$$* \quad * \quad *$$

My mother hates water: she flinches from it as if it is messy. Last night, when I said goodnight to Harriet and went into the bathroom for a bath, I began to remember. I had been in the bathroom on that afternoon many years ago when my mother called to me from the kitchen. It was winter, and the bathroom and the kitchen were the warmest rooms in the house. We spent most of our days in the kitchen, Mum, Verity and me; laundry hanging behind us on the backs of our chairs, steaming and stiffening. I had gone into the bathroom to sail a boat in the sink. The boat was an empty margarine pot. I was holding it beneath the surface of the water and planning to lift it high, full of warm water, to shower my fingers.

It was winter; the winter following the death of my grandfather.

'He's gone to heaven,' my mother would tell me: my atheist mother; my mother lost for words.

We were alone in the world, Mum, Verity and me; all day, week after week, we were alone in the kitchen. It was a long winter.

I went into the bathroom to sail my boat one afternoon, after *Women's Hour* and before *Playschool*, when the day was darkening and there was no evening. I looked through the window of frosted glass at the sky: it was birdless and thick with unfallen snow; it stared back at me, swollen and blind. And then I heard my mother calling to me from the kitchen.

It was a long time ago. I was very small. When I stepped into the kitchen, the door was closed behind me and I was lifted onto a chair. Verity was even smaller than me. She could not walk or talk much but usually she fluttered in a highchair; her bright green gaze filling the room, her soft hands open and outstretched. Now she was sitting across the table from me, but she was sitting very still. There was nothing on the table. Mum walked from the table to the window and took a roll of tape from the sill. She tore a long strip from the roll, lifted it to her lips, placed it between her teeth, and snapped it with a sharp movement of her head. It fluttered briefly before she laid it along the edge of the window and smoothed it flat with her fingertips. Verity watched from beneath lowered eyelids, her gaze unflinching. There was a long, high-pitched whine as each strip was dragged from the roll.

When the window had been sealed, Mum left the roll of tape on the sill and went to the drawers. She opened the bottom drawer

206

and chose two tea towels. Then she closed the drawer, knelt on the floor, folded the tea towels, and tucked them into the gap at the bottom of the door. After rising, she crossed the kitchen to the oven. She opened the oven door, turned the knob, but did not strike a match. There was no boom of heat and light. The oven gaped, dark and cold; and she sat on the floor beside it, hugging her shins; and I looked down onto the bright crown of her dark hair.

$$* \quad * \quad *$$

We did not die. I do not know how or why, but we did not die. Perhaps my father came home early but I do not know because I have never been told.

I remember hospital: the fierce white light burning back my eyelids; the miles of flaking ceiling tiles; the kindly talk all around me eventually from the nurses about going home. And I remember going home, sitting on the back seat of the car, my father's eyes in the mirror above the windscreen, his unkind words: '*You should have done something, Elizabeth, why didn't you do something?*' And I stared into the mirror, into his eyes, and began to hate him.

I think that my mother stayed for a long time in hospital: a different hospital, not the local hospital with the white light and kind nurses. I have a few memories of visits: tall trees in the windy grounds; and a room prickly with cigarette smoke which was not her own because she has never smoked because it is *bad for you*. I do not have many memories of living at home with my father and accompanying him to his office every day, although I remember the shiny black and red numerals of the calendar on the wall behind his desk. I remember trips to London, the seat belt across my chest, the liquorice taste of the traffic fumes. I know that I stayed sometimes with my grandmother because she bought me a vanity case to pack with my nightdress and hairbrush for overnight and weekend visits.

'You're a big girl now,' she said.

Verity was so much smaller than me that she was taken from the hospital to live for a while with strangers and she did not return until after my mother had come home. I suspect that she is unaware of this. She has never been told the truth.

I am a doctor, I know about gas. At medical school I sat through the epidemiology lectures, the lectures that no one else sat through, the paper dart contests. And I watched the lecturer working without the myth of medicine, without the colour-coded cards, the unsent words, as he drew illness and death onto graphs: unbroken lines, morbidity and mortality rates. Epidemiology is the study of public health; but, in medicine, public is a dirty word: in medicine, suffering is unique to the individual, is taken into the healing hands of the doctor. I sat through a lecture on suicide rates and I learned a fact: more than half of all suicides in the 1960s were the result of gas.

So the stories were not unique; or were they? The unbroken line on the graph did not tell of fear and desperation; it did not tell of choice, of the desire for bloodless death, for death at home. The lecturer drew the line, the voices were silent: *A woman's place is in the home; Kinder, Kirche, Kuche; Your wife is in the oven.* The lecturer could not know why death by gas would have been the perfect death for my mother. He could not know that the kitchen was the warmest room in our house, that it was my mother's room. He did not know the whole story; but there is always a story, and this one is mine to tell. My mother would not have wanted to die in water, to drift alone and hatless like her grandmother on the surface of a cold lake. She would have wanted to suffocate on something hot and dry. My mother was a war baby, she knew about gas: gas was the bogeyman of her childhood, the killer of six million people.

'Times have changed,' announced the lecturer at the end of

his lecture, 'and you will never see a case of death by gas oven because the domestic gas supply is no longer poisonous.' So the stories are different now. Gas has been made harmless not by doctors but by the gas board, and no one will ever die now in the way that my mother intended me to die.

My mother intended me to die: strange words. Did she intend me to die? I remember that sometimes she would categorise another person's suicide attempt as a *cry for help*; disdainfully wrinkling her nose, implying that there is virtue only in sincerity. A cry is an inarticulate expression of helplessness. No one likes a cry-baby. No one likes a fake or a failure. In medicine we have the category of *parasuicide*. But what of a cry for help *gone wrong*? Is it a cry too loud, or too soft? Is it a success, or a failure? Is it possible to fail at failure? Nowadays paracetamol is the scourge of parasuicide: taken in haste, repented at leisure. I have seen survivors dying days later in hospital; the physicians in a bedside vigil, frowning with exhaustion under the dead weight of their detoxification- and intensive-care skills. Sometimes I see dying survivors leaving in ambulances for the liver transplant unit, and sometimes I do not see them return. Usually they are teenage girls reconciled too late with their lovers.

So did my mother intend us to die? I don't know; she has never told me. Is it a secret, or is it a lie? I don't know. Is it a deceit? Or a tight-lipped silence? Or the belief that I have forgotten or that I failed to notice, that I am as unknowing as when I sat on the bathroom tiles, too young to be left alone, whilst my mother stood over me and washed her cap in the sink? My mother once told Verity, that *there is a time and place for everything, including knowledge*. Is this the time, is this the place?

Perhaps she has been expecting me to ask: I imagine indignation, and protestations. *You never asked, and what am I, a mind reader?* Perhaps she has been expecting me not to ask, perhaps she believes that children should be seen and not heard.

Perhaps my mother assumes that I know. Death was secret but there were clues: it was *not good for us to hang around here all the time*; it was *not easy for her*; I was *an irresponsible child*. My

209

father still checks rooms for draughts. Verity still avoids the dentist because she is afraid of the gas. My mother was vigilant, never leaving us alone. There was a long and desperate wait for Carrie, for another chance, a *third time lucky*. Carrie means *love*, not recrimination or shame or guilt or all the other things that Verity and I must mean. Carrie is *sweet*, sweet and innocent perhaps; but I am irresponsible and Verity is not to be trusted. I failed, but Verity did worse: Verity was the cause. I remember the bubbling vein on my mother's leg, and the accusation: '*Look what you've done, Verity; I had lovely legs before you were born.*' But Verity was not the cause. My mother's father died, and if she was denied a childhood when he left London for the war and failed to *turn again*, then suddenly she was denied again. She was left alone all day with Verity and me: day after day, week after week, month after month, for the rest of her life. 'It's not easy to have a toddler,' my father once barked at me; and Verity was not an easy toddler: she was slow and pale, vulnerable even to sunlight. We were my mother's responsibility and she took us seriously: '*It's not your life,*' she once told Verity, bitterly, '*it's my life.*'

If she turned on the gas tap, she intended us all to die. I shudder as I recall the ultimate defence: '*I do my best.*' It was my mother's justification for the clothes in which she dressed us, the food which she fed us, the stories which she told us, everything. She would never have considered it best to leave us alone. So she did her best. She tried to kill us when she tried to kill herself.

But she failed and we did not die. I remind myself that we did not die. I walk closer to the water. Bright foam is crackling between the small stones at my feet and running back into the sea in pale veins on the backs of the waves. We did not die; and it is a cold spring morning, more than twenty years later, and I am walking beside the sea, stepping between the waves, remembering and forgetting, playing *Catch-me-if-you-can*.

📖 *flamingo*

Flamingo is a quality imprint publishing both fiction and non-fiction. Below are some recent titles.

Fiction
- ☐ The Things They Carried *Tim O'Brien* £4.99
- ☐ Matilda's Mistake *Anne Oakley* £4.99
- ☐ Acts of Worship *Yukio Mishima* £4.99
- ☐ My Cousin, My Gastroenterologist *Mark Leyner* £4.99
- ☐ Escapes *Joy Williams* £4.99
- ☐ The Dust Roads of Monferrato *Rosetta Loy* £4.99
- ☐ The Last Trump of Avram Blok *Simon Louvish* £4.99
- ☐ Captain Vinegar's Commission *Philip Glazebrook* £4.99
- ☐ Gate at the End of the World *Philip Glazebrook* £4.99
- ☐ Ordinary Love *Jane Smiley* £4.99

Non-fiction
- ☐ A Stranger in Tibet *Scott Berry* £4.99
- ☐ The Quantum Self *Danah Zohar* £4.99
- ☐ Ford Madox Ford *Alan Judd* £6.99
- ☐ C. S. Lewis *A. N. Wilson* £5.99
- ☐ Meatless Days *Sara Suleri* £4.99
- ☐ Finding Connections *P. J. Kavanagh* £4.99
- ☐ Shadows Round the Moon *Roy Heath* £4.99
- ☐ Sweet Summer *Bebe Moore Campbell* £4.99

You can buy Flamingo paperbacks at your local bookshop or newsagent. Or you can order them from Fontana Paperbacks, Cash Sales Department, Box 29, Douglas, Isle of Man. Please send a cheque, postal or money order (not currency) worth the purchase price plus 22p per book (or plus 22p per book if outside the UK).

NAME (Block letters)_____

ADDRESS_____

_____

_____

While every effort is made to keep prices low, it is sometimes necessary to increase them at short notice. Fontana Paperbacks reserve the right to show new retail prices on covers which may differ from those previously advertised in the text or elsewhere.